The Road to Happenstance

Happenstance Chronicles, Book 1
The Mosaic Collection

Janice L. Dick

Tansy & Thistle Press
faith, fiction, forum

The Road to Happenstance

Published by Tansy & Thistle Press, Guernsey, Saskatchewan, Canada

Cover by Think Cap Design

Interior design by Wild Seas Formatting

Author Photo by Carla Lehman Photography

ISBN (ebook): 978-1-7770005-1-6

ISBN (print): 978-1-7770005-0-9

Welcome to
The Mosaic Collection

We are sisters, a beautiful mosaic united by the love of God through the blood of Christ.

Beginning August 2019, The Mosaic Collection will release one book each month for the next twelve months, exploring our theme, *Family by His Design*, and sharing stories that feature diverse, God-designed families. All are contemporary stories ranging from mystery and women's fiction to comedic and literary fiction. We hope you'll join our Mosaic family as we explore together what truly defines a family.

If you're like us, loneliness and suffering have touched your life in ways you never imagined; but while you may feel alone in your suffering—whatever it is—you are never alone!

Subscribe to *Grace & Glory*, the official newsletter of The Mosaic Collection, to receive monthly encouragement from Mosaic authors, as well as timely updates about events, new releases, and giveaways.

Learn more about The Mosaic Collection at
https://www.mosaiccollectionbooks.com
Join our Reader Community at
www.facebook.com/groups/TheMosaicCollection

Books in The Mosaic Collection

When Mountains Sing by Stacy Monson
Unbound by Eleanor Bertin
The Red Journal by Deb Elkink
A Beautiful Mess by Brenda S. Anderson
Hope is Born: A Mosaic Christmas Anthology
More Than Enough by Lorna Seilstad
The Road to Happenstance by Janice L. Dick
Coming soon: novels by Angela D. Meyer, Sara Davison, Johnnie Alexander, Regina Rudd Merrick, and Hannah R. Conway

Learn more at www.mosaiccollectionbooks.com/books

PRAISE FOR
JANICE L. DICK

Janice L. Dick makes fine use of her considerable gift of seamlessly weaving history and faith into the lives of characters that she makes us care deeply about...Her writing reminds me of Janette Oke's, with its clean, honest and heartfelt style. Because her love for her characters and her sympathy for their circumstances shines through, the reader is able to go along on their journey.
— Donna Gartshore, author of Instant Father and Instant Family (Love Inspired)

Author Janice L. Dick is known for her faith-filled historical fiction.

Other Side of the River: With insight, compassion and beautifully evocative language, author Janice L. Dick does for the Russian Mennonites under Stalin what Dale Cramer did for the Amish of Paradise Valley.

Although The Road to Happenstance is a contemporary novel, the town's nostalgic feel lends an impression of stepping back in time, and Matthew's personal struggles are affected by his faith. Savor and enjoy!
— Janet Sketchley, author of the *Redemption's Edge* Christian suspense series

Janice L. Dick is a master storyteller - she takes a simple plot line, builds tension, adds suspense and intrigue, leaving the reader breathless in anticipation of what may happen, and the conclusion is often not which one expects. Enjoy - you'll not want to put the book down until you finish and then you'll wait anxiously for the next book to make its appearance!
— Helen F., reader, researcher

Are you a treasure hunter? You're about to unearth an aggregate that compels you to keep reading – keep searching. Matt Sadler hits the road, escaping small-town gossip while grieving the loss of his wife. Not planning to ever stop, he lands in a mysterious town called Happenstance with its cast of characters: some dubious,

some charming and some beautiful. The unexpected surprises hold him in place [and] catch him up in a web of similar social issues to those he left behind. This story is a treasure hunt that keeps you reading to finally discover the answers. Well researched with accomplished writing. Five stars.
— Sheri Hathaway, writer, speaker, editor

In The Road to Happenstance, Janice Dick has created compelling characters and a plot that kept me turning the pages. I quickly became invested in the biker escaping his past and the quirky sisters who run the local hotel. Happenstance is a town with a few surprises in store for us. You'll be glad you travelled this road.
— Tandy Balson, Inspirational Author and Speaker

Your story gathered me in.
— Carolyn Wilker, author, speaker, editor

Anything can happen in the town of Happenstance, unexpected, comforting and mysterious events too. The author keeps you guessing what might happen next and who you can really trust in this cozy mystery. The setting makes you want to stop in for a visit but at the same time you wonder, like the main character, if you can believe what you hear and see. I would recommend this story to anyone who loves to curl up with an enjoyable, easy reading mystery.
— Carol Harrison, author, speaker, mentor

DEDICATION

To Iffy, who helped me discover the story,

the characters, and the town of Happenstance,

and who has been a true friend and encourager for many
years

To Linda & Lyse because you loved it first

To anyone who needs a second chance at life

1

Nothing figured stronger in Matthew Sadler's mind at the moment than to put as many miles as possible between himself and Reedport. He revved the engine of his 1977 Harley and leaned deep into another curve of the number fifteen highway.

The towers and traffic of the city had morphed into the feigned order and charm of the suburbs, and then to the freedom of farms and fields and open road.

Matt had abandoned a full-face visor for his old beanie helmet and the wraparound shades Ginny had given him on his twenty-first birthday. The wind feathered his new growth of beard and blew the years away. He was twenty-one again and Ginny's arms circled his waist.

Matt's memories short-circuited as he throttled down behind an old blue station wagon.

He tried to revive the image of Ginny's face in his rearview mirror, still young and full of life, her smile flashing wide, auburn curls flying out the back of her helmet.

He slowed again. Darn station wagon. Sunday driver, and it was only Wednesday. He swerved to the left to pass, but a semi-truck and trailer approached from the front, giving him no alternative but to maneuver past the car on the right shoulder. The car also began to turn right onto an access road, and with a muttered curse, Matt sped ahead of it to keep from being hit, struggling to maintain his balance. He glanced in the mirror. The station wagon now tailed him.

With no room to turn around, and a distinct lack of faith

in the driver behind him, Matt persevered, hoping for a place to pull over. The road was scarcely wide enough for two cars to pass, a dirt path with a scattering of gravel on top as a sort of apology. Thoughts of Ginny and Reedport dissipated in his effort to hold the Harley upright.

Ahead of him, a large red building loomed in the middle of the road, an honest-to-goodness covered bridge. As he entered the enclosure, the bike's headlight flickered in the claustrophobic blackness and Matt blinked to clear his vision. He tore off his shades and held the bike steady, concentrating on the faint light ahead. The hair at the nape of his neck tingled as he roared across the bridge.

Emerging again into brilliant sunshine, he jammed his glasses back on. A sign to his right read:

HAPPENSTANCE: A TOWN YOU CAN TRUST.

Yeah, right.

He geared down and checked his rearview mirror. His nemesis still followed. At the sight of a garage with gas pumps, he signaled and pulled off the road.

Matt removed his sunglasses once again and stared at the gas pumps, two tall, round-topped obelisks of brilliant red, with wide windows to view the propellant as it gurgled into the tank. Straight out of the sixties, he thought. He booted the kickstand into place and peeled off his gloves as he dismounted.

"Welcome to Happenstance," a falsetto voice chirped behind him, interrupting his stretch. Matt turned to stare at a large man with oil-stained coveralls and an Exxon cap pulled over scarecrow hair.

"Thanks." Matt shaded his eyes and looked around. "How big is this town, anyway?"

The mechanic, already shooting fuel into the motorcycle, squinted at him. "Oh, big enough, I'd say. We got whatcha want, unless you want what we don't got, and then you prob'ly don't need it. Where you headin'?"

Matt unfastened his beanie, pulled it off and scratched his head. "As far as I can ride."

The man finished filling the bike and returned the nozzle to the pump. He fished a rag from his hip pocket and polished the area around the bike's tank. "Nice bike you got here; almost a' antique." He wiped his right hand on the rag and extended it toward Matt. "Name's Gavin Beresford, but most everbody calls me Bear."

They shook hands. "Matt Sa... Smith." *Ooh, that was original.*

Bear nodded and smiled. "You might wanna tour on up into town, Matt. Nice park to relax in, library if you like readin'. Mrs. Phipps, she makes me wear them little plastic gloves so's I don't get the pages greasy. Can't never get these hands clean." He chuckled, examining his stained fingers. "If you're needin' a place to sleep, we got that too, down to the other end of town. The Happenstance Hotel."

"Thanks, but I think I'll grab a coffee and head out."

"Can't get back to the main road thataway." Bear shook his head as he stuffed the greasy rag back into his pocket. "Have to turn right 'round and go back over the bridge. Best you stay a bit though. Wouldn't want to leave Happenstance without you've properly seen it. The Barlow sisters that own the hotel—Miss Emmaline and Miss Grayce—would love to make your acquaintance, I'm sure. Just seen 'em come into town behind you."

So, his nemeses had names. "They wouldn't happen to drive a blue station wagon?"

"Yessiree. I keep it tuned up so it purrs like a well-fed kitten. Mighty sweet old ladies, the Barlows. Ackshully, Miss Emmaline in't really a Barlow anymore. She married an Osmer, but he's dead. Miss Grayce, she never married. They like comp'ny. Lotsa room at the hotel. Stay a while. Do you good."

Matt's head spun. "Thanks for the advice, Bear. Maybe I'll cruise through before I leave."

"Good idea, Matt. See you again." With a nod and a toothy grin, Bear turned back to his shop and bent over the engine of a sixty-something Ford pickup truck.

Matt pulled his hair into a ponytail and slipped his helmet back on. He climbed aboard his Harley and, with a rebellious rumble, rolled out of Beresford Gas Station and toured up the street. The town of Happenstance had seen fit to pave the section of road this side of the bridge. He wondered why they wouldn't also pave the piece coming off the highway. Maybe that was county property. Whenever a situation like that arose, you could count on a political tug-of-war.

To Matt's left, an apple orchard boasted fruit round and red and so sweet he could smell it from the road. Houses of all description lined the streets in pleasant disarray, like a picture out of a storybook. The street sign read Bridgeway Avenue.

Matt followed it past an old stone church set into a grove of maples. He could see the cemetery behind the church, and off to one side, what appeared to be the parsonage, rather crippled with age. He'd make sure to avoid all three.

Bridgeway turned into Parkview Drive. Matt took a left, following Main Street North around a large oval of grass, paving stone, flowerbeds and wrought-iron benches. The Stars and Stripes waved in the breeze. To his right a vacancy sign hung by one corner at the end of a long lane shaded by more rows of maples and hovering elms, the arrow indicating Happenstance Hotel.

He cruised around the square, spotting Estelle's Esthetics, My Lady's Millinery and Harold's Haberdashery on a side street. Didn't millinery mean hats? Did women still wear hats? Maybe in this town they did. But what the heck was a haberdashery?

A trim male figure with broom in hand waved from the sidewalk in front of the shop. "Must be Harold," Matt muttered as he returned the greeting. What did they do, send out a welcoming committee? He expected a Welcome Wagon representative to leap from the bushes at any moment and accost him with a basket of coupons and spice samples.

He stopped his bike in front of The Waldorf Café. A 1954 Star Chief Convertible Pontiac, painted a deep ocean blue, sat on a concrete pad near the entrance. Its license plate read: PHILS. Matt pushed open the café door into a modest lobby and entered the restaurant.

"Coffee?" The proprietor resembled a middle-aged mafia boss. "We have quite a selection. Please take a seat at one of those tables and Cydnee will bring you a menu momentarily." Scrap the mafia idea, Matt concluded. The speech didn't fit.

Matt eyed the tiny round tables and delicate white tube chairs with candy pink seats. "Mind if I opt for a booth?"

"Not at all. Cydnee! Customer."

"Coming, Mr. Philatopoulos."

That would be Phil, Matt decided as Elvis rocked within the confines of the jukebox. A unique set of salt and pepper shakers, miniature replicas of Big Ben and the Leaning Tower of Pisa, stood sentinel beside the napkin dispenser.

A blithe teenage girl with swinging ponytail placed a coffee menu in front of him. He raised his eyebrows at the selection: Irish Creme, Belgian Chocolate, Mocha, Cappuccino, Espresso, Latte, Macchiato, Colombian, the list went on.

"What's the closest thing to real coffee?"

Cydnee giggled, snapping her chewing gum between red lips. "Like, I totally don't drink coffee, but maybe the Colombian would be the safest." Her voice lifted at the end of the sentence, making it sound like a question. "That's what Mr. Alkmaar orders when he comes in on Tuesdays. He has, like, a dairy just down this road. Makes really good cheese." She tapped her penny loafers on the black and white tiled floor and flicked an imaginary thread from her poodle skirt as Matt considered his options.

"Make it Colombian then please, with fresh cream, if you have it."

"Sure." She hesitated before leaving with the coffee menu. "You sure don't talk like a biker." She giggled again and bounced off toward the kitchen.

Don't talk like a biker. Can't even fool a high school girl named Cydnee.

Matt rubbed his hands over his face. He'd planned to keep riding, but he was so tired. He doubted coffee would give him the lift he needed. Glancing out the front window of the café, he noticed a sign hanging in front of a business across the street: Paradise Realty and Insurance. He could use an escape to paradise, a place where nobody knew his name. Maybe he'd relax a day or two before he moved on, like Bear suggested. He leaned back in the booth and stretched his long legs under the pink table. He'd try not to want what they didn't have. As far as coffee, that wouldn't be difficult.

2

Half an hour later Matt entered the foyer of the Happenstance Hotel and sighed as cool air enveloped him. As his eyes adjusted to the dimness his breath caught. Two curving staircases ascended to the floor above, one leading up from his right and the other from his left, opening onto opposite ends of a balcony that ran the width of the lobby. He imagined fashionably attired men and women watching from above as the younger set danced the Charleston to the stylings of a live orchestra.

He stepped down the two wide stairs leading into the lobby. *You'd love this, Ginny. Big and rambling, and slightly neglected. Kind of like me before you came along.*

He took a deep breath and stared at his surroundings. A room to his right beckoned with cheerful yellow walls, white trim, and natty white wicker furniture. Late afternoon light streamed in the expansive bay windows, dappling flocked wallpaper and sepia photos under convex glass fronts. He took a few steps into the room and leaned over to inspect one of the photos. Two young women from a time long past, one thin and one of more generous proportions, smiled demurely at him from the gilded frame.

He turned his back on the sunlight and approached the long, black, marble counter, helmet in one hand, backpack slung over his other shoulder. A row of flowerpots boasted brilliant pink begonias, and a slim ornamental lemon tree stood at attention, in lieu of a desk clerk, he presumed. He picked up the old school bell that sat waiting and gave it a twitch.

As in the Waldorf Café, he stepped back in time, only this time was earlier than that. Perhaps late twenties, before the crash. Affluence and celebration. The celebration at the Happenstance Hotel had dwindled a good while ago, but he could still sense it.

"May I help you?"

Matt jerked back to the present. Behind the desk stood a tall woman of good posture and well-endowed form. Her thick silver hair lay in waves and coils about her broad face, which was almost devoid of wrinkles in spite of her advanced age. She wore a dark purple gown, almost a rosy brown, with lace at the throat. A pair of wire-rimmed glasses hung from her neck by a gold chain.

"Young man, you will cause me to blush if you keep staring. My, my, it's been a long while since anyone has noticed me so. Makes me think of my Bruce." She touched her eyes with an embroidered hanky she'd pulled from her sleeve. "He's been gone now for thirty years, but sometimes I still expect him to come whistling through the door. He had such a sunny disposition. I believe we made a good pair and I do miss him."

She paused, then took a deep breath. "Now, what can I do for you?"

Matt placed his helmet on the black marble and pulled out his wallet. "Sorry for staring, Miss ahhh, Miss..."

"Emmaline. My name is Emmaline Louise Barlow Osmer."

"Miss Emmaline. I was caught up in imagination, thinking of what this place must have looked like in its prime."

"Very much as it does now, dear, but busier. Since my sister and I have aged since then, we are rather glad it is quieter than it used to be, although we could use a little more business. Do you require a room?"

"Just for a night or two."

"It's cheaper by the week, you know, or by the month." She propped her glasses onto her aquiline nose and pulled a large, worn registry from beneath the counter. "You have your choice of two suites on the main level, one near the conservatory, which is empty I'm afraid, and one next to the chapel, or a series of rooms on the second floor. Besides our own suites, only one other room is occupied on the second floor at this time. Another lodger to keep us company. Of course, there's another apartment on the third level, but it would have to be aired, as it has not been used for some time."

Just then another woman joined the first from a room behind the counter. Matt noted a certain resemblance of face, but this second woman left a much different impression. Everything about her was thin: her face, her hair, her figure. Only her eyes, magnified behind her glasses, showed depth. They were crystal blue, clear and wide, startling against her pale complexion. She smiled at him.

"Good day. I am Grayce Lorraine Barlow. And you are?" Again, the sweet smile and a delicate hand held out to him.

"Matt, Ma'am. Matt Smith." He bowed over her bony fingers. "I'd like to stay for a night or two, if you have room."

"Of course, Mr. Smith." She turned to her sister. "Emmaline, mark down Mr. Smith's name for Suite One on the main floor." She looked up at him. "That's straight down the lobby and to the left, next to the chapel. These are our rates," she pointed to a brochure lying on the counter. "Sign here, please. We will take payment by the week or when your stay is complete."

Next to the chapel. What an uncomfortable coincidence. He returned his wallet to his pocket and signed: Matthew Smith.

"You do have a way with people, Graycie," said Miss Emmaline. "You managed to get all his information in just a few moments."

"Thank you, Emmaline." Turning back to Matt, she said, "You're a nice young man, not the sort of person I'd expect to ride a motorcycle. You cut us off rather abruptly when we turned into town earlier, but we won't speak of that again. Now, follow me, Mr. Smith, and I will show you to your suite." She stepped around the corner of the registration desk and took his arm.

"You have forgotten your helmet, Mr. Smith," called Emmaline, holding it out to him.

"I'll carry that for you, Mr. Smith," assured Grayce, with a smile. "My, my, what a heavy little hat this is. Protects the brain, I expect. Do you worry much about taking a spill on that machine of yours?"

"Not really, ma'am."

Miss Grayce smiled and tightened her hand on his arm as she drew him through the wide hall. He looked down at the top of her head, not understanding the strange sense of protectiveness stirring inside him. He'd left Reedport to get away from the judgmental remarks and accusatory glances, in search of a place where no one knew him. He had no intention of becoming involved with a couple of curious women. Besides, they had almost run him off the road earlier. *Get a grip, Sadler.*

Miss Grayce led him past a spacious room boasting a floor-to-ceiling fieldstone fireplace against the far wall. Two tapestried sofas invited the weary traveler, and plants of various sizes and species leaned in to commiserate. Armchairs sat in comfortable proximity, and odd tables gave place to piles of magazines and books. On the other side of the wide hallway, a dining table waited for dinner with three places set. Matt heard pots and pans clanging in a room beyond and smelled the tantalizing aroma of roasting chicken and something garlic.

Straight ahead, a small sitting room with French doors offered a quiet place to relax and read. Again, books sat in piles on tables and on the floor, and shelves lined the long wall, bursting with tomes of all sizes.

"To our right at the end of the hallway is the conservatory. In former times, it was a beautiful place to sit surrounded by plants and flowers and butterflies. I'm sorry to say it has been empty these many years. We hope someday to resurrect it, but the time has not yet come."

They turned, as cued by Miss Grayce, and advanced to the left.

"This is your suite, Mr. Smith. I hope you will be comfortable."

"Thank you, ma'am; I'm sure I will." Matt threw his backpack on the high, soft bed and set his helmet on the dresser. A worn but cozy armchair beckoned him. He leaned over the desk to look out the window.

"Your own verandah and view of the gardens," said his

hostess. "And there's a full bath."

"Very nice. Thanks."

"You're very welcome, I'm sure. The chapel is right next door. It's open all the time. Avail yourself of the opportunity to search your heart and listen to God."

Matt's lips thinned but he nodded to Miss Grayce. "Do you serve dinner here, or should I go to The Waldorf?"

"The Waldorf? Oh, my dear man, the Waldorf is fine for coffee and snacks and for passing the time, but if you prefer real food, come to the dining room at seven for dinner. We play classical music and light jazz on the phonograph, not that heathen noise that curdles milk. And Johanna's culinary skills are guaranteed never to disappoint. Feel free to wander about and acquaint yourself with our hotel." She inclined her head in a gracious nod and left him alone in the room.

Apparently the third plate at the dining table had been set for him. How had they known he would come? Or were they expecting someone else?

"Am I taking someone's place?" he asked as the ladies arrived for dinner.

"No, dear. There isn't anyone else here, is there Graycie?"

"No there isn't, Emmaline."

"We do have one other lodger, but she is regrettably absent this evening. I wish you could meet her. She's an interesting woman."

"Maybe I'll meet her tomorrow if I'm still here," said Matt.

The sisters shared a glance as Matt pulled out their chairs. He sat, thankful he wouldn't have to make conversation with yet another stranger, although for some reason the Barlows didn't feel like strangers.

Matt's mouth watered when an older, heavyset woman emerged from the kitchen and served them roast chicken, garlic mashed potatoes and herbed carrots. She returned with a spinach salad and disappeared again.

"What brings you to Happenstance?" asked Emmaline, her smile sweet and guileless.

Matt met her gaze. "What brings me here? The two of you,

I'd have to say. I hadn't intended to stop here at all. I've never heard of Happenstance before."

"It's an old historic town. We've been here all our lives," said Grayce.

Emmaline reinforced Grayce's words. "We are glad you have come to stay with us, however you happened to discover our little town."

"Thank you. I toured around the square before I stopped here. By the way, what is a haberdashery?"

"It's a men's store." Grayce sipped her tea.

"Yes," added Emmaline. "Harold is a bit of a literary fellow. He liked the sound of Harold's Haberdashery." She marked out the sign in the air. "He stocks only good quality clothing, of course."

"I'll have to check it out. This is an excellent dinner, by the way."

"It always is," said Grayce.

"Johanna trained as a chef in Germany. She knows how to please the palate," added Emmaline.

"Please give her my compliments."

"I certainly will," said Emmaline. She set down her fork. "What activities have you planned for your stay here, Mr. Smith?"

"I haven't planned anything; I'm just passing through."

"There's a hiking trail in Lakeview Forest, if you're interested in that sort of thing. Miss Wilkinson often goes hiking there."

"Miss Wilkinson?"

"Our other lodger, Miss Veronica Wilkinson. She has a suite on the second floor."

"Did she come in this week as well?"

"Oh no. She's been with us almost six months now."

"She works at Paradise Realty. She loves to hike and she takes a lot of vitamins and teaches exercise classes over at the high school two nights a week. If I were younger, I'd go." Emmaline looked at her sister as she said the words.

"Nonsense," came the reply. "You're far too old to even consider such a thing."

"Yes, but if I were younger I would sign up, no matter what you say."

"Emm, really. Where are your manners?"

Emmaline lifted her chin. "Perhaps Mr. Smith is interested in an exercise class. It's open to everyone, you know."

Matt's mouth tugged at one corner. "I don't think I'd keep up. I'm a bit out of shape of late."

"Of late? Did you used to work out?"

"Emmaline Louise, leave the poor man be."

Emmaline frowned at her sister, and Matt imagined her sticking out her tongue.

The conversation moved from hiking to the weather, and then took a more personal turn again. Matt parried the questions like an experienced fencer, determined to protect his private life. He had never succeeded in silencing the aspersions in Reedport; he did not intend to start the ball rolling here in Happenstance.

After dinner, Matt sat on the verandah outside his suite and stared at the stars. He had no one with whom to share the tranquil beauty, and loneliness descended. Thoughts of Ginny filtered through his mind and he put his hand to his heart to soothe the ache.

Bitterness also return with a vengeance, and his head began to hurt along with his heart. Where was justice anymore? He'd given twelve years to that school and what did he get in return? He hadn't been raised to be a quitter, but they had backed him into a corner. It was either fight or flee, and he was tired of fighting to no avail.

With an effort, he rose from the deck chair and returned to his suite. A John Grisham novel sat on the desk. How did they know his partiality to Grisham's work, or was it happenstance? He climbed into bed and read until the book slipped from his hands.

3

Matt awoke to the smell of bacon. "Ginny." Her name formed on his lips as he scrambled out of bed. He stood there in his boxers, trying to get his bearings.

"Where in the world—ahh, Happenstance." He slumped back onto the bed, heart racing, and held his head in his hands. He hadn't experienced Ginny's presence this acutely for a couple of years. He took several deep breaths and shuffled into the bathroom to splash cold water on his face.

"Can't keep the ladies waiting."

He dressed in jeans and a T-shirt, ran a comb through his hair and pulled it into a ponytail.

"Good morning, Mr. Smith," said Emmaline as he entered the dining room. "Take a plate and help yourself to the buffet on the sideboard. Johanna has outdone herself again."

"Thank you, ma'am."

"Did you sleep well?" asked Grayce.

"Yes, thanks."

Emmaline took her serve. "Are you sure, dear? You look a little pale."

"I slept well." He tucked into his bacon and eggs and tried to deflect the limelight. "Johanna is an excellent cook."

"We are well aware of that. I'm not sure what we would do without her, are you, Graycie?"

"Oh my, no," said Grayce with conviction. "You know I can't cook at all, and it would be an enormous task for you to keep up with it."

Johanna, tall, ruddy and thick, came with coffee. Two cups of the full-bodied brew went a long way to easing Matt's morning memories. He thanked her, and she answered with a mumbled *"Bitt' schön."*

"Our Johanna is very shy," said Emmaline after the cook had returned to the kitchen. "You see, she was quite alone in the world when she came to us fifteen years ago. We were getting too old to manage the hotel on our own, so we all benefited, wouldn't you say?"

"You needn't give Mr. Smith her entire history, Emm."

"Oh, I haven't yet. Besides, he wanted to know, Graycie."

"How do you know that?"

"Well, because I would have wanted to know if I'd been him."

"Which proves one thing...."

Matt drowned his smirk in another draught of coffee. He came up sputtering.

"Are you all right, dear?" asked Emmaline.

He nodded, coughing and choking. "Just...inhaled instead of...swallowing...I'm fine." It had been a long while since anyone had called him dear or showed any concern for him. Happenstance appealed to him, but it also seemed intent on revealing secrets, and that was something he could not allow.

After a stroll around the business district of Happenstance, Matt stopped for a mid-morning coffee at the Waldorf Café. He had left his motorcycle parked in front of the hotel, confident that no one in this sleepy little town would steal it or anything else. It was like a fairy tale village with every necessary amenity and no visible vices.

Mr. Philatopoulos himself stepped from behind the high counter with a pot of coffee and pointed Matt to an empty booth.

"Columbian again?"

Matt nodded and thanked him. "I need a cup of caffeine, the simpler the better." He sipped the rich, hot brew and tried to dismiss his discomfort at several sets of narrowed eyes that turned away when he returned their glances. "How long have you been running this establishment?"

The proprietor set the carafe on the table and leaned against the side of the booth. "It will be twenty-five years this fall. The restaurant was already in operation when I arrived here from Greece, but I altered the menu and redecorated." His hand waved at wall sconces, pillared corners and wreathed mirrors. "Cydnee suggested the coffees last year. Myself, I think it may be somewhat excessive, but it makes people realize we have what they need. No one has to go over the bridge for anything."

"Over the bridge?"

"Out. Away from Happenstance."

Matt frowned. What was it about Happenstance that drew him in? He had planned to be on his way today or tomorrow, but now he wasn't sure he wanted to leave. Happenstance was a quiet reprieve from the fiasco back home.

He did not want to be reminded of Reedport. The thought made him shudder. He was glad he'd left town, even if it had been a spontaneous decision that might result in negative repercussions in time.

"Mr. Smith?" Mr. Philatopoulos stared at him.

"Sorry. Lost in thought."

"Perhaps it would be prudent of you not to linger on that particular thought. It appears to be painful. Sit back and enjoy the coffee. I'll bring you today's paper." He picked up a thin newspaper from the end of the counter and slid it onto Matt's table. "Here you go," he said. *The Village Voice*. By the way, call me Phil."

"Like on the license plate?"

"Affirmative."

"I'm Matt."

Phil nodded, refilled Matt's cup and carried the carafe back to the element.

While conversation droned on around him, Matt perused the paper, which took all of four minutes. *Exercise Classes at School Well Attended*, he read. That would be Miss Veronica Wilkinson's community involvement. *Kids Make Nutritious Snacks*. That brought a silent chuckle. *Heat Wave Linked to High Temperatures*. He shook his head as he finished reading the headlines. He thought of writing a self-help book for journalists: how to make news out of nothing.

He skipped the gossip columns and checked out ads from Wuppertal's General Store and the clothing stores. Library hours were listed as weekdays from ten until five and Saturdays from nine until noon. He'd have to check out the library.

As he sipped his java, the mechanic from the gas station pushed through the front doors.

"Hey there, Matt. Glad to see you took my advice and stayed."

"Me too, Bear. Nice town you have here. The Barlow sisters have already made me feel at home."

Bear slid into the booth across from Matt.

"How are you progressing with that pickup truck, Bear?" Phil asked as he poured him a coffee and topped up Matt's cup.

"Not bad a'tall." He paused to empty four creamers into his cup, and then glanced up at Phil's frown. "Oh, sorry, man. Just used to drinkin' it like I do at the shop, you know."

"At least you aren't polluting an expensive flavored blend."

"There you go, always somethin' to be thankful for. By the way, Matt, there's gonna be a roofing bee over to the reverend's tomorrow. We wanna get that roof sealed up proper-like before it starts leakin' again. Every able hand is needed. Lunch provided. Be there at nine if you wanna help."

Matt hesitated. "I was thinking of leaving tomorrow morning."

"Your choice, but we could sure use the extra hands."

"Okay, thanks for the invite. I'll see what the morning brings." They parted company without a commitment from Matt, but somehow, he already knew he'd be helping the roofing crew on Friday.

Matt spent the rest of the morning acquainting himself further with the town of Happenstance. He stopped first at the library to borrow a thin history of the area, personally recommended by the librarian. Mrs. Phipps scrutinized him over her spectacles and pronounced him fit to handle the book sans plastic gloves. He would skim through the volume this evening and drop it off Saturday on his way out.

He passed *Paradise Realty and Insurance*. A man in a business suit waved at him through the window as he talked on the phone at his desk. A large bank stood adjacent to the realty office. It even offered Interac. At the end of the street on his right, an old-fashioned shingle hung out over the pavement. Clinic...Doctors Phineas and Paul Percy. Again, residences of varied sizes placed themselves at odd angles between businesses.

Matt crossed the street and stood before Harold's Haberdashery, proprietor Harold Haskins. The window displayed a classic three-piece suit, a casual outfit of beige slacks and a lightweight, pale yellow cotton sweater, and a couple of spiffy golf shirts, all good quality, as Emmaline had suggested.

Matt pushed open the door and the ambiance settled on him. It was like a miniature Brooks Brothers, with neat, attractive displays of suits, ties, socks, casual clothing and jackets. The man Matt had seen sweeping his sidewalk the day before, looked up from his newspaper. He smiled and approached, hand outstretched.

"Welcome to my humble establishment," he said. "I am Harold Haskins, proprietor, and you must be Matthew Smith. Pleased to meet you."

"And you," said Matt, wondering how Haskins already knew his name. "Nice place you have here."

Harold accepted the praise, acknowledging it to be true. "How can I help you today? You look as if you prefer casual clothes to suits. I have a new line of khaki pants and knit golf shirts just arrived in."

Matt reminded himself that in his jeans, T-shirt and ponytail, no one would guess he dressed up for work in Reedport. He had fallen into a casual persona and liked it there. "Do you have any ball caps?"

Harold's hand froze on the hanger of a navy knit shirt. He turned to look at Matt. "Ball caps?" He cleared his throat. "I'm afraid you'll have to rely on the farm dealerships for those. Or perhaps Wuppertal's little business." He said Wuppertal's as if it disgusted him to say it, even though that little business was several times the size of Harold's Haberdashery.

"I didn't bring a cap," explained Matt, "and I was thinking of helping shingle the reverend's roof tomorrow. It's too hot to work bareheaded, don't you agree?"

Harold lowered his chin and smiled. "Of course. Follow me, please, and I will show you what you need."

Matt followed Mr. Haskins all the way to the back of the store—about four steps from where they had been standing—to a display boasting everything from a beret to a deerstalker, a fedora and a Panama. But no caps. Matt tried on the Panama and winced. It would keep the sun off, but it didn't suit him. Next, he popped the deerstalker onto his head. Add a moustache and a pipe and he could pass for Sherlock Holmes.

He liked the look of the fedora. Maybe it wasn't him either, but it would provide shade and look unique in the process. He'd have to store it in the side bag of the motorcycle instead of crushing it into the snap compartment like a cap. He might stop at Wuppertal's and pick up a cheap cap for tomorrow, but this fedora had his attention.

"I'll take it."

Harold beamed. "We often don't know what looks best until we've had a chance to experience it. Good choice, if I may say so."

I'm sure. Costs five times as much as a ball cap. He thanked Harold and set off to see more of the town.

My Lady's Millinery and Estelle's Esthetics bookended The Waldorf. Matt continued on around the square past Wuppertal's General Store, the windows of which were papered with sale flyers and offers that promised to be too good to pass up. He looked around for a bit but couldn't find any ball caps, and he was hesitant to lose himself in the bustling aisles weaving between tall stacks of goods.

By eleven o'clock, Matt had seen most of the business section. He returned to the hotel, grabbed his helmet and a sack lunch begged from a blushing Johanna, and fired up his Harley while Misses Grayce and Emmaline stood on the top step of the Happenstance Hotel with their hands over their ears. He walked the bike backwards, turned it around, and headed for the park. The ladies took their hands off their ears and waved.

Matt cruised around the town square and arrived at the park entrance in a matter of minutes, deciding that next time he would walk. He locked his helmet onto the bike, slipped the keys into his pocket and put on his new fedora. He needed a cap. Snapping a water bottle to his belt, he set off into the trees. Perhaps he'd even run into the elusive—and health-conscious—Miss Wilkinson.

Matt stopped to bask in the winking sunlight as it filtered through the canopy of green. The calm of the windless forest descended on him, and he pulled in deep gulps of the pure air. Walking again, his boots made little noise on the bed of fragrant pine needles besides a soft squish-snap with each step. He heard a sharp tapping above him and identified a downy woodpecker, intent on either defending his territory or communicating to his mate that an interloper had entered their woods. A pair of blue jays screeched at each other in avian annoyance, while a band of black-capped chickadees lifted as one and disappeared into the trees. Matt stepped into yet another world.

His mind wandered as he hiked, until a sudden unidentifiable tingling at the back of his neck alerted him to a suspicion that he was not alone. Were there dangerous animals in this forest? He had no way of defending himself against anything bigger than a squirrel. He had never even been a boy scout! He stood still and listened. Just as he was about to chalk it up to an overactive imagination, laughter erupted to his left.

He whirled around but could not locate the sound, until a man separated himself from a thick stand of blue spruce. Matt stood still as the man approached. His age was difficult to gauge, although Matt guessed him to be about thirty. He was tall and slim, with a lean, bearded face and bushy brows, and he wore the only actual pith helmet Matt had ever seen. Even Harold's Haberdashery didn't carry pith helmets. The figure was dressed in khaki, from his hat to his boots, camouflaged from the untrained eye.

"Good afternoon to ye," said the khaki-clad stranger. "Beautiful day, i'n it?"

Matt faltered at the strong Irish brogue, then nodded.

"I'm not meanin' ta stop yer tongue, now. Name's Lysander Patrick Joseph Fitzpatrick III, a.k.a. Sandy. An' you are?"

Matt cleared his throat. "Uh, Matt. Matt Smith." He frowned. "What are you doing out here, if I may ask?"

"Ye surely may ask. I'm dendrologizin'." His lean face broadened with an ear-to-ear grin.

Smart guy. "And how does one go about dendrologizing?"

"Aha! I thought ye might ask. A dendrologist is one who studies trees. I was tempted to say he is a student of trees, which theoretically would mean the same thing, but practically might prove confusin', if not alarmin'."

Matt took a deep breath in sympathy with Sandy's lungs. The man seemed able to talk while breathing in and breathing out.

"Are you with a research group?" Even as the words left Matt's mouth, he knew he should have found a shady spot in which to sit while he listened to Sandy's reply.

"Well I was, ye see, but now I'm on me own. I'm a PhD undergraduate, workin' on me own study for me thesis. Ye see, dendrology is a many-faceted field. Ye have your deciduous dendrologists and yer coniferous dendrologists. Kinda sounds like some sheds their clothes for the occasional washin' and some wears 'em fer life! Ha, ha. And then there's yer temperate dendrologists an' yer torrid dendrologists, an' even the odd frigid dendrologist, but they're as few an' far between as their subjects."

Matt stifled a snort, and then sobered at the realization that there might also be hemispheric divisions of dendrology, and their continental counterparts, but to his surprise, Sandy had stopped talking and stood looking at him expectantly.

"And to think I'd never even heard of dendrology." Matt removed his fedora and scratched his head. "I am here on a specific mission as well." For some perverse reason, he stopped and waited for the question.

Sandy chuckled. "An' what would that be, then?"

"Glad you asked. I came looking for peace and solitude."

"Pardon me for interferin' in that quest. I'll be off."

Matt relented. "No need. You seem a part of the solitude, except for your tongue, that is."

Sandy's teasing eyes twinkled. "Me mam always said as much to me."

The corner of Matt's mouth twitched. "Nice to meet you. I'm off to search out a sunny spot to have my lunch."

Sandy knocked on his pith helmet, as if thumping out a response. He shook his head back and forth. "I'll try to give ye adequate directions."

"Thanks."

"Would ye p'raps be wantin' comp'ny? I'm needin' a bit of a breather from dendrologizin', and takin' ye there would be much easier than explainin'."

"Let's go."

"Follow me," invited Sandy. "We'll find a sunny spot and have a cuppa. Ye say you've brought lunch?"

4

The next morning, Matt walked to the parsonage, arriving early for the roofing bee. He had yet to meet Miss Wilkinson. She had again been "regrettably absent" from dinner the evening before, and had been up and gone to work before he arrived in the dining room for breakfast. Emmaline had seemed disappointed. He did not share her disappointment. He was not in search of female companionship, but his interest had been piqued by the fact that he had not set eyes upon Miss Wilkinson for two days running.

The roofing bee interested Matt. He had some experience in the construction industry, since as a teacher he had summers to work at other jobs, and a little physical exercise might do him good and help out the minister at the same time. The concept of a roofing bee surprised him. He'd read about "bees" in grade school, but he hadn't supposed people still had them. A person came to expect the unexpected in Happenstance.

Matt passed the church on his way to the parsonage. *Our Redeemer Community Fellowship*, the sign said. *Worship Sunday 11:00 a.m., Sunday School 10:00 a.m. Bible Study Wed. 7:30 p.m. Everyone welcome in the name of the Lord.*

A bell tower overlooked the old stone edifice, like a beacon calling the lost and weary to refuge. Matt admitted to being weary, but he drew the line at *lost*. He was not lost, only in transition. It seemed God had deserted him in his hour of need, and he had ceased to call on Him since then. Not that he didn't believe; he was disillusioned.

Matt retreated in the direction of the parsonage where a crowd gathered. By nine o'clock, the yard buzzed with activity. A crew of locals piled shingles at the side of the house. Matt looked forward to some manual labor, but he dreaded the personal questions he knew would accompany the work, and hoped he'd be able to field them all. He recognized one person: Gavin Beresford.

Bear called him over and introduced him to Karl Collins, from Paradise Realty and Insurance, the man who had waved at him through the window.

"And this is Bob Rampole, retired plumber."

Matt followed Bear's introductions and shook Bob's hand.

"Over by the truck is Mr. Alkmaar. Has the dairy west of town. And Donald McDonald here works on the oil rigs, a month in and a month out. His wife is Maisie down to the hair salon."

"Good day to you," said Donald with a solid slap on the back. "Appreciate you coming out to help, being new and all."

"Not new, just passing through."

"Yeah, we all have our stories. I'll tell you mine sometime." Donald saluted, grabbed a ladder from his truck and settled it against the shabby little house. "See you on the roof."

Bear nodded toward a scowling older man standing near the pile of shingles. "That there's Morris Craddock, teacher at the high school. He'll tell you what to do, but you don't have to listen. Nobody does."

"Maybe that's why he's sour."

"Maybe, but it ain't helpin' matters any."

Morris Craddock approached Matt, his scowl deepening. "Newcomer, are you? Hope you can help and not hinder."

"I'll do my best, but it's been awhile since I was up on a roof."

"Are you planning on helping or jawing?"

"Pardon me?"

"We have a lot of work to do here, mister. Whoever you are and whatever you've done in the past, you may as well get busy as stand here trying to entertain one who needs no entertaining."

Matt turned to Bear in surprise, but the big man had moved away. Matt pressed his lips together and walked over to the other side of the building. A couple of workers were already on the roof, ripping off the old shingles, which rained down in rapid succession to the flowerbeds below.

"You knuckleheads are ruining Annaliese's flowers," shouted Morris Craddock, following Matt.

"We'll clean it up as soon as they're done," said Bob Rampole, who had sauntered over beside them.

Craddock hollered something else but no one paid attention.

"Don't listen to old man Craddock," whispered Rampole. "He whines like a saw blade and his words are as sharp. What brings you to Happenstance?"

"Just passing through," Matt said again. "Nice place."

Rampole grinned. "I stopped by for a tank of gas—that was twenty-five years ago. Just never got back on the main road, you know? Nice of you to help out today. You working up or down?"

"I'm good with up. I've worked a bit of construction here and there."

"Great. At my age I prefer good old terra firma beneath my feet." He squinted at Matt. "Does your wife let you wear your hair like that or do you have to sneak out and do it later?"

Matt fingered his ponytail. "I'm sure my wife wouldn't mind, if I had one."

"Hmm. Well, good for you. Did you bring tools?"

"No. I'll have to borrow."

"Here you go," said Rampole, handing him a brand-new ripper. "I'll start picking up these shingles before old man Craddock bursts a blood vessel."

"Thanks. Talk to you later." Matt climbed a ladder and began to work.

The crew finished stripping off old shingles in short order and began applying tarpaper and new shingles. By noon they were ready for a break. The minister, introduced as Reverend Otto Selig, raised his hands and blessed the food. His wife Annaliese, and Maisie McDonald, served sandwiches and fresh veggies. Maisie had stopped by on her lunch hour, bearing fresh doughnuts from the bakery.

"Bless you, darlin'," said her husband Donald. "How'd you know I was hungering for a fresh chocolate glaze?" He grabbed her and kissed her full on the lips, to the entertainment of the rest of the crew. Some whistled, others called for more. Old man Craddock huffed and turned away, mumbling about loose morals.

"Give 'em a break, Morris," said Bob Rampole. "They've been married ten years."

Laughter floated through the group, and Matt felt more at home than he had in a month of Reedport Sundays. If he could avoid answering their questions, he could stay a bit longer.

In the afternoon, the men got to work with their air-nailers. Soon row upon row of new, green Weather-Alls covered the parsonage roof. By late afternoon, most of the men had to leave for one reason or another: Mr. Alkmaar, whose first name was Jerry, had to milk his cows; Karl Collins needed to check in at the realty office; Donald McDonald had to go home to the kids until his Maisie finished work; and Morris Craddock was exhausted from a long day of giving orders no one followed.

"You look done in, Mr. Smith," said Emmaline when he arrived for dinner. "Did they work you too hard?"

"No." Matt eased into a chair and flexed his fingers. "I'm not used to handling a ripper all day or climbing up and down a ladder."

"Well, you relax and eat some of Johanna's fine cuisine, and you'll feel much better. Did they feed you over there?"

"They sure did. Too much. Nice group of people."

Three plates waited to be claimed. "Is Miss Wilkinson not coming?"

The sisters glanced at each other, smiles in their eyes, and Emmaline answered. "Not tonight, dear. Miss Wilkinson won't be back until tomorrow; she had to make a business trip, you know. She works for Karl Collins at the realty office. I'm sure the two of you will get along well." She smiled again.

Great. Matchmakers. "I don't suppose I'll be here long enough to get to know her. I had planned to leave tomorrow, but I may stay over the weekend. Come Monday, I'm off."

Emmaline's brow furrowed, but Grayce smiled serenely and offered him another roll.

Matt's legs ached after the day's work clinging to the roof like a monkey, but he knew he needed a bit of a walk to loosen up before going to bed. He took a stroll around the hotel grounds, retired early and slept through the night.

Mid-morning Matt headed over to the Waldorf for a coffee. The place was empty. He grabbed a copy of the day's paper, hot off the press, still smelling of ink, and took it to his booth.

Having run out of headlines and ads before he ran out of coffee, he started in on the gossip column written by Belvina Rampole. Must be Bob's wife. As he scanned the column, his eyes widened to find his own name there.

Newcomer, Mr. Matthew Smith, currently residing at Happenstance Hotel, has been seen hiking in Lakeview Forest and riding his loud motorcycle around the town square. When not keeping villagers awake and alert, Mr. Smith has been looking for a certain young woman who is also staying at the H hotel ...

"What?" Matt threw down the paper in disgust. He could almost hear the buzz around town. Everyone would be talking about his alleged romantic interests. "Aagghh!" What a disastrous way to begin a quiet stay.

Phil came trotting out of the kitchen, grabbing the carafe as he rounded the corner of the counter. "I'm sorry, Matt. I forgot how quickly coffee cools."

"No, no," Matt assured him. "It's not that."

"Then what?"

Matt nodded his head in the direction of the now-abandoned newspaper. "That thing says I'm spending my spare time out chasing some woman."

"Better one than many. I doubt our citizens would approve of that. One woman, however, is romantic."

"I have not been chasing anyone. I admit, I am curious about Miss Wilkinson because although we are both staying at the hotel, we have not met, but I'm not at all romantically inclined nor so desperate that I need to chase unknown women."

"Perhaps you should have more coffee. You look somewhat frazzled. Myself, I find the heat does it to me."

Two women entered the café then, a slim woman whose long red curls hid her face as she talked on her cellphone, and an overweight woman of about sixty. The older one wore her bottle-blonde hair piled up on her head, and sported a too-tight pink track suit. She smiled and fluttered as she caught Matt's eye. He nodded and looked away. If anyone knew he had acknowledged this woman, there would be another article in Belvina's column. He'd better leave the café before he did something else newsworthy. Better yet, he should pack his bags and leave Happenstance. Nothing held him here. He would get out, go over the bridge and never look back.

The women picked a skinny pink table in the middle of the room and balanced themselves on the pink vinyl seats. The large woman's lavish form hid her chair from view. Matt hoped it would hold her weight, at least until he left. The other woman sat with her back to Matt, her cellphone still tight to her ear.

Phil shot Matt a glance as he greeted the women. "Good morning, ladies."

"Good morning, Mr. Philatopoulos," said the large woman, as he poured their coffees.

"Anything else today? More cream, Belvina?"

Matt did a double take. Belvina? Belvina Rampole? If he didn't leave here at once, he would strangle her with his own hands and someone else would have to write it up in *The Village Voice*. Leaving his change on the table, he ducked past the women as they buried their heads in their menus.

When Matt appeared at the hotel for dinner that evening, the ladies waited for him in the dining room. There were four places set.

He nodded. "Ladies."

"Mr. Smith. How was your coffee?"

"The coffee was good. The article in *The Village Voice* was scandalous."

"We don't have a lot of news, Mr. Smith," said Emmaline. "I'm sure your arrival has piqued the interest of many. Why I was talking with Belvina just yesterday and she said—"

"Emmaline, I'm sure Mr. Smith doesn't want to know everything you and Mrs. Rampole discussed. As soon as Miss Wilkinson arrives, we will be served."

"You mean the woman I've never seen but apparently stalk all over the park? The fabled—"

As a woman entered the room, Matt shot to his feet, his eyes wide, his face pale. "—Miss Wilkinson?"

5

Instead of a stranger, his late wife Ginny approached him, or at least the closest thing to a double he had ever seen. Her mass of spiraling auburn hair, unsuccessfully restrained by a clip, spilled over her shoulders as she advanced toward him. He must be dreaming. No, this woman was taller than Ginny and moved in a deliberate, casual manner.

"Mr. Smith, whatever is the matter? You look as white as a sheet."

Grayce's voice jolted Matt back to the present. He realized he still stood gripping the edge of the table, his mouth hanging open. Taking another look into the woman's face, he saw sea-green eyes, not Ginny's brown ones, and this face was bronzed by the sun, not pale and sprinkled with freckles as Ginny's had been.

He held up his hands, palms out. "I'm okay. I just... you look very much like someone I know...knew."

She smiled. "I hope that's a good thing. You sure you're okay?"

"Yeah. Just déjà vu."

"Let's start over then. You must be Matt Smith. I'm Veronica Wilkinson, but I'd be pleased if you'd call me Roni."

Matt calmed himself. Roni was the woman with Belvina at Phil's that afternoon. He remembered the hair but hadn't seen her face. He reached out to shake her hand. "Pleased to meet you, Roni. Word about town says I've been chasing you around the park."

The Barlow sisters gasped, but Roni let out a hearty

laugh. She pushed her unruly hair back, grabbing it in one hand the way Ginny used to do. Matt denied the fresh ache in his heart and focused on what she was saying.

"I thought you might have left town already, Matt. Mind if we eat while we talk? I'm famished."

Over beef stroganoff and fresh broccoli with creamy cheese sauce, Matt and Roni sat opposite and enjoyed a pleasant conversation with each other and the ladies.

After dinner, Matt and Roni moved to the parlor, while the sisters attended to a bit of business in their office behind the marble counter. They had conspired together after dinner, not quite concurring as to what business they needed to see to. He winced at his sore muscles as he sank into the chair opposite Roni.

"Let me guess. You didn't warm up before the roofing yesterday." Roni kicked off her shoes and crossed her ankles on a tasseled foot stool.

"How does one warm up for a roofing?"

"You should come to our exercise classes." The smile on her face told him she was joking. "A few stretches always ease the muscles. You are welcome to come, but I need to tell you there are no other men at present."

"And I'd look terrible in a leotard and tutu."

Roni's laughter sparkled into his soul, devastating his attempt to focus.

"We do not wear tutus, but yes, you would look terrible." She wiped a laugh-tear from her eye and set her empty dessert dish on the low table between them.

Matt smiled, his eyes sweeping over her face, her hair. "I'll remember your advice the next time I take part in a roofing bee."

Roni chuckled. "Only in Happenstance. So, what brings you to our fair town?" She watched him from behind a tumble of fiery curls.

"That is the first question in this place, isn't it?"

"I guess I've fallen in with the locals."

"To be honest, I'm just passing through. I've already stayed longer than I'd planned. No, let me rephrase that: I did not intend to come here at all. I didn't even know *here* existed."

"I know, right? But I felt at home almost as soon as I arrived. There's something welcoming about this place." She sat back against the cushions and pulled her legs up under her.

"I'll tell you one thing that isn't welcoming," said Matt, hands clasped behind his head, "and that's the gossip column in *The Village Voice*."

Roni rolled her eyes. "Dear Belvina. She means no harm, and you and I know there's nothing to the rumor."

"You refer to it as a rumor, but once people see it in print, they consider it fact. Do you realize how many people believe those so-called newspapers at the check-out aisles of grocery stores? People are gullible. They'll believe anything."

Roni tilted her head and observed him. "So why do you care what anyone thinks? You're just passing through. There's no reason for you to respond with such intensity to a bit of meaningless gossip."

Matt stared back. His chin came up. "Some people go a long way on what they call meaningless gossip. Over time it becomes malicious. It's an observation."

She toyed with her bracelet. "I'll give you some people, but not Belvina. She's a kind-hearted woman with a vivid imagination. She lacks confidence and she's lonely. Bob's always busy with some project or other and she needs something to occupy her time. She would never harm anyone on purpose, and I'm sure she would be chagrined if she knew how her words had offended you."

"Yeah, whatever."

"You're cynical." Her eyes held compassion. "What made you that way?"

"Nosy people," he said with a faint smile.

"Touché."

They settled into silence. After a while Roni said, "I don't suppose I can ask you how long you're staying."

"You could, but I have no idea." Matt leaned back into the cushions. "Maybe a couple more days. It's relaxing here." He didn't understand why he kept extending his visit.

"Don't I know it." She stood, picked up her discarded shoes, and smiled down at him. "Take your time and enjoy the journey. It's nice to have someone nearer my age here at the hotel to talk to. The ladies are a bit dotty."

Matt stood with her. "Do you think? I find them endearing."

"I'm sure you're right. Well, I need to do some reading and get my beauty sleep. Good night."

"Good night. Thanks for the visit." He picked up the dessert dishes and took them to the deserted kitchen.

Slouching into the deck chair on his section of verandah, he stared out at the stars. He could feel the blood vessels at the base of his neck contracting as a dull pain spread across his skull. How would he manage to relax enough to fall asleep? It wasn't every day you saw your late wife walk through the door. He had to get a handle on this. She wasn't Ginny.

6

A light knock woke Matt. He sat up to sunlight streaming through his window. His headache reminded him of a fitful night.

The knock came again.

"Yes?"

"Mr. Smith, are you coming to breakfast? We are waiting for you." Grayce's voice barely penetrated the oak-paneled door.

Oh man, he'd really slept in. "I'm sorry, Miss Grayce. Please start without me. I'll have a cup of coffee and a piece of toast later."

After a pause, she answered, "Very well."

Matt couldn't believe the lousy night he'd had. Even after such a relaxing visit with Roni, all he could think about was her likeness to Ginny.

Pull yourself together, Sadler. He rubbed his face and shuffled into the bathroom for a wake-up shower. He watched the soapsuds slide down the shower walls and disappear into the drain and wished he could wash away his confusion with such ease. He decided to go for a good long ride on the Harley after breakfast.

When Matt walked into the dining room, Roni and the Barlows were still sipping their coffee. Misses Grayce and Emmaline looked at him with concern. Roni brightened at his entrance.

"Well, sleepyhead, it's about time you got up."

His heart hammered in his throat again at the sight of her,

but he managed to bid good morning all around.

"The ladies invited us to attend church with them this morning," said Roni. "I mentioned the plans we made last evening to go for a guided tour of the park."

Matt frowned and tried to read her eyes, but she gave no hint. What was she up to? Had he missed something in his mental fog?

"I'm sorry." He turned to Grayce and Emmaline. "Perhaps we can go with you another time."

"We would like that," said Emmaline, but he read disappointment on her face.

Roni winked at him.

"Good jelly," he raised his last bite of toast in a salute to the kitchen.

Grayce gave her sister an I-told-you-so glance and Emmaline raised her chin. "I made the jelly. Sometimes I feel the need to create something nutritious and delicious. The apples are from our own trees behind the house. We have the best apples, even better than those from the grove on the south side of town."

"Some people think the south orchard apples superior in quality, Emm."

"Well, they're wrong then, aren't they?"

Matt smiled in spite of himself. "Thank you for breakfast. I guess we're off to the park. See you at dinner."

Roni rose as well and caught up with Matt in the hallway. "Matt, I hope you're not mad at me for that."

"You caught me off guard. At my age, I'm used to making my own decisions."

"Sorry. Are we on for a hike around the park or shall I find another companion?"

"Let's do it." He couldn't refuse to spend time with her. He hoped he'd remember to call her Roni and not Ginny.

An hour later, Matt and Roni pedaled through town on two antiquated bicycles ferreted from the chaos of the shed hidden on the west side of the hotel. Matt guessed the bicycles had last been checked over by Emmaline's late husband, Bruce, thirty years before. All the tires were flat, but a bicycle pump hung on a nail on the wall. Matt made use of it and they were on their way.

They turned north up Parkview Drive. Roni smiled at him, her eyes hidden by dark glasses. "It's such a gorgeous day, I couldn't imagine sitting in that cold stone building listening to a doddering old man preach a boring sermon."

Matt remembered the little country church he had attended with his grandparents, a small white clapboard structure with neither steeple nor bell tower. The tall stained-glass windows had created a mosaic of the sunlight as it slanted into the sanctuary.

He had sat near the front with his friends, in easy view of his grandparents. He hadn't always paid attention, but he never created trouble, as some of the others had. He remembered Bobby Chimmers counting out M&Ms for his friends and dropping the box. The contents spilled and rolled, scattering the attention of the congregation. Gramps questioned him about his part in it later, but when he said he hadn't been involved, Gramps believed him. Gramps and Amma always trusted him to tell the truth, and he didn't want to disappoint them.

Maybe that was why it had been such a shock to realize the whole school and then the entire town of Reedport labeled him a liar. The actual accusation was more damning to his career, but the lack of trust hurt him more. He'd never been able to adjust to their misplaced sense of justice. He wished he could go back and do everything differently—not that he'd done anything wrong. No one could accuse him of misconduct.

No, he hadn't wanted to go to church this morning. The church in Reedport had given the most disappointing response to his professional catastrophe; they believed the rumors instead of him. He had to admit, though, they were supportive earlier, when Ginny became ill. Church folks were great comforters in times of sickness and death, but give them financial ruin or marriage problems or a besmirched reputation, either real or rumored, and they fell all over themselves, clucking their tongues and tripping over judgmentalism. He didn't want to set himself up again.

"Does your silence mean you'd rather be in church, Matt?"

"Nope."

She swerved to avoid a pothole. "I don't need church. I get along fine on my own. I think that's the key to life anyway: do the best with what you have because you're the only person you can count on."

"Sounds like cynicism to me."

"Not cynicism; realism. That's how you survive in this world."

"Dog eat dog, right?"

"Pretty much. So where do you come from, anyway?"

Here we go again. "Couple day's ride up the road."

"Sorry, I won't ask that again. Are you single, or do you have someone waiting somewhere?"

He looked over at her, but she was smiling into the breeze.

"Single."

She looked over at him and shook her head. "Let me guess. She left, and took you for all you're worth, and now you're bitter."

He kept pedaling and forced the words out from between clenched teeth. "She died."

Roni remained silent a few moments. "I'm sorry, that was tactless of me."

"Whatever. It's been a long time."

"Guess I am a bit cynical. I've always fought my own battles. No one ever stuck up for me, so I decided not to count on anyone."

"Once bitten?"

"Something like that. But let's not spoil a great day with negative thoughts. We're here to enjoy and relax."

They pulled into the parking lot and left their bicycles leaning against the rough rail fence. Matt shouldered the food pack and Roni draped her camera and binoculars around her neck.

"I wonder where we'll find our self-appointed park warden, Sandy."

Matt forged ahead. "We won't find him, he'll find us when we least expect it. Stop looking for him." He put a finger to his lips.

"Matt Smith," said Roni in a stage whisper, "I swear there's a sense of humor in you somewhere. Relax and let it out. I won't ask any more deep questions."

"We are going to suffer tomorrow," said Roni as they dismounted their bicycles and pushed them back toward the shed, "but what a great day."

"Sandy may have annoying manners, but he's an excellent guide," returned Matt, closing the door of the shed and heading up the steps to the hotel.

"And what a sense of humor. He makes me laugh every time I meet him. You could take a lesson." She glanced at him from the corner of her eyes.

He frowned. "What, and spoil my reputation?"

"Matt, you are teasing behind that frown."

"Well, I'm famished, and that's the truth. Meet you in the dining room in half an hour."

She saluted and trudged up the staircase. "If I make it to the shower."

Matt went to his room next to the chapel. A shower would feel like heaven right now, followed by a good meal and time to read before bed. A simple life. Just what he'd been looking for.

He entered the dining room ahead of schedule to find six places set. Six? He heard the Barlow sisters greeting people at the front entrance and heard them all approach the dining room.

"Mr. Smith, we were sorry you missed meeting Reverend Selig in church this morning, so we invited him and his wife to dinner. Now we can all visit together."

Bingo. The Hound of Heaven is after me again.

"Nice to see you again," said Matt. He cast a glance at Roni as she walked into the room. She smiled and greeted them too, but he sensed her heart wasn't in it.

"Thank you for all your help at the roofing bee," said the reverend. "I'm sorry I wasn't able to add much to the effort. My dear wife won't allow it."

Annaliese reminded Matt of his grandmother. When they were introduced, she reached up and patted his cheek. Just like Amma had often done.

"My Otto, he cannot anymore work hard with his hands.

37

Is his artritis, you know?"

Reverend Selig shrugged. "Annaliese knew if I showed up at the site I'd end up helping anyway, so she locked me in my study."

"The study door has not a lock, Otto. I ask you please to stay from the outside work away, this iss what happens."

He smiled at his wife, and Grayce ushered everyone to a chair. Their pleasant conversation as they ate complemented Johanna's creative cuisine.

"Miss Emmaline tells me you have been enjoying the beauty of the park," said the reverend when the meal was over.

"We have," answered Matt. "Roni and I just returned from there."

"Yes," concurred Roni, "and I must excuse myself. I'm beat."

Matt's eyes followed her out of the room. He had to force himself to concentrate on the conversation.

"Have you met the infamous Professor Fitzpatrick?" Reverend Selig asked after Roni had gone.

"Sandy? Oh yes, and he's unique. Have you ever been the victim of one of his sudden appearances?"

Selig chuckled. "He is a character."

"Mysterious he iss," twinkled Annaliese. "You not can know from where he next pops up."

The similarity between the Seligs and his grandparents wrapped Matt in bittersweet nostalgia. *She's as sweet as Amma's cinnamon buns, and he is anything but doddering.* Again, the strong sense of memory rose to overwhelm him. What was it about this place?

Later, Matt settled into the deck chair on his verandah to read the *Happenstance History* he had picked up from the local library and was soon engrossed in its pages. He propped his feet on the railing where the paint had peeled. Happenstance had not been a boring town in the old days, but a bustling community dealing with issues of political and economic significance. The inhabitants of the town had varied from poor farmers and trappers to businessmen and entrepreneurs like the Barlow family, who had amassed their fortune in import and export.

Matt recognized a certain latent aristocracy in the sisters. Now he knew where it came from. He marked his place in the book and went inside, weary of slapping insects. He glanced at his wristwatch. Almost midnight. He crawled into bed and slept all night without waking.

Next morning, Matt felt more rested than he had in a long time, but for the muscles exercised riding and hiking the day before. He decided to take a spin on his motorbike after he had eaten something. It might keep him from seizing up entirely.

Roni didn't show up for breakfast. He assumed she either had an early morning at work or couldn't get out of bed after their hike yesterday. In spite of his wish to maintain a safe distance from everyone, he had given her a place in his thoughts, and his heart had taken steps beyond his control. He reminded himself she was not Ginny. He needed to think of something else.

He was eager to talk with the ladies about the *Happenstance History* he'd read last night.

"Your history is amazing," he said to Misses Grayce and Emmaline once the breakfast blessing was given.

"Well!" said Grayce in return. "I realize my sister and I are aging, but we are not as yet historic figures."

Matt's mouth tilted. "Not the two of you. I mean Happenstance. I borrowed a book from Mrs. Phipps at the library and read more than half of it last night after the Seligs left."

"Oh, I see. That's better then."

"The book said this hotel used to be Barlow Manor. When did it become Happenstance Hotel?"

Emmaline opened her mouth but Grayce spoke first. "It was a matter of expediency, my dear Mr. Smith. Hard times come upon us all in this life."

Emmaline took her opportunity when Grayce stopped for breath. "It was the crash of '29, you know. Papa had imported a large shipment of goods from Italy, but then no one could afford to buy anything, as you know, but the exporters demanded payment. Papa was never the same after that. Mama worried about his health, but even Prohibition didn't keep him from drifting to alcohol for—"

"Emmaline! We do not speak of our family's vices in public." Grayce turned to Matt. "Suffice it to say our father lost his fortune with the stock market crash. He died soon after, and Mother was left to devise a way to keep body and soul together for her family. She chose to rent out rooms in our home. There are certainly enough of them."

Ah, he drank himself to death and left his young wife to deal with the consequences of his actions. Matt wondered how the community and the church had reacted to that ultimate faux pas. "It must have been difficult for you all."

"One does what one must. Difficult times require strong faith and character. Our mother had both."

"And passed them on to her daughters. Were there other children?"

"No, just Emmaline and me."

Emmaline ventured to re-enter the conversation with a glance at Grayce. "I was two years of age when our papa passed away. Graycie was five. What we know we learned from Mama. She worked hard to make sure the hotel ran well and we had what we needed. Our grandparents—Papa's parents— lived with us and helped where they could."

Grayce took up the baton. "Emmaline and I assumed operation of the hotel when Mother fell ill with tuberculosis in the fifties. She recovered and lived here with us until she died in 1993."

"Yes," laughed Emmaline. "She was 88 and still bossing us around—never mind telling me off, Graycie, I'll speak my mind. You're just like Mama, always telling me what I can say and what I can't."

"Don't start, Emm, you know it's bad manners. I'm sure Mr. Smith doesn't wish to hear us quibble."

Matt was about to say he enjoyed it, but he desisted in the name of propriety. It was a catchy thing, propriety. It suited the sisters and the hotel, and Happenstance itself. Perhaps one acquired it with time. Whatever the case, he wouldn't be here long enough to assimilate much of it himself. The thought saddened him. He fought the urge to care about the Barlows, little girls grown up without a father. He had been a potential father who had never had his own children.

What is with you, Sadler? Snap out of it.

"I'm going for a ride on my motorbike. I'll be back for dinner and then I want to finish reading the book. I plan to leave tomorrow."

"We're sorry to hear you are planning to leave. Are you taking Miss Wilkinson on your motorcycle ride?"

"No, ma'am. I haven't seen her today and I don't even know if she likes bikes."

Concern etched itself in Emmaline's features, but she smiled and bid Matt a good day. As he walked down the hall to his room he heard her voice behind him: "If I were twenty years younger, I'd join him. I would ride a motorbike."

"Fiddle, you would! Twenty years? You'd better make that forty. You wouldn't have been able to manage it."

Matt shook his head, a slight smile playing at his lips, as the conversation rose and fell behind him.

Matt retrieved his helmet from his room, eager for a good ride. He hit the steps in anticipation of the wind in his face. Time for a spin to blow out the cobwebs.

He idled into Beresford Gas Station for a fill-up and found Bear half hidden in the bowels of a truck engine. He revved the Harley and Bear popped up, bumping his head on the raised hood of the old pickup.

"Dang!"

"Sorry, man."

Bear broke into a grin at the sight of Matt. "No worries," he said, rubbing his head. "I was wonderin' when I'd get me another look at that bike of yours."

"Here she is. What's the matter with that truck?"

"It's the wrong make, that's whatsa matter. Won't start. Can't even get the darn glow plugs to work. It'll turn over, but there's not enough juice to start her."

"Diesel?"

"Yup. Usually a good thing, but sometimes you get a lemon. Then you might as well make orange juice."

"Lemonade."

"Whatsat?"

"When life hands you a lemon, you might as well make

lemonade."

"Words of wisdom, Matt, words of wisdom. Where you headin' today?" They walked over to the gas pumps and Bear topped up the tank of the Harley.

Matt adjusted his helmet. "I'm not sure. I need to unleash the fury, you know?"

Bear squinted at him against the sun. "Yup. Every once in a while a man's gotta do that." He hung up the nozzle and replaced the gas cap. "Good road north of town. Follow Parkview 'til you meet the 85. It's a two-lane road, but it winds through the trees real pretty and there ain't much traffic."

"I thought you couldn't get out of town except by crossing the bridge."

"Well, not if you wanna get back on the main highway. If you're lookin' for a nice jaunt up the road, then the 85 is the ticket."

Matt's curiosity got the better of him. "How far does it go?"

"How far does what go?"

"Highway 85."

"It curves east toward Oblivion Point."

Matt let out a laugh, then realized Bear was serious. "Oblivion Point. Right. Well, I'm off to the great unknown." He climbed aboard his bike. "Any gas stations on the 85?"

"Coupla small ones. Just gas, no mechanic, no food."

Matt headed north and then east. He would carry on at least as far as Oblivion Point, maybe ramp off the edge of the world.

He had ridden a couple of hours when he stopped for gas. He remembered how Ginny used to grab the squeegee and clean the windshield while he filled up the gas tank. Then she'd run into the station washroom while he paid and be ready to take off again, her arms tight around his waist as they leaned into the corners. She'd loved cornering, although she'd never driven the bike. She lacked a sense of balance. Besides, the bike was way too big for her. That was okay with Matt; he liked her behind him. After a while she'd sit back and lean on one armrest so she could see past his helmet. He'd found the armrests at a salvage yard and installed them himself. She flipped one up to dismount and snapped it down again as a bit of security when she rode....

Why was he thinking of Ginny again? Ever since he'd come to Happenstance, ever since he'd met Roni.... He grabbed the squeegee and cleaned the windshield with vigor, then jammed on his sunglasses and roared back onto the road, wondering if Roni liked bikes.

The tour down Highway 85 had cleared his head, leaving him with a fresh perspective. He'd enjoy Roni's company this evening, then head off into the wild blue who-knows-where in the morning. He knew he'd have to go back to Reedport at some time to see the whole thing through before the new school year began, but he dreaded that. There was time to postpone the return for a while.

The bike started misfiring on the way back to Happenstance and slowed to forty miles per hour, then worked up again to sixty. He breathed a sigh of relief until it happened again a few miles up the road. He hoped it was just dirty gas, but motorcycles tended to be finicky things, no matter how tough they looked. He relaxed as he putted back into town.

Funny how all roads led to the town he had never heard of less than a week ago. He stopped for a coffee and Danish at the Waldorf Café before heading back to the hotel. Bear had been right about two things anyway: the gas stations on the 85 did not offer food, and the highway ended at Oblivion Point. It ran up to a T intersection and then the 752 continued east and west. Kind of like his life: *Dead end. Whatcha gonna do now, Sadler?* Jim had told him to be back when school started again after summer vacation, but he didn't want to work in that environment anymore.

The idea of getting to know Roni stirred in his mind like the cream in his coffee. He had come here without meaning to; maybe he should hang around a bit and see what transpired. On the other hand, maybe he should pack his bags tomorrow and leave as planned before something bad happened. That seemed to be the pattern for his life.

Besides, this look-alike thing with Roni and Ginny was playing with his mind. His relationship with Ginny could never be recreated. Nothing could be that sweet. At least he didn't think so.

Yeah, he'd pack his bags and leave this surreal place called Happenstance and continue on the main road away from Reedport. It had been a good, if brief, respite from the world.

7

After finishing his coffee, Matt climbed on the Harley and turned the key. He back-walked out of the parking spot and started the engine. The bike revved and sputtered, revved and sputtered, sputtered and died. Perplexed, he backed it closer to the sidewalk again, told Phil why it was there, and hoofed it to the hotel.

The lobby was as deserted as it had been the day he arrived. The lemon tree still stood at attention.

He leaned over the counter and found the number for Beresford Gas Station on a *List of Important Numbers* beside the phone. He dialed, drumming his fingers on the black marble. The phone rang four times before an answering machine picked up.

Beresford Gas Station, Gavin Beresford here. Well, I ain't ackshully here. I'm prob'ly under the hood of some vehicle. Please leave a message and I'll call you back soon as I can. Beeeep.

Matt left a message. He hoped Bear checked his voice mail once in a while. It was almost quitting time. His plans for leaving might have to be adjusted. With a sigh of resignation, he hung up the phone and went to his room.

Matt thought he heard voices and followed the sound out his verandah door. The Misses Barlow sat in worn canvas lounge chairs under a large, tattered umbrella on the lawn, engaged in what appeared to be a serious conference. He decided this was as good a time as any to tell them he was leaving. As he approached, they shared a look and turned as one to greet him.

"Mr. Smith. We were just talking about you. Do join us." Grayce indicated a chair across the table from her.

"We like to get to know our guests," said Emmaline. "Tell us something about yourself."

Matt sat back and tried to hide his irritation. "Not much to tell. I'm on a leave of absence. I wanted a change of scenery and time to relax."

"And do you find our establishment relaxing, Mr. Smith?"

Matt wondered how to describe his experience here. "The suite is comfortable, the food is excellent, and I enjoy your company. This place is interesting, if a little strange, but I'm afraid I won't be around to figure out why. I'm planning to leave in a day or two."

Emmaline sat forward in her chair. "Have we done something to offend you? Have I asked too many questions?"

"No, it's nothing anyone has done. I didn't plan to stop here in the first place. I need to carry on, but it's been a nice break."

"We've come to enjoy your presence with us," said Grayce. "When do you plan to leave?"

"I had thought tomorrow morning, but my bike won't start and I can't get hold of Bear. I'm stuck until I get my wheels back."

"Oh dear," said Emmaline. "I thought since Miss Wilkinson was here—someone closer to your own age—you'd be content to stay longer."

Matt caught the twinkle in Emmaline's eyes. He fingered his ponytail. Lately he'd felt older than what his driver's license stated. Forty was frightening, but after that, man, you were aiming at fifty.

"Roni's nice to visit with, but I'm not looking for romance." The twinkle disappeared like a faint star. Matt hated to disappoint Emmaline, but he didn't fancy a full-figured, silver-haired cupid fluttering around him, flinging arrows indiscriminately.

"Don't you ever wish to marry, Mr. Smith?" she asked,

innocence in her eyes.

Grayce frowned at her sister and Matt sighed. "Like you, Mrs. Osmer, I have loved and I have lost. I'm not looking for a replacement. Besides, I'll be leaving any day. A companionable friendship however, would be acceptable."

"I'm sorry to hear of your loss, Mr. Smith. If it isn't too forward of me to ask, how long have you been alone?"

"Ginny died about five years ago." He clasped his hands on the table in front of him as Ginny's angel face materialized in his mind. He wanted to reach out and stroke her hair, touch the tip of her turned-up nose. Funny how the memories grabbed you without warning at the least appropriate times.

Emmaline dabbed her face with her embroidered hanky, and Grayce's discerning eyes reflected sympathy in their crystal blue depths. She leaned forward and placed her hand on his arm. "My dear Mr. Smith, please accept our condolences."

"Call me Matt. Mr. Smith sounds way too formal."

Emmaline twinkled again. "Oh, we couldn't. But perhaps Matthew would be acceptable."

He chuckled in spite of himself. "That would be fine."

"Well then, Matthew," smiled Emmaline, "I must see how Johanna is doing with dinner. Thank you for the visit."

Grayce rose to follow her sister. She stopped beside Matt's chair and patted his shoulder. "Time heals all wounds, Mr. Smith." He watched her sweep across the lawn toward the house and wondered what sorrows her life had held. Would she still be on his side if she knew what had happened in Reedport? He hoped she would—and if Grayce was, Emmaline would be also—but he had no intention of revealing that secret.

Matt couldn't stand the thought of sitting in his room alone after dinner. Since Roni was busy with her exercise class and the ladies were playing bridge, he pulled on a light jacket and strolled over to the Waldorf. Maybe he'd meet someone there who would help him forget his sorry life. He'd never been one to drown his sorrows in alcohol, but strong coffee would help.

"Matt, come on over here." Donald McDonald waved from a corner where he and Maisie shared a booth with Gavin Beresford and Bob Rampole.

Matt sauntered over and pulled up a chair at the end of the booth.

"Hey. Good to see you!" said Donald with his usual heartiness.

"And you. Say, Bear, did you get my message?"

"Yeah, your Harley ain't firing right. Nearly tripped over it on the way in here." He grinned. "I'll take a look at it first thing tomorrow."

"Thanks, man." Matt noticed Maisie leaning into Donald. "Who's looking after your kids tonight?"

"Cydnee. They love her."

"You're kidding. She doesn't look like the babysitter type."

"Oh, she is. She has brains, too," said Donald. "She hides them so kids at school don't make fun of her."

"Why would kids make fun of her for bein' smart?" asked Bear. "Seems like somethin' you'd be proud of."

"Been to a high school lately?" asked Matt. "It's not cool to be too smart."

"Geez, I shoulda postponed my education a few decades. I'da fit right in."

"So, what are you folks up to tonight?" asked Matt.

"This is as close to a party as you can find in Happenstance on a Monday night, eh, Bob?"

"Yeah-up. Used to have the occasional dance at the Orchard Grove, but that's all closed down now."

"Where was that?"

"Over behind Harold's. Nice little restaurant with a horsehair dance floor. You don't see anything like that anymore."

"Horsehair?"

"Under the hardwood. Yeah-up. Lotta short-tailed horses there for a spell." Bob snorted at his own joke.

Matt ordered a latte and leaned back in the chair. "Where do you folks eat when you don't want to eat at home?"

"Well," said Maisie, lowering her voice and glancing toward the kitchen, "if you want Italian, there's Wong's over on the west side of town." She cut a piece of chocolate swirl cheesecake with her fork.

"And pizza," said Bob. "Wong's has great pizza, and they deliver. They have Chinese, too."

"The best place was The Orchard Grove, though," said Maisie, as Donald and Bob rolled their eyes. "It's back in the apple orchard near the river. Very classy—"

"—and expensive," finished Donald. "You can leave a good-sized roll of cash if you have drinks and all."

Maisie ignored him. "They had live entertainment on weekends. Sometimes it was a pianist or a sax player, or a classical guitarist. And sometimes a band so you could dance."

Donald hooted. "You mean *you* could dance. I can't dance, my lady, not even to please you."

"You could take lessons."

"Do I have to, love?"

She smiled and patted his cheek. "Not if you don't want to, darling, but I do love to dance. Do you dance, Matt?"

"I used to."

"What happened?"

"Lost my partner. Haven't tried since."

Maisie leaned across the table and patted his hand, then cozied up to Donald again.

Bob chimed in. "Hey, what did you folks do on the weekend?"

They talked of relaxing and going to church and mowing the lawn. Of spending time with family. Matt told them he planned to hike in the park again the next day while Bear fixed his bike. After the others left, Matt stayed until he saw Phil flip the OPEN sign to CLOSED. The walk in the cool night air cheered him and he managed to fall asleep within minutes.

He dreamed he was sitting in The Orchard Grove with his arm around Ginny—or was it Roni? They rose as one and danced the night away on the horsehair floor until a man resembling Phil, wearing a bright green shirt printed with shiny red apples, flipped the OPEN sign to CLOSED. Then they took the long way home through the orchard, a classical guitarist accompanying them as they walked. Matt threw a wad of bills at the man and he left them alone.

8

When Matt stopped by the Waldorf after his hike the next afternoon, Bob was there drinking coffee and shooting the breeze with Phil. Matt slid into the booth and turned a mug right side up.

"You look somewhat fatigued, my friend," said Phil as he topped up the steaming brew.

"Ahh!" Matt sat back and stretched out his feet under the table. "Just walking in the woods. It's a great place to unwind, you know?"

"You unwinding alone or with someone?"

"No, just me. I like my space."

"None of my business anyways." Bob drained his cup and held it out for more. "I heard that maybe you were spending time with—"

"You are beginning to sound distinctly like your dear wife, Mr. Rampole," said Phil as he poured the coffee. "Anything new from the town council meeting last week?"

Matt appreciated the rescue. Reminders of Belvina caused his blood to boil, and his heart rate hadn't decreased enough yet to risk that.

"Same old, same old. Gotta find somebody to replace Craddock at the high school but he won't quit. Dadblamed stubborn, that's what he is. Can't handle the stress, can't get along with the kids or the other teachers, has to keep taking sick days. I don't know how we'll be able to convince him to retire."

"What's wrong with him?"

"You haven't heard? He has depression. Some days are better than others."

"How long has this been going on?"

Bob took another slurp of java. "Since his wife died. Hasn't been the same since. Nope. Terrible business. There was this accident, see..." Bob pulled up to the table and held his cup with both hands, eyes on his one-man audience. "Morris and Madeleine were headed back from a little jaunt up to Oblivion Point, a Sunday drive, you know. They loved to do that together.

"They were a nice couple. She was always his girlfriend, you know? Well, they're driving along the 85, coming up to the Point when this semi comes from the east and he's signaling, but doesn't slow down at the T intersection. I guess Morris was sure he'd slow down."

Matt sat back with his own coffee between his hands, trying to distance himself from what he imagined was coming.

"So Morris, he thinks the guy's gonna slow down in time to turn. He pulls onto the road in front of him, but the trucker has no intention of turning. Somehow his signal was busted and wouldn't go off by itself, and the truck's loud enough he doesn't hear it. He doesn't expect the car to turn on in front of him because he doesn't know he's signaling.

"Well, Matt, that semi plowed into Craddock's car at a good clip. Lucky they were wearing their seat belts, but they were both still hurt real bad. The car was one of those old Oldsmobiles with the long tail end, that's what saved them at first. Crunched right up to the front seat. Morris, he was hurt pretty bad, legs broken, head injury, internal bleeding, stuff like that. Madeleine fared some better, a concussion and shock."

Matt grimaced, thinking of the bitterness in Morris Craddock's words at the roofing bee and remembering his grandfather's words: "Don't judge; you never know everything about a person."

Bob continued. "They'd both been in the hospital for a week, but Madeleine couldn't seem to pull herself together. They operated on Morris and he started to stabilize, but Madeleine just up and died one night. Surprised everybody, even the doctors. Guess the shock was deeper than they thought. Morris got better physically, but after his wife died, his light went out, you know? Never was the same again. Used to be a good teacher, one the kids respected. After the accident, he was nasty. Yelled at the kids, threw chalk and brushes when he got real mad, stuff like that. And then he started to have these attacks of depression where he can't work. Can't even get up and get dressed. Just stays in bed for days."

Matt imagined why Morris might have chosen the path of least resistance, of giving up.

"Now Matt, I'm as compassionate as the next guy, and I don't wanna kick a guy when he's down, but we can't have somebody like that teaching the kids. It isn't fair to them. Josiah's gonna have a talk with him as soon as he can. Tell you one thing, I'm glad it isn't me that's gotta tell him to quit."

Matt shook his head. "I feel sorry for him. What's he supposed to do? Now he at least has a purpose when he's feeling well. Quitting might kill him."

Bob pressed his lips together and stared into his cup. "Yeah-up, I know." He glanced at Matt. "Got any suggestions?"

"Not offhand. By the way, who's Josiah?"

"Josiah Wuppertal. Mayor and owner/operator of Wuppertal's General Store."

"Oh. I haven't met him yet."

"Well, you should. Josiah's a good man. So anyway, the next question is: who are we gonna get to fill Morris' place? We don't have any extra instructors. Got a couple of supply teachers, but they don't want full-time."

It was Matt's turn to purse his lips and stare into his cup. What he had done for a living in Reedport was no one's business, and he wasn't looking for a job.

Bob swirled the coffee in his cup, gulped it down and said he had to go. "Nice to see you, Matt."

"Bob."

Matt walked to the counter and picked up a copy of *The Village Voice*. He carried it to his booth, scanning it for his name. To his great relief, it did not appear. Better to know for sure, instead of finding out after everyone else had already seen it.

He sat back in the booth and sipped another cup of coffee, looking for someone with whom to visit, now that he was sure he had not been slandered in the newspaper. Bear hadn't come in this afternoon, at least not when Matt was here. Maybe he was concentrating on finishing the bike job. Donald McDonald was babysitting the kids until he was flown north again to the oil rigs. Bob Rampole was looking for a replacement for Morris Craddock, and Phil was busy ordering supplies at one of the round pink tables, hunched over a long list and checking off items one at a time. Matt thought he might even welcome Morris Craddock, but the man didn't waste time socializing.

Maybe he should wander down to Harold's, but he had nothing to buy. One didn't require an extensive wardrobe to live a casual life in Happenstance. If his bike were in working order, he would hop on and leave Happenstance in the dust. He'd go "over the bridge" for good, destination unknown.

As it was, he was here until the Harley came back to life, and time was way too heavy on his hands. He had been busy in Reedport. Always papers to grade, class projects to evaluate, extra-curricular sports events to organize and attend, and until five years ago, there had been Ginny to come home to.

He was about to leave the café, when the door burst open and Roni breezed in. She spotted him and smiled, and his heart skipped a beat.

"Hi." She slid into the bench opposite him and grabbed a cup. Phil jumped up to pour coffee for her and then resumed his work.

"Thought I might find you here. I'm on my coffee break, so I don't have much time, but I was wondering if you'd give me a hand with something."

"Well, I don't know. I'm kinda busy."

She grinned and swatted his arm. "Don't you even want to know what it is I need help with?"

"Forgive my bad manners. What kind of work do you have for me?"

"I don't need help as much as company. Morris Craddock is selling his house on the south side and I thought you might want to come along with me when I talk to him."

"When did Morris decide to sell? I talked to Bob Rampole a few minutes ago, and he said the guy won't quit his job and they don't know how to break it to him."

Roni raised her finely arched eyebrows. "Hot off the press: Josiah Wuppertal went to see him this morning and after lunch Morris called Karl about listing his house."

"Now you want to feed me to the lions. Do you know what he thinks of me? He believed that trash Belvina wrote about me chasing you around the park, for heaven's sake."

"Matt, Morris thinks the worst of everyone. I happen to know he is a bona fide card-carrying chauvinist and I thought it might help to have a male member of the species with me."

"What about Karl? It's his business."

"He had planned to go himself, but he just called on his cell phone and told me he's been delayed up in Foggy Plain. Couldn't get back in time to talk to Morris."

"And you believed him?"

" 'Tis not mine to question why; he pays my wages."

Matt sighed and frowned. "You sure know how to back a guy into a corner. Okay, let's go."

"Great. The coffee's on me." She left some change on the table and waved to Phil. "My car's at the office."

"Too far to walk from the hotel this morning?"

"I knew I'd have to take it out. Thought it would be easier to have it at work."

He glanced over at her as they climbed into her VW coupe, her hair corkscrewing this way and that, falling forward to cover half her face. She looked familiar and he liked spending time with her, even if it was to visit Morris Craddock.

Roni started the engine and strains of *Chicago* filled the car. She backed out of the parking spot and pulled into the street heading south around town square while he tried not to stare at her profile. Different, yet similar.

"I thought we'd better get out there before Morris changes his mind."

Roni parked in front of a small cottage, white stucco with green shutters. She knocked on the windowless door and sent Matt a nervous smile. He answered with a thumbs up as Craddock opened the door. Matt put his hands behind his back and let Roni do the talking.

"Good afternoon, Mr. Craddock. I'm Veronica Wilkinson from Paradise Realty and Insurance, and this is Matt Smith." She offered him her hand but he ignored it.

"I know who you are. Brazen woman."

Her face paled, showing the determined line of her lips. "Pardon me, Mr. Craddock, but I would prefer it if we could conduct this interview in a courteous manner. It would be to your benefit, I assure you."

"That why you brought your heavyweight along?"

Matt swallowed his snicker with difficulty. He'd never been called a heavyweight in his life. Ginny had always encouraged him to eat better so he'd gain some weight. He'd put on a bit coming up to forty, but lately he'd needed to cinch in his belt a notch.

"He's along as a witness if we have some paperwork to sign," said Roni. "That saves you the hassle of coming into our office."

"Hassle. What kind of a word is that? The Queen's English is in dire straits these days."

Roni followed him into his kitchen. She took the documents out of her briefcase, laid them on the table and explained the details to Craddock. He listened with occasional incomprehensible mutters.

Matt used the time to glance about the room. The adage, "a place for everything and everything in its place," came to mind. He was sure not even dust dared to touch the furniture. A growing gloominess seeped into his soul as he sat there wondering if this was the kind of future he was headed for. He was relieved to witness Craddock's signature on the contract so they could leave.

"This deserves a reward," Roni said. "How about an iced cappuccino at Phil's?"

"You're the boss, lady. I'm just a witness."

"All right then, Phil's it is. Maybe we could even work in a piece of pie or chocolate cheesecake."

"A little close to dinner, isn't it?"

She hesitated a moment, glancing over her shoulder before pulling into the street. "Spoilsport. But you're right. I do adore Johanna's cooking."

After a brief stop at The Waldorf, Roni dropped Matt off at the hotel and headed back to the office to finish up the paperwork on Craddock's house.

"Ladies," said Roni after dinner, "why don't you have a seat in the parlor and I'll bring your tea."

Emmaline batted her eyes at the unexpected attention and took Matt's arm. Grayce followed, refusing to accept his help and remained silent.

Matt settled them into their favorite chairs. "You are fortunate to have such a caring tenant," he commented.

"Yes, Matthew," said Emmaline. "Miss Wilkinson is good to us. Tea in the evening and even in the afternoon if she's at home. We're fortunate, aren't we, Graycie?"

Her sister sat with her lips pressed into a thin line. "Very fortunate, I'm sure."

Matt wondered that her facial expression negated her words. "Is there a problem, Miss Grayce?"

She glanced up at him, her clear eyes calculating her response. "She does more than we ask for." Grayce smoothed her skirt with a thin hand and added, in a stage whisper, "Not that we weren't managing quite well before."

Matt's eyes darted to Emmaline's face, but she remained unaware of her sister's comments.

Roni walked in with a tray holding two china cups with saucers, and two mugs. Matt reached to help, but she evaded him.

"Just let me set down this tray, Matt. Here you go, Emmaline." She handed her a cup and saucer painted with dainty pink roses. "And for you, Grayce, the periwinkles."

Roni sat and accepted the mug of coffee Matt passed to her.

"My, but this is strange tasting tea," said Emmaline. "Quite strong. Do you like it, Graycie?"

"It's not the same brand as yours, Emmaline," said Roni. "I gave you organic herbal tea. Grayce's is Earl Grey."

"I like Earl Grey, too."

"I'm sure you do, but I thought it might be good for you. Different folks need different kinds of tea."

"I was not aware of that," said Grayce. "Would you care to explain why?"

"Really, Graycie. Don't bite the hand that feeds you."

"I am not even nibbling, Emm. But I want to know the contents of what you're drinking."

"Ladies, please don't argue. I'll be happy to tell you what's in Emmaline's tea. It's an infusion of herbs for relaxation. If you would prefer Earl Grey, I can get you some."

"No, no, dear. Don't trouble yourself. I will get used to this."

After the sisters had finished their tea and retired upstairs to bed, Roni settled back on the sofa and turned her head to look at Matt. "Is your coffee okay, or don't you like that brand either?"

"Easy there, Roni. It's fine. What's with this tea business anyway?" Matt took Roni's empty mug and set it on the tray with the china.

"I suppose it was my fault. I shouldn't have tried to get something by them without preparation. I thought the tea would be good for her. They have given me a pleasant home at a reasonable rate, and I want to give something back, you know?"

"Emmaline seems grateful, but what's with Grayce?"

Roni pursed her lips and looked to the doorway through which the sisters had departed. She turned back to Matt. "I don't know how to say this, and maybe I shouldn't say it at all, because I don't know all the facts."

"Well, now you have me on the hook. Spill it, Roni."

She sighed. "Well, I've been here longer than you have, so you may not have noticed, but Grayce's behavior can be strange at times."

"Strange? Give me a for instance."

"Well, there are inconsistencies in her behavior. At times she seems as clear as a bell, but other times, like tonight, she recedes into herself and offers little by way of conversation, or else her words become sharp."

"I'm sure we all feel that way sometimes."

"Yes, but this is different. I'm worried she may be at the beginning of Alzheimer's or dementia."

"Because she doesn't feel like talking or she snaps at you,

she's got Alzheimer's? Isn't that a bit of an overreaction?"

Roni looked away and dabbed at her eyes. Matt reached over and took her free hand.

"Hey, hold on there. I was just disagreeing; nothing personal."

Roni sniffed, and her attempt at a smile failed. "I guess I've come to care for them over the past six months and I hate to see them going downhill."

"Grayce had a bad day and there's nothing wrong with Emmaline. Instead of worrying about it, why don't you suggest they go to the doctor? Let an expert diagnose the problem, if there is one."

She withdrew her hand and turned to him with frustration on her face. "You don't see what I see. There is something wrong with Emmaline. She has a heart condition and she's overweight. And you've never tried to suggest anything to Grayce Lorraine."

"I don't think I've had the opportunity at this point, no."

"Well, it's a tricky business, let me tell you. She has a suspicious nature, and if she doesn't want to do something, she just won't do it."

"Want me to try?"

This time she smiled at him. "You'd do that, wouldn't you? You are a gentleman. But maybe you're right. Maybe I jumped to conclusions, exaggerated what I saw out of concern. I think we should watch them for a while, not mention it abroad, and see how it progresses."

Matt returned her smile. "Let's. Now promise me you won't worry about it anymore."

"I'll try." She stood and stretched. "I'm tired enough tonight to go right to sleep."

Matt pushed himself off the sofa and joined her in the hallway. "Good night, then. I hope you sleep well."

"Thanks, you too. 'Night."

Matt turned toward his room.

"Matt?"

He stopped and looked back.

"I'm glad you're here."

They stared at each other for several moments before Matt managed to respond.

"Me too. See you tomorrow." As he entered his room, he decided he had meant what he said. Maybe it was a good thing the bike wasn't working. Maybe he'd stay a bit longer, see what happened.

9

"I think I'll take a walk around town later this morning," said Matt to Grayce at breakfast. Emmaline and Roni were in conversation about exercise classes and herbal teas. "I have to see how Bear's doing with my bike, and I need a new ball cap. The classy fedora Harold convinced me to buy leans toward overkill."

"Go to Wuppertals'," said Roni, looking up. "They have everything, and it's cheap."

"Price or quality?"

"Both."

"Josiah Wuppertal does us a great favor by stocking such a variety of items," Grayce pointed out. "Without the General Store, we would be forced to go over the bridge much more often."

"Josiah's the mayor," added Emmaline. "A busy man, but he always takes time to show friendship."

"Thanks for the tip, Miss Emmaline. By the way, I need to do some laundry. Do you have facilities here at the hotel, or is there a laundromat downtown?"

"We have our own facilities," Grayce answered. "In the cellar. But we seldom venture there. Mrs. Friedlund picks up our laundry on Monday mornings."

"There used to be a laundromat in behind Estelle's," said Emmaline, her conversation with Roni on hold, "but it's closed."

"How about I drop off your stuff at Mrs. Friedlund's?" offered Roni.

"I can do my own laundry. Just point me in the right direction and I'll be fine."

"I do not approve of men doing their own laundry," said Grayce.

"In my situation, I've been forced to do the unthinkable."

Emmaline glanced at Grayce, and Grayce frowned back. She sighed and said, "I suppose that would be permissible."

Roni excused herself and left for work, while Matt followed Emmaline. She led him downstairs while Grayce hovered at the door to the basement.

"Just show him the basics, Emm, while I watch the desk. We don't want him stuck down in that dark place any longer than necessary."

"I am quite capable of instructing Matthew as to the use of our laundry machines." They descended the stairs arm in arm, Matt matching his steps to Emmaline's.

"Now, Matthew, here we have our state-of-the-art washing machine."

The washer, resplendent in red, looked archaic to Matt.

"It was brand new when we bought it, you know. Poppy Red was all the rage, along with Avocado Green and Harvest Gold. I think it's lovely. Much more creative than white. Graycie says white is more serviceable, but at the time, she humored me, because I was grieving for my Bruce. I still think of him when I see it."

"And this must be the dryer." Matt decided Emmaline needed a bit of a prod out of her reverie.

"Pardon me? Oh, yes, the dryer. A practical white. We compromised, Graycie and I. *Objet d'art* for me; utilitarian for her."

"Are you almost done down there?" The voice of Grayce trembled down the stairs.

Emmaline gave Matt precise instructions on the workings of the laundry machines and they ascended the stairs together, her arm through his. Grayce stood at the top waiting for them.

"Well, Emmaline, did you get lost on the way to the washer? Let us leave our guest to his laundry."

Matt thanked them and went back to his room to collect his clothes. Since reading the *Happenstance History*, he had acquired a new interest in the hotel. Grayce had told him to make himself at home. He decided to take her up on it. He tucked a flashlight into the laundry bag.

While the ladies were distracted by their favorite game show, Matt ran down the basement stairs with his small sack of laundry. The light switch at the top of the stairs had activated one lonely bulb above the washer and dryer and another beside the stairs. He threw his few items into Emmaline's outrageously-red washer, turned the dial to Quik Wash, low water level, and proceeded to acquaint himself with the basement of Barlow Manor.

The laundry facilities took up the southeast corner of the large stone basement, flanked on the east wall by a set of indoor clothes drying racks about seven feet long, and on the south wall by a narrow folding table.

Matt shined his light toward the stairway and saw again the pantry Emmaline had pointed out to him. He lifted the drop latch and pulled the door open. On three sides, shelves held an array of cans, jars and boxes of edibles. A partition in one corner concealed a cold storage bin the size of a shower stall. He peeked inside and discovered it to be almost empty but for a few unidentifiable vegetables that smelled of decay. Matt heard the whirring of the washer as it spun his clothes.

On the other side of the staircase, two ponderous chest freezers purred as Freon flowed through their metal veins. The lid of the first protested with a squeal as Matt lifted it. Inside, several boxes of meat wrapped in butcher paper lay in the bottom third of the space. The second freezer held baked goods and frozen vegetables. The entire contents of both freezers could have fit into one smaller version with room to spare.

The washing machine ceased its mad spin and settled in to fill with rinse water. Continuing his exploration in the northwest corner of the room, Matt discovered an antique wood/coal stove. It was connected to the outside by a stout stovepipe, which, to Matt's guess, vented near his room one floor above. The warming oven held a variety of dusty jars and utensils.

A wide wooden table sat next to the stove. It was covered by a faded red-and-white-checked tablecloth and several thousand empty egg cartons, nestled one inside the other. A large hairy spider crawled out of one of the cartons, and Matt amended his find to *almost*-empty egg cartons.

He moved along the north wall to a wardrobe standing about seven feet tall. Double doors fronted the unit. He pulled them open. The dim light from behind him illuminated a storm of dust motes, and the accompanying mustiness made him cough.

The washer spun again and finished its cycle with a loud beep. Matt closed the wardrobe doors; he'd have to wait to examine the contents until another time. The strength of his flashlight dimmed, and he switched it off as he moved across the center of the room toward the washer. His eyes had not yet adapted to the darkness and he walked smack into the furnace, which sat like a sentinel in the middle of the dark space. The metal was cool, but the collision created a resounding boom that he was sure could be heard halfway to downtown. He bit his tongue to stop the flow of words that threatened to spill out.

"Are you all right down there, Mr. Smith?" He recognized Grayce's voice.

Matt controlled his snappish response with difficulty. "Physically I am fine, but my psyche has experienced considerable bruising." He located the washer and transferred his clothes to the dryer.

The voice of Miss Grayce was silent for a moment. "Well, come up as soon as you can, dear."

"I'm coming right up."

The sisters squinted at him when he reached the top of the stairs. "Are you all finished?"

"My clothes are in the dryer," Matt answered Grayce's question. "You could use better lighting down there, you know."

"We know," said Emmaline, "but we send our laundry to the cleaners as a rule, so we seldom venture down there, although Miss Wilkinson seems to enjoy doing her laundry in our basement."

"Does she?" The fact surprised him. He thought of her as more the type to send out the laundry if there was an option.

"You never can tell with people." Grayce's simple words

sounded like a warning.

Matt set out on foot around the town square and south down Bridgeway to Beresford Gas Station. He met Bear coming out of his shop.

"Hey, Matt. Howzit goin'?"

"Not bad. What's the latest on my Harley?"

Bear winced. "I got good news and I got bad news. Which do you want first?"

"What's wrong with it?"

"Coils are shot."

"That's not a big job, is it?"

"No, but we might as well change the plugs while we're at it. Gotta keep this shovelhead runnin'. That's the good news."

"What's the bad?"

"I gotta order in the parts. I phoned around. They don't have 'em in Foggy Plain or even in Athens. Gotta get 'em from outta state. Could take a bit."

"A bit?"

"Few days, maybe a week."

Matt blew out his breath. "Great. Guess I won't be leaving for a while then."

"You make it sound like you're ready to ditch this joint. Hurts my feelings."

"Don't be so sensitive. This is a great place to visit, but I have to get on with my life and I'm not accomplishing anything here."

"Your gettin' anxious won't make the parts come any sooner. May as well save your energy for somethin' worthwhile."

"Like what?"

Bear scratched his head and pulled his cap down solid again. His eyes lit up. "Like helpin' the reverend and his wife with their renovatin'. They want to fix up their house but they need help. Asked me, but I never seem to be able to get away."

Matt shrugged. "Maybe I'll talk to them about it if you don't get the bike parts soon. I don't want to start something and then leave in the middle of it."

"Okey doke. I'll let you know what's happening with the

bike soon as somethin' does."

Matt plodded back up Bridgeway toward Wuppertals' lost in thought. *Just call me Mr. Good Fortune. Run off the road by two elderly ladies, forced into a make-believe town, bike breaks down, no parts this side of the Pecos, an invitation to remodel the parsonage, what next? The measles?*

As he approached the General Store, he half expected to see Josiah Wuppertal up on his stepladder, pasting more specials and ads on his already plastered windows. He suspected the "plaster advertising" worked or the mayor wouldn't do it.

Morris Craddock stood scanning the latest deals and Matt snuck into the store, hoping he hadn't been spotted. He didn't want to risk being taken to task for wasting time buying a ball cap when there were more important things to do.

Inside the store, Matt searched for ball caps, but nothing had a definitive department in the old warehouse store. After wandering around for a few minutes, he spotted some women's straw gardening hats hung in behind the hoes and rakes. Perhaps if he looked for baseball gloves and bats he would find the caps.

"Good day to you, Mr. Smith. What can I help you with this morning?"

"Good morning. Mayor Wuppertal?"

"Name's Josiah. The mayor job is something I do because they asked me to." His gnomelike face sparked with personality.

"Josiah it is. Call me Matt." They shook hands. "I'm looking for a ball cap, nothing special, anything to keep the sun off, except bright orange."

"Not bright orange? Not a hunter?" Josiah dodged his way around displays and shelving units to a spot beside the fishing tackle. Matt hurried to catch up, stopping to rescue several soccer balls that had escaped their mesh enclosure. Josiah picked up a gray cap with a leaping fish on the front and handed it to Matt. "Try this one. I got gray, black and red." Josiah disappeared, then reappeared moments later with a yellow cap sporting a leaf insignia on the front, and another dark green one that said *Happenstance—A Town You Can Trust.*

Matt knew which hat he wanted. He pulled the green one onto his head and peered into the full-length mirror outside the change room. "This is great. Just what I was looking for."

"Want to take one of the fishing hats too, in case you misplace the green one?"

"No, this is good, thanks."

"Anything else I can help you with? You need a pair of cargo pants, or the ones where you zip off sections as the day warms up? Good sellers, those." Wuppertal moved about his store at a brisk pace as he talked, always with an eagle eye on the cash register at the front. "I got some new T-shirts in yesterday, all colors. Should be one that matches the hat."

He picked up an olive-green T and handed it to Matt, who winced at the color combination. Ginny would have forbidden it. "No, Josiah, I think I'll just take the hat today."

"Give you a break on the cap if you take the T-shirt too."

Matt shook his head no. "Maybe next time."

"Suit yourself. Five ninety-five plus tax..."

Matt paid for the cap and pulled it on as he walked out the door and down the street. He stopped at the Waldorf for a quick coffee and then at the library to pick up another book. He had finished the Grisham novel and was close to done with *Happenstance History*, and he hated being without a story to distract him.

"I am enjoying the *Happenstance History*, Mrs. Phipps. I had no idea this town was involved during the civil war and temperance."

"You'd never know to look at us," said Earlene Phipps, "but we are an important part of history. I set aside another book for you. It's about trees of the area. I thought you might be interested, with all your wanderings in the park."

Matt eyed her, wondering if she was referring to the alleged incident of him stalking Roni, or just the fact that she had heard he loved to hike. She looked innocent enough as she handed him *Trees of America's North-central States* by Maribelle Knowles.

"This book must be returned in three weeks," she said, "or you're subject to a fine of five cents per day. I hate to charge, but we have to keep our books in circulation. I've stamped the return date on the bookmark inside the front cover. Don't lose it, Mr. Smith."

"I won't, ma'am." Matt bowed his way out of the library and headed home for lunch. Home? Where did that come from? With a shrug, he took the path toward the hotel.

Later that afternoon, Matt slipped down to the cellar to recover his clothes from the dryer. On his way back up the stairs, he met Roni coming down. She froze mid-step, her eyes wide.

"What were you doing down there?"

"Um, laundry. You have a problem with that?"

She flashed him a smile and eased her grip on the handrail.

"No, of course not."

"Good. Laundry seems to be a touchy subject around here. How was your day?"

"Great." She smiled too brightly and moved past him down the stairs. "See you at dinner."

He wondered what she wanted in the cellar. She hadn't been carrying any laundry. Grayce's words came to mind: You never know about people.

That afternoon, Matt took one of the old bicycles and Knowles' *Trees of America's North-central States*, and pedaled to the park. He enjoyed the afternoon checking the book against the information Sandy had given him and concluded that Sandy knew his trees.

He returned to the hotel for dinner to find an ambulance backed up to the main entrance, double doors open. He dropped the bicycle beside the driveway and raced up the steps into the lobby.

10

Voices floated down from the second floor. Matt took the stairs in giant leaps, wondering if Grayce was as frail as she looked, or Emmaline as weak as Roni thought she was.

Grayce herself stood at the door of one of the upstairs suites while Gavin Beresford and Donald McDonald lifted an unconscious Emmaline from the floor to a stretcher.

"What on earth happened?"

Grayce turned and reached out to him with both arms. "Oh, Mr. Smith, we don't know. My sister must have collapsed. I don't know how long she has lain here alone."

Matt wrapped an arm around Grayce. A robust gentleman with a shock of white hair stood next to the stretcher, a stethoscope dangling from his neck. "I'll phone ahead to the hospital," he said.

"Thank you, Phineas," said Grayce as the man excused himself and descended the stairs.

"She was taking her afternoon nap," said Grayce, her voice weak with anxiety. "I came upstairs to see why she hadn't come down; she doesn't often nap this long."

"Don't worry; Gavin and Donald know what they're doing. I'll come with you to the hospital."

As the two men left the room with the stretcher, Bear suggested Matt follow them with the Barlows' car. "That way you can bring 'em back home once Miss Emmaline gets checked out."

"Good idea, Bear. May I bring your car, Miss Grayce? Would you like to ride with me?"

"No dear, I'll stay with my sister." She scrounged in a drawer and handed Matt a set of keys. "You can use these; they're Emmaline's."

Matt offered his arm to Grayce as they descended the steps, then stopped and held her by the shoulders for a moment. "I'll be right behind you. At the hospital they will know what to do for Miss Emmaline."

Grayce gave him a wobbly smile and patted his arm. "I don't know what I'd do without you right now, Mr. Smith."

Johanna appeared in the lobby, and Grayce went to her. "Don't worry, dear. They will take good care of our Emmaline."

Matt escorted Grayce down the steps to the ambulance where they watched as a still, silent, chalk-faced Emmaline was loaded into the back of the vehicle. Matt helped Grayce into the back seat and ran for the Barlows' car as the ambulance sped off down the long lane and onto Main Street North.

He backed the station wagon out of the old carriage house and followed the speeding ambulance past the church and down Partridge Avenue. One week ago he had been forced into Happenstance by the very car he now drove. He shook his head in disbelief and pushed the accelerator to the floor in an effort to keep up with Donald McDonald's expeditious driving. He wanted to be at the hospital for Miss Grayce when they arrived.

Matt vowed after Ginny died he would not enter another hospital unless they had to carry him in. So much for vows. He stopped at the admitting desk.

"Hello?" He leaned over the counter to find an empty office. He pressed the bell and waited.

"They're busy with an emergency," called a voice from a room nearby.

Matt peeked in the door of the nearest room. A boy of about ten lay on the bed, one leg encased in a foot-to-hip cast, held aloft by a series of cables and pulleys.

"Hi. Were you talking to me?"

"Yes, sir. There's no one in the office because the

69

ambulance just came in with an emergency. An old lady is having a heart attack or something."

"Heart attack?"

"Well, I don't know for sure, you know, but it's, like, something with her heart."

"Thanks, buddy. I'm with the old lady."

"You her son?"

"Uh, no. Just a friend. Where would I find the emergency room?"

"Go around the office and turn right. It's at the end of the hall. That's where they brought me in. I been here for three weeks already. Two to go." He mustered a brave smile.

"Hey, hang in there. Once my friend is settled, I'll try to drop by before I leave."

The smile lit his eyes. "Gee, thanks, mister. I'll be here. Oh, you might wanna watch out for the nurse in charge."

"Thanks for the heads up." Matt walked around the office and took a right. He ignored the AUTHORIZED PERSONNEL ONLY sign and reached the emergency room just as Bear and Donald wheeled Emmaline in. Poor Grayce tottered behind, her face almost as white as her sister's. Matt moved toward her.

"I'm sorry, sir, you're not allowed in here." A wiry woman in a brown cotton pantsuit printed with white bunnies approached him, clipboard in hand. "Please go to the waiting room beside the office."

"I've come for Miss Grayce."

"We will contact you as soon as we have examined her."

Matt called Grayce. She looked up in surprise, which turned to relief as she recognized him. "Mr. Smith."

"Come to the waiting room with me, Miss Grayce. I'm being evicted."

"I must insist you remove yourself immediately or I shall have to call security," ordered the nurse.

"All right, already, I'm going." Under his breath he muttered, "Genghis Khan." Matt took Grayce's arm, and led her from the emergency area. He hoped Bear and Donald would stay a bit to make sure The Khan took proper care of Emmaline.

"Would you like a cup of coffee, Miss Grayce?"

"What's that?"

"Coffee," he repeated. "Would you like a cup?"

"Oh. Yes, I suppose. Thank you."

Matt looked around the waiting room but could find no coffee or pop machines. He settled Grayce into an aquamarine vinyl chair and poked his head into the boy's room.

"Hi again. Any idea where I could get a coffee?"

"Probably the restaurant across the street. What's your name?"

"My name's Matt. Don't they have a snack counter or a kitchen here?"

"Yeah, I guess they do, 'cuz they feed me once in a while. I'm David Johanson." He gestured toward the name slot screwed to the wall above his head. "I'd help you, but I'm kinda' hung up here." He grinned.

Matt smiled back. He was about to return to Grayce without coffee when he noticed a large comfortable rocking chair in the corner of David's room. "Would you like to do something useful, David?"

The boy lifted his head, eyes excited.

"I'm going to bring Miss Grayce in here. Her sister was brought in by ambulance with an undetermined condition and I need someone to look after her while I hunt up some coffee or tea."

"Sure! Bring her in. My folks don't come on Wednesdays."

Matt ushered Grayce into David's room and introduced the two. He pulled the rocker close to David's bed and helped Grayce sit. "I'll be right back with some coffee."

They were already chatting as he left the room in search of the kitchen. He found it, as deserted as the rest of the place. Right now, some of Roni's tea would probably be better for Grayce, but he didn't have any. He followed his nose to a carafe on a large industrial coffee machine. He left three bucks on the counter by the machine, filled two styrofoam cups with coffee, and grabbed a can of cola from the fridge.

David beamed at the cola and Grayce thanked him for the coffee.

"Doesn't taste like they make a fresh pot every twenty minutes," Matt quipped. "Are you the only patient here,

71

David?"

"Almost. I started out in Athens—that's an hour or so from here—but it was too far for my parents to drive every other day, so they got me moved closer to home. Since it's summer holidays, they try to keep the hospital as empty as possible. I heard someone say the health unit is trying to close this place."

"Why ever would they do that?" asked Grayce.

"I don't know. They want us to go to Athens, but that hospital is always overfull. That's where I started off, and I had to lie on a bed in the hall for two days before they found me a room."

"The joys of downsizing," said Matt.

"My folks say if they would fire a few of the administrators they could afford to hire nurses who actually take care of patients."

Grayce glanced toward the door. "I'll check the office," said Matt.

The nurse hadn't returned and he tiptoed down the hall and peeked through the emergency room doors.

"Out, out," ordered Genghis. "I'll be with you in a few moments."

Matt was relieved to see another nurse as well as Dr. Percy in the emergency area with The Khan. He thought he heard Emmaline's voice, weak but calm. Bear and Donald had disappeared, no doubt ordered back from whence they came. He returned to David's room to report.

Matt and Grayce returned to Happenstance Hotel after midnight, without Emmaline. He accompanied Grayce up to her room and said goodnight. As he started back down the stairs, a whispered voice stopped him.

"Matt, how is everything?" Roni advanced from her room farther down the hall.

Matt glanced at Grayce's room and motioned Roni downstairs. She tightened the belt of her robe and followed him to the dining room. He tried not to think of Ginny in her bathrobe.

Two cups of hot chocolate waited on the table.

"Did you request hot chocolate?" asked Matt, eyeing the steaming cups.

Roni wiggled her eyebrows and whispered, "Maybe Johanna's psychic."

With mutual shrugs, they sat opposite each other and wrapped their hands around the mugs.

"How is Emmaline? I was shocked when I heard."

"They've stabilized her and she's awake, but they don't know yet what happened. It looks like a heart attack, but she said she's been doing so well."

"At her age, anything can happen." Roni drank some chocolate.

"We will all be her age someday. There still has to be a reason."

Roni frowned. "No clues?"

He shook his head. "They will be starting with a battery of tests tomorrow to determine the cause of her collapse. Until then, we wait. Poor Grayce. She's exhausted."

"I believe it. I was worried when I got home from work and Johanna told me what had happened. I stayed around the hotel all afternoon and evening in case you called."

"Sorry. I didn't think to leave a message."

"Don't worry. I'm glad you were here for them. Poor dears."

They sipped their drinks in silence, then Roni covered Matt's hand with one of hers and said, "Don't worry, Matt. She's in good hands now. Get some sleep and you can check on her tomorrow."

"Yeah. Hey, thanks for staying up with me for a while."

"No problem. See you at breakfast."

As they walked out the dining room door, Roni took Matt's arm and placed a kiss on his cheek. "Chivalry isn't dead after all."

He watched her climb the stairs, then locked the front doors of the hotel and checked all the lights on the way to his room.

He lay awake for at least an hour, staring at the ceiling, worried about Emmaline and Grayce, and remembering the interminable days and nights in the hospital caring for Ginny. He hadn't been good in that kind of situation, but you did what you had to do. Just like he was doing now.

A few times his thoughts flitted to the boy in the hospital, David Johanson, and how excited he was earlier when Matt brought Chinese takeout for all three of them. They'd had a little party there, although Grayce couldn't fully enjoy herself while Emmaline lay in serious condition one hallway over. But they needed to eat something while they waited.

Dr. Phineas Percy, solicitous and positive, had found them in David's room. He'd taken over from The Khan, and let them speak with Emmaline for a few minutes before they left for home. "Mrs. Osmer is going to be fine," he assured them. "We will continue testing her, and I'll be in touch as soon as I know anything."

"Thank you, Phineas," Grayce said. "We should go home now, Mr. Smith."

Now, lying in bed after a long and anxious wait at the hospital, Matt drifted to sleep with the memory of Roni's kiss on his cheek. What was that all about?

11

Since neither Roni nor Grayce appeared at breakfast, Matt decided to take himself for a walk downtown. He met Bear at the Waldorf and joined him for coffee.

"What's the latest on Miss Emmaline?" the mechanic asked between slurps of coffee.

Matt told him. "It seems her heart is not as strong as she thought. Do you remember her ever having similar problems?"

"No sir. She's had a heart condition, but it was under control. Other than that, she's always been as healthy as a horse. Came as a big surprise when the old ticker gave out."

"It always does. Sometimes it's harder on the family than on the individual."

Bear held his cup of coffee near his chin and watched Matt. "What makes you such a' expert on people?"

Matt returned his stare. "Experience. I've worked with a lot of people in my life."

"Social worker?"

"Might as well have been."

"Not tellin', huh?"

"I didn't come to Happenstance to whine about myself. I'm worried about Grayce. She seems to be the one in charge, but she's lost without Emmaline."

Bear sipped his coffee. "Good thing you were there for Miss Grayce yesterday."

"Yeah. What is it with Happenstance? The more I try to mind my own business, the more I become involved."

"Yup, life can be strange that way. In this town everbody cares about everbody, even the newcomers. Why, Roni stopped by for a fill-up on her way to the park yesterday after dinner, said she had to get away from the worries about Miss Emmaline."

"That's strange. She told me she sat at the hotel all evening and worried."

"Just tellin' you what she told me. Well, I gotta get back to work. See you around."

Matt watched Bear stride out the door and wondered why Roni had lied to him. Maybe she was overtired, and he couldn't blame her for wanting to get out of the house.

Matt picked up a few things at Wuppertal's and Hanson's Market for Grayce and carried them back to the hotel. The place was as quiet as the cemetery behind the parsonage. He located Grayce in the little office behind the counter, poring over a ledger at the weathered oak desk.

He knocked. "May I come in?"

"Of course." She looked at him over her spectacles. "I have been reviewing our reservation list." She sighed. "It seems we have no reservations whatsoever. No one comes here anymore."

"What am I? Chopped liver?"

"You did not have a reservation, as I recall. You showed up out of the blue."

"Isn't that the truth? And it's soon time I popped out again."

Grayce leaned forward and her large eyes widened. "Mr. Smith, you aren't going to leave me now, are you? I am not in the habit of begging, but I don't know how I would manage without you."

"Don't worry, Miss Grayce, I won't desert you. Why are you concerned about reservations? Could you manage more people here with Miss Emmaline in the hospital?"

She sighed. "We need the income."

"I don't want to pry, but do you rely on the hotel income to survive? Doesn't yours and Emmaline's social security keep you above water?"

Grayce laughed, a sharp laugh. "It may have at one time, but there were Bruce's medical bills to pay after he passed away, and then, more recently, the renovation charges."

"Renovation charges?"

Grayce hesitated. "I don't suppose I can expect you to help if you don't know the facts. After Bruce died, we found ourselves dealing with some rather unscrupulous people who said the hotel needed extensive refurbishing. I don't believe it was ever that serious, but we were forced by the department of safety to bring the hotel up to modern standards. That included a new roof, new steps at the entrance, and bathrooms in every suite. When you begin moving inner walls, Mr. Smith, one thing leads to another.

"The bills kept mounting but our income remained the same, thus Emmaline and I accumulated debt, on which we pay regular interest fees. They are higher than our meager social security, so yes, we need income from paying guests. And now with Emmaline in the hospital and having tests, there will be more expenses."

Matt sat thinking. Somehow the ideas, the assistance, now had to come from him. Was that why he had ended up here in Happenstance? To help two elderly ladies save their home?

"Do you advertise the hotel?" Matt asked.

"Mr. Smith, Happenstance and the hotel have been here a long time and we've never yet had to advertise." She tapped her pencil on the desk again. "Although, there used to be a sign up on the main highway two miles from the access road. The sign blew down in a winter storm and was never put back up."

"What happened to it?"

"I believe Mr. Beresford brought it back to town in his tow truck. He may still have it."

"Well, why don't we put it up again? I'll talk to Bear and see if he has it. Then I'll get him to help me dig it back in where it was. I know it's not much, but it's a beginning. We'll think of more as we go."

Grayce smiled. "Thank you, Mr. Smith. I am unable to do things like that on my own, and now that Emmaline is not here, I can't seem to think straight." She put her pencil down on the desk. "I'm too old for this."

Her hands shook as she removed her glasses. "Aging is not a pleasant process, Mr. Smith. One is forced more and more to depend upon others, and when one has always been an independent person, that is a difficult transition."

"You're not alone, Miss Grayce. Miss Emmaline will be back soon, and Johanna is always here, and now Roni. I don't think she's planning to go anywhere."

"I will not depend upon Miss Wilkinson."

"What? Why not?"

"I am uncomfortable with her."

"You are? Why? She seems concerned about you and Miss Emmaline."

Grayce sat straight in her chair and fixed her eyes on Matt's. "I have a feeling about Miss Wilkinson. I can't put my finger on it."

"Has she said or done anything to make you feel that way?"

Grayce paused. "It's more what she hasn't done, I think. She has not—until you arrived—spoken to either Emm or me other than when it was unavoidable. But now she insists on bringing us tea and making us comfortable in our favorite chairs. We've been quite comfortable until now, all on our own, and Johanna makes better tea than Miss Wilkinson. And Emm falls for it. The same thing happened to Belvina Rampole. She began attending Miss Wilkinson's exercise classes and they became fast friends overnight. I have been unable to discern Miss Wilkinson's motives."

"You think she has a hidden agenda?" Matt sat down in the antique love seat across from the desk and drummed his fingers on the armrest. "I'm sorry you feel that way, but we don't want to judge her without all the facts. That can have far-reaching effects."

Grayce stared at him. "Is that what happened to you, Mr. Smith? Were you judged unfairly?"

Matt looked past her out the window. "Yes. But most of them had their minds made up without any evidence. I didn't have a chance."

"So you left?"

He looked back at her. "What else was I to do? How long do you live with everyone talking about you behind your back?"

"I did not mean to imply you had done the wrong thing. I, for one, am more thankful than I can say that you were led to Happenstance."

"*Led* to Happenstance?"

She returned the registry book to the top drawer of the desk. "I do not believe in coincidence, Mr. Smith. Not for a moment."

The telephone rang then, startling them both. Grayce answered it, her hands shaking again.

"Hello? ... Yes, this is Miss Barlow... Is she? That's wonderful ... We shall come in to see her this afternoon." She glanced at Matt for confirmation and he nodded. "Thank you for calling." She hung up the phone.

"Emmaline is still under observation and there are more tests to complete, but she is feeling quite well."

"Excellent. Let's eat lunch and go visit her."

"I do miss her very much, even though we don't always see eye to eye."

"I know. I envy your relationship. I have no siblings."

Grayce slipped her arm through his as they left the room. "That's unfortunate. It's always healthy for a child to have at least one sibling if possible. However, it happens as the good Lord wills it."

"Does it? Even Miss Emmaline's illness?"

She hesitated for a brief moment. "Yes, it does. Nothing comes to us but our heavenly Father allows it, and He is aware of how much we are able to bear."

"Is He ever wrong in this?"

"In how much we can bear? Only in our eyes, Mr. Smith. He knows the end from the beginning."

"Meaning?"

They sat down across from each other at the dining table and Johanna brought in pasta salad on lettuce, and toasted whole wheat bread with cheese.

After a brief prayer for the food, Grayce reached for her toast, then paused to explain. "Our lives, as I see it, are like a stage play. We each have our parts. We are not puppets; there are no strings attaching us to the Director. We are given basic scripts as we go and are invited to follow them." She took a bite and chewed before speaking again.

"Sometimes we assume we are capable of creating a superior plotline to the one given to us, but since we don't know the end of the play, our feeble attempts cause chaos for ourselves and others. Our Director knows best, and if we follow the script, we come out with the appropriate ending and fewer fumbled scenes along the way."

"Very well spoken, Miss Grayce. I had not thought of it that way. My disagreement comes with the fact that I may not like the ending the director has chosen." *Alzheimer's? Dementia? I don't think so, Roni.*

Grayce sprinkled Parmesan on her salad. "That is a matter of faith. When once you come to know the One in whom you trust, you can relax in the faith that He has your best interests at heart. If you follow his lead, the ending will be a reward. If you don't, there are appropriate consequences."

"Kind of a thin line to walk, isn't it?"

"Perhaps, but if you consider the options, it is the best possible place to be. Have you ever seen a picture of a jungle bridge that spans a deep, roaring river canyon?"

Matt nodded. "You mean it's better to hang onto a frightening swinging bridge than to fall into the canyon below?"

"Exactly. There is safety on the other side."

Matt thought about that as they ate. If life was a bridge, he had no choice whether or not to step out on it. His bridge had begun to swing when Ginny died, but it had eventually stilled again. However, when the accusations came in at work, his bridge had swung wildly. He hadn't cared if he fell or not. But, however close he had come to letting go, he still held on. And now Grayce needed him to help her do the same, and perhaps he needed her, too.

Matt watched Grayce relax as they drove to the hospital, and decided to spend a little time with David Johanson so the sisters could visit in private.

Emmaline sat on her bed, face rosy, eyes shining as they entered. She reached out her arms to Grayce and they hugged through tears.

"Dear, dear," said Grayce, wiping her eyes. "No propriety at all."

"Dash propriety, Graycie. It's so good to see you. Matthew, how are you? Thank you for bringing my sister."

"I'll let you two visit for a while. I'm going to say hello to David."

"You do that. Poor child can't even sit up."

"I'm okay, Mrs. Osmer," called David from the next room. "I'm getting used to it. My brother brings me lots of comics and I get to watch TV anytime I want."

"You are a real little soldier," Emmaline called back, her voice quavering with the effort.

David was grinning when Matt pulled up a chair beside his bed. "She's a nice lady. I'm glad she's here. Too bad we can't share a room."

"You'd like that, wouldn't you?"

"Yeah, but she might not. And when my family comes in to see me it's a real zoo. That's what my mom says."

Matt laughed. "I'll bet it is." They chatted on about David's family, his sports interests, his hope to get in on a bit of the summer before it ended.

"I wish someone else my age would come in here too, but I wouldn't want them to be very sick."

"I don't blame you. Well, I'd better spend some time with Miss Emmaline."

"Thanks for the visit, Matt. See you tomorrow, I hope."

"You bet. Oh, here. I brought you something."

"You did? What? Oooh, cool. A skateboarder magazine. I'll have to hide it from my mom because my skateboard is the reason I'm in here. I missed a boardslide."

Matt winced. "You're lucky you didn't hurt more than your leg. Sorry, I didn't know what happened."

"That's okay. I'm not gonna stop skateboarding because of this."

Matt gave him a high five and returned to Emmaline's room. The sisters sat in pleasant camaraderie, Grayce crocheting a pillow cover while Emmaline leaned back into the cushions with her eyes closed and a smile on her face.

"Serenity personified," whispered Matt as he entered the

room.

"We are quite comfortable with silence," said Grayce, "at least I am."

"Graycie, you can talk with the best of them," countered Emmaline, her eyes still closed. "Don't believe her, Matthew."

"Don't go spreading untruths, Emm." Grayce turned to Matt. "When we were children, Emmaline would be talking when I fell asleep at night, and when I awoke in the morning, she was still talking. Her tongue is always the first thing to wake up."

"Pshaw, Graycie, you used to beg me to tell you stories. I had to obey you because you were older."

"Don't be ridiculous! You never did a thing I told you to do."

"Ah, but you did tell me what to do. She was a tyrant, Matthew."

"Truce, truce," laughed Matt. "They'll never let you go home if you can't get along with each other."

They all jumped at a knock on the doorframe.

"Excuse me," said a teenaged girl in a pink and white striped apron. "I've brought Mrs. Osmer's dinner."

"Thank you, dear. Put it right here," said Grayce.

"Better bring it to me, or my sister will eat it," corrected Emmaline.

She seemed so much herself again, except for the fatigue, that Matt wondered how serious the illness had been. Had she suffered permanent damage? What had caused the problem in the first place? He decided he would talk with Dr. Phineas Percy.

After they'd returned home, Matt left Grayce sitting in the parlor, and he walked down the long lane and out onto the street that led to Alkmaar's Dairy. He wondered what was up with Roni; he hadn't seen her since the night before. Right now she would be at the Paradise Realty office, but he walked past it and turned in at the clinic.

An automatic Avon chime announced his entry and a middle-aged receptionist asked what she could do for him.

"I'd like a word with Dr. Phineas Percy if he's not too

busy," he said.

The receptionist checked the day's schedule. "He is seeing a patient at the moment, but there may be a bit of a break between this one and the next. Mr. Moyer is usually late. Please have a seat and I'll let the doctor know you're here."

Matt leafed through a worn but colorful copy of *Farm & Ranch Living* and tossed it back onto the coffee table. The receptionist reappeared and motioned him into a room. "The doctor will be right with you."

Matt thanked her and sat, leaning his elbows on his knees. He'd hated doctor's offices since he was a kid. Waiting inside the exam room was like playing hide and seek, and knowing it was only a matter of time before someone would pounce in and scare you to death. He heard footsteps, but they continued down the hall outside his room. Then a rustle of paper and the door burst open. He'd been found!

"Hello there," said the doctor.

Matt stood.

"I've seen you somewhere, haven't I?"

"At the hotel, when Miss Emmaline collapsed. I'm staying there."

"Ah. Thank you for your kindness in looking after Grayce. We've known each other for a long time. Now, what can I do for you, Mr. Smith?"

Matt reminded himself he was no longer eight years old and sat down in his chair, crossing one ankle over the other knee. "I've come about Miss Emmaline. We'll be bringing her home soon, and she seems to be her normal self again. We were wondering—Miss Grayce and I—if you had found anything that would hint at a reason for Miss Emmaline's illness."

Dr. Phineas pursed his lips and tapped his pencil on the clipboard as he leaned against the counter. "Again, let me tell you I am impressed by your kindness and consideration for the Barlow sisters. The problem is I can't tell you anything. First of all, the lab has not yet sent me the reports or test results, and when they do, the law of confidentiality prevents me from divulging the information to anyone other than the patient. I can tell you right now that Emmaline has been stable and that her episode has me baffled, but further to that I cannot help you. I hope you understand."

"Of course. I've become their self-appointed guardian. I was hoping you might have formed some sort of preliminary opinion when you checked her out."

"It wouldn't be wise to suggest something that has not been proven, Mr. Smith. Bring Emmaline here to the clinic when she gets home. Make an appointment with Sylvia on your way out. Oh, and bring Grayce along too, while you're at it. She pays better attention than Emmaline."

"Yes, we shall come for her tomorrow morning. Thank you. Goodbye."

Matt heard Grayce's words and walked into the parlor as she hung up the phone. "Miss Emmaline's ready to come home?"

"Yes, it seems so. Just one more test tomorrow morning and she will be free to go."

"Have they found out what was wrong with her?"

"They won't say anything over the telephone. I expect we will have to see Dr. Phineas for the report."

"I just talked with him and he said to bring her in when she gets home."

Grayce rose and reached out her hand to Matt. "My dear Mr. Smith, you are a Godsend. Bless you."

He offered her his arm. "Glad to be of service, my lady."

12

Emmaline wept when they drove up to the hotel late Friday morning. "I've missed my home and all of you." She grasped her sister's hand as they walked up the steps. Matt supported Emmaline on her other side.

"No need to worry anymore, Emm. You are back where you belong."

Grayce's voice sounded high and fragile to Matt. He worried as much as Grayce about the outcome of the tests. They all would have to wait until Dr. Percy received the results.

They settled Emmaline into a comfortable chair in the parlor and brought her a cup of Earl Grey tea and some shortbread cookies fresh from Johanna's oven.

Matt remembered coming home from the hospital after Ginny died. People from the church had kept knocking at the door, bringing casseroles and cakes and loaves of homemade bread. They came with their offerings of food to their gods of guilt and duty and pity, but he would rather have been alone. He had accepted their oblations for Ginny's sake, but he couldn't eat anyway, couldn't swallow past the enormous lump of grief.

Eventually, the gifts tapered off and Matt felt like the walls and ceilings would close in and crush him, like on the old episodes of *Get Smart*. Except that on TV, "86" and "99" always managed to escape the crush at the last moment. What had hurt the most was that these same people who had reached out to him in his grief didn't believe his innocence in the school scandal. He sometimes wondered if even God believed him.

The hum of Roni's VW bug alerted Matt and the ladies to her arrival as they sat ready to begin their lunch. She marched into the dining room with a cheery smile on her face, but stopped in her tracks when she saw Emmaline.

"Home already, are you Emm? I'm so relieved. You're looking great." She moved around to Emmaline's place and kissed her cheek, bringing a smile to the older woman's face and a frown to her sister's.

"*Miss Emmaline* has just arrived home from the hospital and is still weak from her illness."

"Oh, I'm sure it will take a while to get back to yourself. You relax and we will take care of everything else."

"*We* can manage on our own, thank you," said Grayce. Hurt and surprise showed on Roni's face.

Johanna stepped into the room with another place setting for Roni, and Matt attempted to fill the awkward silence that followed. "Soup's getting cold. Why don't you sit down, Roni, and we can talk while we eat."

After a few minutes of strained conversation, Roni said to Matt, "You should come out for a hike tomorrow. You need a change after sitting around in that sterile hospital room."

"I'd consider it, but Miss Emmaline has an appointment with Dr. Percy tomorrow morning."

"On Saturday?"

"He said he'd be at the office anyway doing reports, and made an exception for her."

"Phineas is right around the corner, Matthew," said Emmaline. "We can manage that. You need to get out and exercise. I believe Grayce and I shall relax in our lawn chairs tomorrow. We can drive to the end of the lane and around the corner to see Phineas."

"Absolutely not," responded Roni. "I will take you to the appointment and then go for a hike. I'm sure Matt won't mind waiting."

Grayce glanced from Matt to Roni.

Matt stepped in again. "Don't worry about the

appointment, Roni. You sleep in on your day off; I'll take the ladies to their appointment."

"That will be fine, Mr. Smith," said Grayce with obvious relief.

Matt noted Roni's hesitation, but she agreed to his suggestion. Maybe he was getting too tied up in the Barlows' business. They had survived more than eighty years without him. Lately, though, he couldn't get the thought of Miss Grayce's financial worry from his mind. What if the hotel was in as bad shape as Grayce seemed to think it was? What would she and Emmaline do without the Happenstance Hotel? And what would Happenstance do without it? He believed this whole episode with Emmaline had brought Grayce to the point of considering her future, with or without her sister. As Grayce implied, aging wasn't for cowards.

That afternoon while the ladies were napping, Matt stopped at Paradise Realty and Insurance on impulse. Roni was alone in the office. She clicked out of whatever computer program she'd been using and swiveled her chair to face him. He thought she looked a bit flustered, but she recovered and gave him a wide smile. His throat constricted for a moment as it always did when he looked into Roni's face. The green eyes and lack of freckles reminded him again that this was not his Ginny.

"What a nice surprise!" she said, her frown belying her words. "What brings you to our humble office this fine afternoon?"

Matt took a chair across from her desk and relaxed into it. "Lack of something better to do."

"Oh, don't flatter me."

He smiled, then sobered. "I thought of you laboring away here, and decided you needed a break. And I enjoy your company."

"Ah, that's better."

He leaned forward. "Roni, has Karl ever said anything to you about the status of the hotel?"

"What do you mean?"

"I mean is it covered by insurance? Are the Barlow sisters

secure there? Is there a chance they could lose the place if they don't make their payments on time?"

"I have no idea. I assumed they were financially sound."

"I'm not sure. There haven't been any summer guests, other than you and me, and there are old bills and now Emmaline's hospital stay and tests to pay for. I was wondering if, as an insurance agent, you had any idea if they could be in danger of losing the hotel."

Roni stared at him. "Are you serious? Who would take away the hotel from two little old ladies? Are you sure there's reason to worry? Maybe Grayce is a bit over the edge after Emm's—sorry—*Miss Emmaline's*—collapse. I wouldn't worry, Matt."

"Grayce is over eighty years old, never married, her sister may have a serious heart condition, and they have no income besides social security. They may have reason to worry."

"If they need to save some money, maybe they could let Johanna go."

"She depends on them for her livelihood. And how would they survive? As I said, Grayce is eighty-something and Emmaline isn't far behind. Besides, that wouldn't be enough of a saving, I'm thinking."

"Just brainstorming." Roni touched Matt's arm as he rested his elbows on her desk. Electricity sparked, surprising him. Had she felt it too?

"Matt, don't worry. I'll talk to Karl, see if there's a problem. He's quite familiar with the legal end of things."

She leaned forward and kissed him. He stared at her, stalled in mid-thought. Silence filled the spaces where their words had been.

"Sorry," she said. "Guess I misread the mood."

He blew out his breath, trying to rein in his emotions. "No worries." He changed the subject. "The Barlows seem so defenseless."

Roni paused at Matt's comment. "Yeah. I worry about them, but maybe this is one way we can help. Let me look into it. Well, I should get back to work if I'm planning to finish this report by tonight."

"Right. See you at dinner."

"I look forward to it." Her eyes said more than her words.

Matt and the Barlow sisters returned to the hotel after their Saturday morning appointment, much sobered by the doctor's words. Matt, who had paced the waiting room while they spoke with Dr. Percy, waited to hear the report.

"She is well enough, Mr. Smith," began Grayce, "but we need to discuss something with you. Would you please step into our office?"

"Is there a need for secrecy?"

"Please, Mr. Smith."

Matt followed her through the door and let her close it behind them. Emmaline sat in a rocking chair in the corner, Matt dropped into one of the leather armchairs and Grayce took a seat behind the desk to preside over whatever pronouncement she proposed to make.

13

"Now Mr. Smith," Grayce began, "my sister and I have been discussing her sudden and unprecedented illness, and we want to know what you think."

"What did Dr. Percy say? What did the tests show?"

"My present health is much improved since Wednesday," said Emmaline.

"That's obvious. What caused—"

"Digitalis," said Grayce. "Emmaline has traces of digitalis in her bloodstream."

"Does her medication contain digitalis?"

Emmaline opened her mouth to speak, but Grayce beat her to it. "She's on a mild heart medication which contains a minimal amount of digitalis, but it is nowhere near the amount needed to cause a collapse such as Emmaline experienced. We take no other medicines or supplements."

"Aside from my slight heart condition, we've always been perfectly healthy."

Matt paced the floor in front of the desk. "There has to be some sort of explanation."

"There's the tea."

Matt stopped and faced Grayce. "What did you say?"

Grayce sat up straighter and fixed her eyes on his. "The tea. Miss Wilkinson began giving Emmaline a special herbal tea—"

"—for my constitution—"

"—and then she collapsed."

Matt narrowed his eyes and shook his head at them. "I

can't believe you would even think such a thing. First of all, you have nothing to go on but conjecture, and second, Roni would never do such a thing. In fact, she has been going the extra mile for you both."

"Well, you never know about people."

"So you've said. Miss Grayce, with all due respect, that is a slanderous statement. I've been getting to know Roni since I came to Happenstance, and I don't believe she would ever do anything to harm anyone."

"I told you we shouldn't mention it to him," said Grayce to Emmaline.

Grayce sat at her desk and toyed with a pen. "What then would you suggest we do, Mr. Smith? Dismiss the apparent coincidence that Emmaline drank the tea and fell ill? Let it go in case we hurt Miss Wilkinson's feelings? This is my sister's health we are discussing. Emmaline takes only that one medication, yet she has enough digitalis in her system to endanger her life. What other explanation could there be?"

Matt sat back in the chair facing the desk. "Perhaps Emmaline took an extra dose. It happens."

Emmaline stood from her chair. "Would you two stop talking about me as if I'm not here. I did not overdose on my pills. They are sealed in my bubble pack."

"Overdose. You watch too much television, Emm. We are not suggesting you are a drug addict, only that you might have taken two pills in one day by mistake."

"Well, I didn't."

Grayce's brow lowered in thought. "Even when you weren't feeling like yourself?"

"No, not even then. I'm very careful with my medication. Besides, two pills would not have created that effect."

Matt stood again, and put his hands in his pockets. "I'll talk with Roni about the tea. There has to be a reasonable explanation for all of this."

"I wish you wouldn't mention it just yet," said Grayce. "I don't think she would take well to such an accusation."

"I'm sure you're right about that. We'll keep it under our hats for the present, but I don't think we should judge without facts. Now, are you ready for lunch?"

"I am," said Emmaline. "No more hospital food for me. It

is good to be home."

"That is the tenth time you've said that today," grumbled Grayce. "Try to vary your comments."

"Oh fiddle. Let's make it eleven times." Emmaline's eyes twinkled with humor.

When Matt had seated them at the dining table, Roni joined them for soup and individual omelets. The tension remained, but Matt was glad for her presence.

Matt and Roni left for their hike as soon as they had finished lunch. Sandy did not materialize, and Matt found himself distracted by Roni's presence.

She walked through the woods with a reverent air, now and then marveling over the sweet moist aroma of decaying plant matter or the variety of birdsongs in the air. As Ginny would have done, she collected intricately-shaped leaves from the forest floor to press between the pages of a heavy book, to be found at a much later date and enjoyed again. They wandered through the trees in a comfortable silence and appreciation for the gentle dialogue of nature.

"What are you thinking?" Her words interrupted his thoughts.

"This and that."

"Can you be more specific?"

He kicked at a tree root. "The past."

"Tell me. Where'd you come from and where were you going when you stopped in at Happenstance?"

Matt sighed, weary of playing the deflection game, yet still hesitant to tell all. "Doesn't matter where I came from. I needed some space. Just hopped on my Harley and took off down the highway, no particular destination."

"You must have had powerful reasons to run. Are you in trouble with the law or something?"

Matt flinched. "I've never done anything that warranted trouble with the authorities. I needed a change of scenery."

"You told me your wife died. Ginger?"

"Ginny."

"Yeah. Is that why you left wherever it is you won't tell me about?"

"No."

"Anything you *can* tell me?"

"I was raised by my grandparents after my parents were killed in a car accident."

"How old were you when they died?"

"Five."

"I'm sorry, Matt. That must have been rough."

"I suppose it was at first, but Gramps and Amma took good care of me, tried to raise me as they thought my parents would have wanted."

"Lucky you. My mom dropped me off on a doorstep when I was three and my dad never saw me. I had the questionable privilege of growing up in foster homes."

Matt grimaced. "Was it as bad as what we hear?"

"Worse. But that's behind me now. I got outta there, worked hard, got an education, and never looked back. If you spend too much time in the past, you risk missing the present."

Matt sighed and smiled. "You're right, oh Wise One. I'll try to pay attention from now on."

Roni returned his smile and slipped her hand into his. "Sounds good to me. What do you see in your future?"

"You make it sound like I'm a prophet. I'm not sure what I'll do or where I'll go when I leave Happenstance."

"How long do you think you'll stay?"

"Not sure. It depends."

"On?"

"When Bear gets my bike fixed and how long it takes Emmaline to get back on her feet."

"That's all?"

He looked up into the leaves and shrugged. "How about you?"

"You have a knack for diverting attention from yourself, Matthew Smith, but I'll play along. I don't know either. It depends."

He grinned at her. "On?"

She shrugged and mimicked his nonchalance. "On whether or not I have a reason to stay."

"You mean your job?"

"In part."

"The welfare of the Barlow sisters?"

"Of course. In part."

Matt scratched his head. "Why on earth else would you want to stay? Oh wait; I know. The beauty of the town itself."

She laughed aloud and punched him in the arm, then linked her arm in his. "Matt, you are infuriating. Doesn't our friendship mean anything to you?"

"Sure it does. You're like sunshine after rain."

Roni's smile vanished. She stared at Matt and took a deep breath. "No one's ever said anything like that to me."

"Well it's true. I've been in this fog for so long I've forgotten how to laugh, how to enjoy life. Thanks to you, I'm beginning to remember."

She blinked rapidly and pushed her curls from her face.

"Hey there, Miss Wilkinson, that's supposed to be a positive statement. Don't fall apart on me."

He reached out and tucked her hair behind her ear, his hand lingering on her cheek. His eyes held hers. It had been such a long time... He leaned in and kissed her gently.

Roni's eyes misted. "You never cease to amaze me, Matt."

He grinned and whispered, "Yeah, I like that about myself."

She chuckled, then reached her arms around his neck and closed her eyes. He was about to repeat his previous action when he sensed a presence. Roni opened her eyes, now full of questions, and drew back.

He held a finger to his lips and the truth dawned on her. She stepped back from him.

"Come on out, Sandy," called Matt. "Enough spying."

Sandy stepped out from among the trees to their right, hands over his eyes. "Is it safe to look now? I'll not be interruptin' a memory in the makin'."

Matt snorted and Roni rolled her eyes. "Sandy, you do beat all. How long have you been watching?"

"My dear lady, I am no voyeur. I was mindin' me own business when I came upon a scene so touchin' as to pull me up short. I covered me eyes to preserve me innocence—"

"Yeah, right," said Matt, laughing. "How are you doing with your thesis?"

"Ah, a comforting change o' topic. Very well, thanks.

Should have most o' me research compiled by end o' the month. Then it's off to the big city to write it up."

"Do you have time for a coffee break?" Matt took Roni's hand and walked behind Sandy as they headed toward a clearing overlooking the lake.

"I do. Join me for a cuppa an' tell me how the Barlows be doin'."

As Sandy stepped ahead, Matt winked at Roni and she squeezed his hand.

That evening after dinner, Roni headed out to the school for one of her exercise classes, and Matt played a game of Scrabble with the sisters.

"Have you two been relaxing this afternoon?"

Emmaline glanced at Grayce. "Well, physically we have. Mentally we've been worrying."

"About Roni's tea?"

"About our financial situation," added Grayce.

Matt cleared his throat. "Yes. Listen, do you think you might be worrying too soon, and without reason? I mean, who would take away the hotel from you? You've lived here all your lives."

"It happens all the time these days," said Grayce. "I read about an incident in New York City where an elderly couple was evicted from their mobile home. They had been running the trailer park, but when they had to stop due to health reasons, the next manager forced them out and they had no place to go."

"That was New York," said Matt. "This is Happenstance. Different story. Besides, no one would have reason to force you out."

"The fact of the matter," said Grayce, "is that we need funds to maintain this old monstrosity."

"Don't call it a monstrosity, Graycie. Mother would be horrified."

"She'd be horrified to see the state we're in, after all the effort she poured into this place all her life."

Matt suggested they come up with some tangible ideas of how to keep Happenstance Hotel afloat. "Better to think in concrete terms than to worry in abstract."

Grayce was the first to offer a suggestion. "Mother always told us necessity was the mother of invention. She was never one to give up. You know, Emm, we might let Mr. Hainsford go. He should be retiring anyway."

"I think he stays because he doesn't want to leave us in the lurch, but Graycie, I hate to think what our lawns would look like without dear Mr. Hainsford. I suppose we could hire some of those young people who come around offering to do yard work. "

"I wonder what Papa would say if he knew his daughters had come to this juncture."

"He didn't worry about us when we were children. I don't see why we should consider his opinion now."

"How uncharitable, Emm." Grayce pursed her lips. "But you have a point. Mr. Smith, have you inquired of Mr. Beresford as to whether he has the old highway sign for Happenstance Hotel?"

"Not yet. I'll ask him the next time I see him."

"We could take out an advertisement in *The Village Voice*. Its readership extends beyond the town itself."

"And we could create a website advertising our hotel." Emmaline looked pleased with herself. "I'm sure we could hire someone to do it for us."

The sisters continued to make suggestions and Matt jotted them down on a slip of paper. When the ideas waned, Matt sat back with his coffee and looked around him.

"This is such a beautiful old place. It features in the *Happenstance History*, but I'd love to hear more from you. Do you have any other books about it in your personal library?"

"The book is old and the hotel is now quite ordinary. What you have discovered is sufficient, I'm sure, Mr. Smith."

"We do have the journals, Graycie. We could show him—"

"Emmaline Louise, those are personal."

"But that's what he asked for, personal stories."

Matt's head swiveled from Grayce to Emmaline and back. "What journals? What are you talking about?"

"It's none of your...not something that would interest

you."

"If I'm out of line, forget it. I just thought I'd ask."

Grayce puckered her brow at Emmaline and rose stiffly. She left the room and returned with a large hardcover notebook. The maroon cloth covering had rubbed off in places, exposing the cardboard beneath. With another disapproving glance at her sister, Grayce handed the volume to Matt with reluctance.

"There was only one in our library. There should be two of these. Have you taken one out, Emm?"

Emmaline shook her head. "I haven't looked at them in years. I can't imagine where it would have got to."

Matt opened the cover with care, considerate of the fragility of the pages and binding.

14

The notes were written with ink in large, looping letters, the first entry dated August 12, 1922...

> *The Diary of Amanda Eugenie Rutherford...*
> *The weather has been unseasonably warm in Chicago this summer. I look forward to my trip out west, away from the clamor of the city. It will be the first time I will be traveling without my parents and siblings, able to manage on my own—with Carlo's help, of course. The real reason I have to go is because of Jonas. He's been pressing the issue of marriage, and I don't think I can marry that man. Papa and Mama think he's wonderful, so kind and decent and hard-working. I think he's tiresome. If I should have to live with him, I would die a long, slow death. Carlo says I am being melodramatic, but he understands, I know he does, or he would never have invited me along.*

"Who's Amanda?" asked Matt, looking to the Misses Barlow, who sat on the edges of their respective chairs watching him as a canary would keep an eye on the cat.

"The writer is our mother, Amanda Eugenie Rutherford Barlow," said Grayce. "She was born in Chicago in 1905."

"That would have made her about seventeen years of age when she wrote this."

The Barlow sisters nodded, and Matt returned to his

reading.

> *I'm looking forward to the adventure of heading out west where everything is simple and fresh. And no Jonas. Carlo says I will like Barlow Manor.*

"Ah yes, Barlow Manor, just like the *Happenstance History* book said. Later known as Happenstance Hotel." Matt noted the uncertainty in Grayce's eyes.

> *Carlo recently purchased a brand new Essex automobile for our journey. It will be a long drive, but most interesting, I'm sure. The Essex is all enclosed, so it should be quite comfortable.*
> *Carlo says I will also like William Richardson Barlow. We have corresponded several times in the last year, and I've come to enjoy my written visits with William. Carlo and I will be staying at Barlow Manor for a month or two.*
> *I don't imagine Happenstance, small as it is, will have any motion picture theaters or private clubs, but that's just as well. Mama and Papa would not approve. Papa says we need to cling to our traditional morals and values and that the government is in support of that move. Papa says it's because we have a President who's a Republican! I don't have much interest in politics and know very little about President Harding, besides the fact that his name is Warren G. and something about a campaign slogan referring to "a return to normalcy."*
> *I'm not sure how Carlo convinced Mama and Papa to allow me to accompany him out west. He is not at all traditional.*

"Who is Carlo?"

"He was a—" began Emmaline, but Grayce interrupted her.

"He was our mother's cousin."

Matt wondered what Emmaline had wanted to say. He returned to the script and imagined Amanda to be a willowy girl, tall for her age, with large eyes and silken hair.

I am eager to see William. He is my senior by almost ten years, but that doesn't seem to matter in these modern days. I hope he treats me as an adult, not a child as Papa and Mama are prone to do. I haven't told Mama about our correspondence because she worries about everything. If she knew how much Carlo drank sometimes, she would never let me go with him. But he is always a gentleman with me and, as my protector, he has promised to take good care of me.

Matt looked up at the ladies. "If it's all right, I think I'll take this to my room. I want to read more, but you both look weary." He stood and offered a deep bow. "Good night, my ladies."

Emmaline giggled.

"Our knight in a white golf shirt," said Grayce, with a crooked smile. "Good night. Don't keep us waiting at breakfast."

"I shall be on time."

Matt relaxed against the goose down pillows and again opened the journal of Amanda Eugenie Rutherford Barlow.

August 15, 1922

Mama is worrying again. Ever since she heard about Carlo's recent indiscretion at a downtown speakeasy, she has been talking about "temperance" and the Prohibition Party. Even Papa rolls his eyes. I think he trusts me more than Mama does; perhaps she remembers what is was like to be seventeen, and it gives her reason to worry. Frankly, I don't care what either of them thinks. Mama says she would feel better if Jonas were going too, but that would not be appropriate, and I am ever so thankful for that.

We've had a change of plans since Carlo's recent faux pas: we will be traveling by train, and Miss Goodmason is to accompany me. I would have enjoyed driving out in the Essex, but at least we are still going.

I must go now or Mama will demand to know what I've been doing. I have been enlisted to help prepare and hang flowers to dry in the attic. I love the sweet stale smell of the flowers and the mustiness of the attic, but I do not like marching up and down all those steps. Mama says it's good for my figure, though, and I do want to look my very best for William.

September 4, 1922
Carlo and I—and Miss Goodmason, of course— arrived in Happenstance weary from a long train journey. When I took my first steps on solid ground, I must have looked like a drunken sailor. I find it difficult to explain our arrival in Happenstance. The Barlows sent a car to the station in Athens to fetch us. We turned off the main thoroughfare and followed a narrow dirt road through a long, covered bridge. It was as if we were entering another world; my skin prickled as we crossed the bridge. Yet everyone and everything, while not on par with Chicago, looked normal.

Matt understood her feelings about this strange place. He plumped his pillows and continued reading.

My excitement knew no bounds when we turned into the long oak-shaded lane of Barlow Manor. Carlo remembered to help me out of the automobile, and I remembered to act like a young society woman from Chicago. William and his parents and sister, Lilian, were waiting for us on the front porch of the manor. We were properly introduced all around and then a maid showed me to my room, a small but adequate suite on the main floor next to the chapel. Miss Goodmason stays in a little room connected by an adjoining door. I'm not sure what she does with herself when she's not helping me dress or fix my hair.

I was charmed by my accommodations, but even more so by the young Mr. Barlow. He came for me at dinnertime and escorted me to the dining room as if I were a grown woman—which I am, of course. Carlo and William were very excited to see each other. They act like long lost brothers. They met during the Great War, so Carlo told me, and have always kept up communication.

September 12, 1922
Even though I was determined to make this trip out west with Carlo, for a change of pace, I thought I would miss Chicago, but something happened to me as I crossed the bridge into Happenstance. I can't explain it, except to say that for some reason, I think I was meant to be here. My friends would laugh at my silly notion, but I can't escape the impression that I am somehow tied to this place.

I am also becoming attracted to William. He is different from the young men in Chicago, quieter, but not shy. He is self-possessed in the way that he seems to know what he wants from life. He is already a successful partner in his father's import/export business. Carlo told me William thinks I am a real dish. Mama would be scandalized by his slang, but I find him quite dashing in his own way.

Last night we danced together almost all evening at a party given by the Barlows. Afterward, we walked through the conservatory and out onto the lawn, and stood under the stars. William pointed out many of the constellations to me and we talked of life and his plans for the future. He asked if I had plans for my future. I said I appreciated a challenge and hoped I would find one, that I did not wish to live out my life prancing from party to party and fête to fête. He smiled at me but did not say anything else.

September 25, 1922
William and I enjoyed a drive in his automobile around Happenstance and area, and then stopped for an elegant dinner at a riverside establishment within sight of the bridge. We drank champagne and ate stuffed quail and Mediterranean side dishes. I think William does not want to think of the time when I will leave Happenstance, and neither do I. I wish I could think of an excuse to stay, but at present, there is none. But perhaps there is reason to return.

September 26, 1922
William is always charming and attentive when Carlo isn't around, but the two of them sometimes forget about Lilian and me when they are involved in one of their discussions. I suppose their friendship goes back a good while and they have common experiences that bind them together, but I dislike being excluded from anything. Lilian doesn't appear to be offended by it. I believe she has no higher aspirations than to become a wife and appear with her husband at social events. Well, I am not that easily satisfied. I want an interesting life and a husband who loves me as more than a consort.

September 30, 1922
We've had several parties during the month we've been in Happenstance. I wish I could share some of these times with my friends back home. The Barlows hire small orchestras for the dances. They set up in the sunroom and their music drifts across the main hall and into the drawing room. I love the dancing best, especially when William is my partner. Carlo dances very well, too. Lilian

*is enamored of him, so I don't tell her about all
the young ladies he wines and dines in Chicago,
or of the questionable places he frequents. Let her
hold the dreams into the future until she finds
someone more fitting for her.*

*The days here in Happenstance have not all been
exciting, but I enjoy the peace of this place. On
quiet evenings, we listen to the radio. Mr. and
Mrs. Barlow are personable but set great stock
in propriety.*

Matt smiled. He laid aside the journal and switched off
the light, somewhat disappointed that it was a memoir of
teenage romance instead of a revelation of Barlow Manor
history. He could not, however, prevent the dreams that
resulted from his readings.

He dreamed of dancing with Amanda Eugenie
Rutherford in the front hall of Happenstance Hotel, and of
standing under the stars with her. He dreamed of walking into
the conservatory and finding it alive with plants and birds and
enormous butterflies, and then Amanda was no longer
Amanda but Roni. When he recognized her, she floated away
from him with the butterflies, leaving him with a wink and a
smile.

Roni was not at breakfast on Sunday morning when Matt
showed up.

"She said something about sleeping in and then meeting
Belvina for brunch," said Emmaline.

He sat across from the ladies and helped himself to
waffles with bumbleberry sauce. "I swear I will double my
weight by the time I leave here."

"Nonsense," said Grayce. "You are far too thin. You need
to pick up a little for your health."

"Look who's talking," said Emmaline. "You've turned into
a shadow, a fog. One day you will dissipate with the rising of
the sun."

"Emmaline, you exaggerate. I've always been thin.
Besides, at my age, what does it matter?"

"It matters to us that you stay healthy," said Matt. "Eat up now, ma'am." He gave her a wink, and she raised her eyebrows and dropped a dollop of whipped cream onto her waffle.

"Will you be accompanying us to the service this morning?" asked Emmaline.

Matt's fork paused halfway to his mouth. He wasn't sure he was ready. How did one re-invent a trust that had been bruised? Did he want to set himself up for that again?

"I hadn't thought about it. I don't think I'd fit in."

"Nonsense. Everyone fits in at *Our Redeemer*."

"Don't you have a family pew or something?"

"We used to," said Emmaline, "but Reverend Selig forbids it. He says we come to worship, not to establish our status."

"I don't know...."

"You don't have to worry about what to wear; most anything goes. You can even wear your ponytail. No one will ask you to leave."

"Emm, for heaven's sake use some tact. I'm sorry, Mr. Smith."

"It's all right. I...suppose I could come this time."

"Good then. We leave at 10:35 sharp."

When Matt entered *Our Redeemer* with the ladies at 10:43, he expected he would feel out of his element, but Donald and Maisie sent him warm smiles from the pew where they sat with their three children, and he noticed Bob and Belvina near the back. Her head swiveled like that of a horned owl, and her eyes behind her rimless glasses looked as large. Obviously, she was not brunching with Roni.

Old Man Craddock appeared, much to Matt's surprise. He spoke to no one, but sat alone on a back pew, his head bowed.

The Misses Barlow led Matt to a seat near the center of the sanctuary, "away from the draught of the windows and noisy children." He noticed Harold Haskins near the windows, and Earlene Phipps with a man Matt assumed to be her husband, a quiet looking, well-behaved sort.

Annaliese Selig sat alone on a front pew. Other parishioners filed in and found seats.

The congregation rose when Reverend Selig walked in through the vestry door.

"Let us pray," he said, and proceeded to acknowledge and address a God who was, according to the reverend, both Almighty Judge and Friend of Sinners. The paradox wasn't lost on Matt. He'd experienced many strange things in Happenstance since his arrival, and this followed the pattern.

To Matt's surprise, young Cydnee from the Waldorf approached the microphone, and after her habitual giggle, she tucked her gum into her cheek and proceeded to sing with the voice of an angel.

As the service flowed by, a gentle comfort began to trickle through the barrier of frustration Matt had built up. He closed his eyes and let the song drift through him. Music always stirred him and opened his heart to the deeper emotions.

The song finished too soon and Cydnee returned to her seat. Reverend Selig read the Scripture and expounded on it, not as one who had learned facts from a book or a school, but as one who spoke from experience, from faith, from assurance that what he said was true.

After the service, the congregation traded pleasantries in the brightness of noonday and drifted off to their respective homes for Sunday dinner. Did people still make fried chicken and mashed potatoes on Sunday as Amma had done?

Matt was overcome by nostalgia. He sent Grayce and Emmaline ahead in the station wagon while he sauntered home, deep in thought, hands in the pockets of his chinos. Ever since he'd come to Happenstance, God had pursued him in a quiet but insistent manner.

Matt shook his head. What was it about this town that stamped its mark on a person? Not only did he feel different, his thoughts also changed gears. Happenstance seemed like a beacon in the dark night of his struggle. People accepted him, and even Ginny's physical likeness had been resurrected in the form of Roni. It all worked together to ease the old ache in his soul.

As Matt turned in at the long hotel lane, his mood lightened. He hoped he would find his way out of this valley to a higher plain. And as much as he had thought to avoid it, his feelings for Roni had grown. Her smile, her eyes, her kiss, all seemed to lift him from the pit of his past. Perhaps she would be at lunch after all.

To Matt's amazement and delight, Johanna served crisp fried chicken, a steaming bowl of mashed potatoes, and creamed corn for lunch. She had also made a green salad.

"I can't believe this," said Matt. "I thought the days of Sunday dinners were past."

"We still have to eat on Sundays," said Emmaline.

"Yes, but such fare. Just like my grandmother used to make. I'm going to guess the dessert is fresh apple pie."

Grayce glanced at Emmaline, who beamed at him. "From our own trees, you know."

"Have I died and gone to heaven?"

"Mr. Smith, we do not jest about such matters. Happenstance Hotel is real enough and can be pleasant, but this life still holds too many disappointments to be heaven."

"Sorry, Miss Grayce. Food can create such nostalgia."

Emmaline spoke up. "They say smell is the most nostalgic of the senses; perhaps taste is next."

"Who are *they*, Emm? Who says these things?"

"Oh bother, Graycie, I don't know and I don't care. I read it somewhere."

"How do you know it's true?"

"Perhaps I made it up on my own, in which case it may not be truth at all, but pure conjecture." She lifted her chin in triumph and Grayce snorted.

"You are a piece of work, Emmaline Louise."

"Why, thank you."

Johanna placed a piece of still warm apple pie topped by a scoop of vanilla ice cream at each place.

"This is perfection, Johanna. You cook fit for a royal court."

"*Danke.*" Johanna turned away, her face reddening, and returned to her private sanctuary.

"You see, Matthew, you should not leave us yet. Johanna has more special recipes she wants to try out on you."

"She does?"

"Oh yes, she told me."

"Does she speak? I haven't heard more than two words from her since I arrived. I'm glad she talks to someone."

Matt savored each bite of the pie. The apples were tart with just enough sugar, the crust melted in his mouth, and the ice cream crowned it with cool smoothness.

The rest of the day passed pleasantly. He puttered around the shed and cleaned up what he could, then took a pedal on one of the antique bikes before dinner. He thought he might try to restore it in the upcoming week.

15

Monday morning Matt sauntered over to the Waldorf for coffee. He decided to take the long way home and stop at Beresford Gas Station to check out the situation on his Harley.

He stood outside the doorway of Bear's office while the mechanic finished a phone call. When he heard him end the conversation, he walked in and took a seat on the old straight-backed chair Bear had wired together.

"I know what you're gonna ask, and I got a' answer. That was the bus depot on the phone. Your bike parts came in. I was afraid they wouldn't come till Monday night, and then I have a car and a three-ton truck to look at."

"Do you have to pick up the parts now?"

"That was the plan, but seein' as you're here, would you want to go?"

"Sure."

"You can use my truck."

Matt jumped into Bear's restored 1962 Chevy half ton and purred down a side street to the bus depot a few blocks east of the gas station. He had never understood why the bus lines insisted on hiding their depots in the back parts of small towns. How did the drivers manage to navigate all the back alleys and turnarounds?

The box of coils and spark plug wires on the seat beside him gave Matt a sense of relief. These were the items that would get him on the road again. Now he wasn't sure he was in a hurry anymore. He and Roni didn't have anything official going on, but there were definite possibilities, and he didn't want to leave the Barlows in their current situation.

"How soon will you get to this?" he asked Bear when he got back to the shop.

"Tomorrow if possible, but I might not finish till Wednesday."

"It would be good to get the wheels under me again, but don't stress about it. I need to make sure the Barlow sisters are okay before I leave town anyway."

"Well that's good news if anything is, Matt."

"By the way, do you still have the Happenstance Hotel sign that used to be out on the main road?"

Bear pushed out his bottom lip and frowned. "I think I might. Why? You wanna use it? Needs a bit of work."

"Would you have some time soon to help me put it back up on the highway? The hotel has been empty so long Miss Grayce is getting worried."

Bear shrugged. "I guess I could do that. Oh, and I forgot to tell you, the reverend asked if we'd be willing to help him remove wallpaper tomorrow morning. I can't make it if I'm gonna fix that Harley."

"What did you tell him?"

"Said I was sure you would, even if I couldn't make it."

"How could you offer my services like that? I told you I didn't want to start anything I couldn't finish." *Are you listening to yourself, Sadler?*

"You got other plans?"

"I don't get it. People keep trying to organize my life for me."

"Do it yourself, others wouldn't have to." Bear smirked as he turned on his air compressor, cutting off any response. Matt walked himself back downtown, mumbling all the way.

Thanks to Bear's generous offer on his behalf, Matt hiked over to the parsonage as soon as he had finished his toast and coffee the next morning. He knocked on the door and entered at Annaliese's call. His olfactory sense was stirred by the smell of baking apples, cinnamon and sugar.

" 'Morning. Gavin Beresford said you had some wallpaper that needed to be removed."

"Oh jah. The roofing bee, it made a good roof for my Otto and me. No more rain seeping through and shplinking in pails over all the house. Now the inside we need to fix."

"I'm glad to hear the roof is snug. Tell me where to start with the wallpaper and I'll get at it."

"My Otto, he will first help you move furniture from out the way. He has to the church gone to bring something over. I make for you a cup of coffee and äpfel strudel, hot from the oven she iss."

"I should earn my reward first," said Matt, pulling up a chair and leaning on the tabletop, "but if you insist."

"Jah, I insist!" Annaliese chuckled and bustled about her small kitchen. The strudel was delicious. He was licking the last crumbs off his plate when Reverend Selig limped into the room.

"Ah, while the cat's away... She doesn't let me have many of those delicacies."

"Iss not good for you, my love, but enough you have to keep your belly round."

"Thanks for the reminder. Matt, we may as well get busy, since I'm not going to get any special treatment here."

"Ach, you Otto! He all the time teases me. You go now, work." Annaliese prodded her husband into the living room while Matt followed.

The wallpaper needed redoing. It had warped and wrinkled and folded with time, and was beginning to let loose in places. Matt detected spots where it had been glued back on. Maybe it wouldn't be too difficult to peel off.

"I'll move the furniture, Reverend," said Matt.

"Are you sure? Perhaps I should trot on down to Wuppertal's and rent his wallpaper steamer while you're at it. That would make the job easier."

"You don't need a steamer. Ginny and I figured out that a spray bottle filled with warm water and a touch of soap works best. If you get me a pail of hot soapy water and a sponge, I'll presoak an area at a time and then start with the spray bottle and a putty knife."

The reverend shrugged and headed back to the kitchen. "Whatever you say, boss."

Matt moved the couch and chairs into the hallway and the

old cabinet stereo into the middle of the room. By the time he had finished, the reverend was back with the needed supplies.

"There now. You have me curious, Matt. Since you won't let me help you, I'll sit here in the doorway and you can tell me about Ginny."

Maybe it was the nature and vocation of his listener, but as Matt soaked and peeled, sprayed and scraped, his tongue loosened and his guard fell. It was refreshing.

Matt arrived back at the hotel in time for lunch. He was surprised to find Roni there as well.

"Fancy meeting you here," he said as he pulled out a chair for her. "At least I can rest in the assurance that you will return now and then for food."

"Oh yeah." Roni passed the French bread to Emmaline. "How are you feeling, dear? I haven't had much time to pamper you this week."

"We manage to take care of each other," said Grayce, her lips tight.

Roni sobered. "I'm sure you do. I just meant I missed you both."

"What, and you didn't miss me?" Matt asked.

Grayce stirred her soup but didn't get any of it to her mouth. Frowning, she spoke. "Have any of you seen my glasses? I wear them most of the time, but I took them off to clean them, and now I can't remember where they are."

Roni stopped buttering her bread. "When did you last have them, dear?"

"She wore them this morning when we watched *Jeopardy* in the parlor," said Emmaline. "I remember because I said we would soon need to buy a larger screen TV."

"Did you look in the parlor?" asked Roni.

"Of course we did." Grayce snapped.

Matt stepped in to ward off a confrontation. "I'll go look again right after lunch."

"I hope you find them. I'd help, but I have to get back to work or Karl will have a fit. If you haven't found the glasses by dinnertime, I'll order a new pair tomorrow. I can pick them up in Athens on my next trip."

"Thanks. Have a good afternoon," said Matt as Roni whisked out the door.

Matt looked across the table to Grayce, whose face was taut with barely disguised fury, and Emmaline's brow creased with worry.

Grayce's eyes bored into his. "There. Did you see? She treats me like a child, as if I lack the ability to think for myself. All I did was to ask about my glasses. Do you think Miss Wilkinson has never mislaid anything? My word!"

"Calm down, Graycie. You are going to pop a blood vessel." Emmaline patted her arm, but Grayce jerked it away.

"Calm down, my eye. I do not enjoy being humiliated, and in my own home."

Matt pursed his lips and tried to find the golden words that would dispel the tension. He gave up. "I'll go look for your glasses."

He returned from the parlor in a minute, holding the missing item. He handed the glasses to her with a tentative smile. "They were on the end table beside your chair."

Grayce stared at the glasses, then at Matt. "I looked there. They were not there before." She reached for them with shaking hands.

"Oh dear," said Emmaline.

"Don't 'oh dear' me, Emm. We both looked and you know they weren't there."

"Yes, but perhaps we missed them...although I don't know how we could have."

"You believe us, don't you Mr. Smith?"

Matt came around behind them. "How about you both go upstairs for a nap. You are tired from all this strain. And don't worry about the glasses. It's not important."

"You don't believe us."

"I didn't say—"

"It was implied." Grayce rose from the table. "I am not sleepy. I will be in the office looking through our financial records."

Matt pulled out Emmaline's chair and she headed upstairs after giving him a tight, worried smile. He was about to head out the door when he heard a cry from Grayce. He ran into the office to see her standing at the desk, tugging at the drawers.

"Miss Grayce, what is it?"

"These drawers are locked. I never lock them. There is a key, but it is not where it should be." She turned to face him, worry troubling her features. "It's that Miss Wilkinson. She has locked away the books."

Matt stared at her. "Why are you accusing her? Why would she even bother about the books?"

Grayce sank into the chair and wrung her hands. "She offered to do some of the bookwork for us. You talked to her about the hotel's insurance policy. She said she needed to look at some of the books in order to figure it out. She took them with her to the office, but told me she had put them back. Now I can't even check if they did come back."

"Why wouldn't she return them? And maybe she thought you locked them away for safety. Where do you keep the key?"

Grayce raised her chin and met his eyes. "You think I misplaced that as well? I assure you I did not. The key is kept in this pencil box in the narrow drawer. It has its own space, but it is not there. Would you like to check?"

Matt dropped into the chair in front of the desk and stared back at her. "Miss Grayce, I am as confused as you are by this whole situation. I'll talk to Roni when she gets home, but I know she had no part in this."

Grayce rose as if in pain and walked toward the door. "I'm going upstairs. I will see you at dinner." She turned and gave Matt a hard stare. "I will find proof."

Matt raised his eyebrows. What did she mean by that? Proof of what? How did things get sticky so fast and how did he land up in the middle of it? He left the office, closed the door behind him and headed for his room. Maybe an hour of Amanda's journal would prove an interesting escape from the current situation.

> *October 15, 1922*
> *This sojourn in Happenstance would be perfect, but for the fact that Carlo and William keep disappearing. For long periods of time they are gone, leaving me to visit with William's parents and Miss Lilian. William's sister is a nice girl, but*

rather prudish and inexperienced. I'm afraid my friends would laugh at her. She thinks Carlo Vittorio Farini is the living end. She's absolutely smitten by him and I'm embarrassed to say he deceives her roguishly, because I happen to know he doesn't care for her at all. I must speak to him about it. But now, I must tell about what happened yesterday. It has me in emotional tatters.

Last evening, after a game of bridge, Carlo left the drawing room with the excuse that he needed to go out for a breath of fresh air. William accompanied him. I assumed they wanted to smoke. I hadn't come all the way from Chicago to be left out of whatever it was they were doing, and I'm not afraid of smoke, so I followed, telling Miss Lilian that I needed something from my room and would return in a moment.

Carlo and William did not go outside at all; they slipped down the cellar stairs with candles in their hands. I tiptoed after them, and discovered their secret: there is a hidden room at the far end of the cellar, and past that, tunnels. I was not so bold as to follow them into the narrow passageway, but waited until Carlo returned to the hidden room.

Matt's imagination exploded. Hidden room! Tunnels! That's what Grayce hadn't wanted him to know. But why? What were the tunnels used for? Were they still open? He turned the page in anticipation.

16

When Carlo emerged from the tunnel, I asked him what he was doing. Forgive me, but I will never in all my life forget his reaction. He jumped so high he dropped his candle, which extinguished on the dirt floor, plunging us into total darkness.

Before I knew it, he had grasped my arms and pinned me to the wall. I was too stunned to speak, but I must have cried out, because he realized who it was he held against the rough wall. He released me but would not allow me to leave. He asked me what in heaven's name I was doing down there—actually, his language was stronger than that—and made me promise I would never say a word about this to anyone. I think I am fortunate he didn't strike me senseless before he recognized me. My heart still hammers at the thought of that possibility. I think Carlo was afraid, too, of what he might have done to me.

I've never seen Carlo so angry. I was afraid and couldn't help but cry. He apologized and I'm sure he meant no harm; he's always been a gentleman. I said I forgave him, but I didn't like the fact that he had treated me with such roughness.

He made me promise I would never let on to William that I knew about the tunnels, and sent

*me upstairs with another promise that he would
tan my hide if I ever set foot in the cellar again.
That comment was not spoken like a gentleman,
I think. I said I wanted to be in on whatever they
were doing and he threatened to send me back to
Chicago on the next train if I ever mentioned the
matter again.*

*Why was he so angry that I knew of the tunnels?
What were they doing down there? Will William
ever tell me about it? Of course, I didn't tell
anyone, except for this record, because I am old
enough to be trusted with secrets. If it's that
important to Carlo and to William, I can honor
my promise. But I still wonder. Perhaps I will
investigate on my own, when Carlo and William
are away. They were talking of going over the
Bridge this evening.*

Matt intercepted the sisters as they came downstairs mid-afternoon. Grayce looked somewhat better after a rest.

"I have some questions," he said. "Would you please join me in the parlor?"

They shared a glance and nodded.

"What is on your mind, Mr. Smith?" asked Grayce after they had seated themselves.

"This." He pointed to the journal beside him on the sofa. "I've discovered some pretty interesting stuff in here."

The ladies cast concerned looks at each other.

"Your mother mentions something about tunnels. I've read up to the part where she discovers Carlo coming out of one."

Grayce shook her head. "You see, Emmaline Louise, what comes of divulging too much?" She turned her attention to Matt. "I'm afraid Emmaline has erred in offering the journals to you, Mr. Smith. There are certain...family affairs we do not wish to dredge up at this time—or ever. Would you care to sit out on the lawn with us for a spell?"

"You just want to sweep this down the stairs?" asked Matt, disappointment coloring his words.

"Downstairs! How did you know?" Emmaline stared at

him with incredulity.

"Know what?"

"Oh bother. This is running completely out of hand," said Grayce.

Matt leaned forward. "The tunnels are still downstairs? They've never been closed up? Miss Grayce, why don't you tell me? I understand about keeping secrets. They can destroy you or help you, depending on how you deal with them." *Maybe you should listen to your own advice, Sadler.*

"It all began long ago as a humanitarian effort." Grayce's first whispered words gained strength as she told the tale. "As you know, Mr. Smith, before the civil war, many slaves fled their masters in search of freedom in the north and in Canada. Happenstance stood in the path of some of the escape routes.

"This mansion was known, in those days, as Barlow Manor. My great-great grandfather, Robert Austen Barlow, had a strong wish to help those unfortunate people whom history treated with such cruelty. In the 1840s, he had secret tunnels dug beneath the house and out into the forest so the slaves could hide and rest and continue on undetected."

"He built the conservatory and the chapel at that time also," said Emmaline, "to distract from any suspicions."

"Yes," continued Grayce. "According to older journals, dozens of fleeing slaves used Barlow Manor as a station in the underground railroad in those days, although most traffic traveled east of here. It became quite dangerous after the Compromise of 1850."

"Why would that become a dark secret?" asked Matt. "I would be proud of such a heritage."

Grayce looked at Emmaline and then at Matt. "We would be proud of those days too, but the tunnels have since been used for detestable purposes. I don't know quite how to tell you...I...."

"Rum-running," said Emmaline. "That's what it was, Graycie; rum-running."

Grayce placed her hand on her forehead and sighed. "Yes, Mr. Smith, Emmaline has spoken the truth. Our own mother, Amanda Eugenie Rutherford Barlow, was the one who found it out."

"She caught Father in the act," said Emmaline. "It's all in

the journals."

"Ladies, this is fascinating stuff. What a great story."

Both sisters stared at him in horror. "Mr. Smith," said Grayce, "we must trust you to keep this in confidence. We do not wish anyone to be reminded or informed of it. We prefer to leave the past in the past, and that includes the tunnels. And don't forget to ask Miss Wilkinson about the desk key. I wish to have access to our own records."

"Yes, Miss Grayce."

Matt met Roni as she turned her car into the lane. He jumped off his bicycle and motioned for her to roll down her window. She frowned at him, punched the volume button on the stereo and buzzed the window down.

"You missed me that much?"

"Couldn't wait for you to park the car. Listen, I want to warn you. Miss Grayce is ticking."

"You mean like a bomb?"

"Yup."

"Why? Did she lose something again?"

"Her glasses were where she left them, on the table beside her chair. But now the key to the office desk is missing. She says she never locks it, and when she tried to get the financial records out, she couldn't. She is pretty ticked, to put it mildly."

"Do you see?" Roni slapped the side of the car. "She's not capable of handling the books. Besides, there are serious issues with the finances that need to be straightened out before we can fit a better policy to the hotel. I'm willing to work with them in my off time, but she has to allow me to do the job."

"But they are her books. I'm sure she appreciates your concern—"

"Don't kid yourself. She does nothing of the kind. Emm—sorry, Emmaline—is grateful, but Grayce is a real pill, as they would put it. I'm tempted to throw the books back into the desk and let the ladies fend for themselves."

"You women are playing with my mind. I'd have sworn Grayce was as sharp as a tack, but you keep seeing the inconsistencies, and I don't know what to think. Listen, let's go up for dinner and talk afterward. Maybe we can go for a walk or something."

"Sounds good to me. Beat you back." She rolled up her window and stepped on the gas, leaving Matt in the dust. He pedaled back to the hotel deep in thought.

Dinner passed in stony silence on the part of Grayce. Emmaline batted out a few sentences and Matt tried to field them, but they rolled out of bounds. Roni commented on mundane things and finally gave up.

When dinner was over, Matt suggested he and Roni go for an evening walk, and they excused themselves. They strolled the length of the oak-sheltered lane, then around the square, stopping from time to time to talk, or to point out something of interest. On their return, they walked around the side of the house to the beautiful grounds sloping from the manor to the woods.

Matt stopped and stared at the darkening sky, thinking of Amanda and William. "I can never get enough of the night sky."

Roni stood near him, looking up as well. "I recognize the Big Dipper. The rest are just stars to me."

"It's a good place to start. The Big Dipper is part of the Ursa Major constellation, also known as the Big Bear."

"Impressive. Where's the Little Dipper?"

He stood behind her and pointed over her shoulder. "Look a little more toward the middle of the sky. See that bright star there? That's Polaris. It marks the tip of the handle of the Little Dipper."

"Oh, I think I see it. What's that constellation there to the left?"

Matt focused on where Roni pointed. "I believe that is Cassiopeia. And way over there is Orion. See his belt?"

She turned to face him and put her hand on his chest. "You are a veritable wealth of information, Matt. Where did you learn it all?"

He stared into her luminous eyes, enchanted by the way they reflected the starlight. He couldn't tell if they were brown or green. His heart beat faster and his mouth went dry. He had no intention of telling her that astronomy was one of Ginny's interests.

Roni smiled at his apparent unease. "Don't you want to watch the stars, Matt?"

Matt traced the outline of her jaw with his finger. "I can see them in your eyes. May I kiss you?"

He didn't wait for her response, but knew it in the way she returned his kiss. Heart racing, he pulled away to look at her again. A mosaic of emotions shone in her eyes as he looked deeply into them. She seemed at a loss for words.

"What were we talking about?"

"I think Orion."

"Oh yes. Orion."

Dreams were unkind to Matt that night. Ginny's face materialized and then dissolved among constellations, while Matt scraped wallpaper off the sky so Roni could see the stars better. After several hours of tossing and turning, he snapped on the light and pulled the journal from under his bed. Perhaps Amanda could distract him from his wearying dreams.

October 20, 1922
Soon it will be time for me to return to Boston, but although I miss my friends and family, I do not look forward to leaving Happenstance. I have developed a strange but strong affinity for this town, this manor, these people, and I feel I shall forever be incomplete without them. Most of all, William.
Yesterday I confided to William that I have been more or less engaged to Jonas for some time now. Everyone expects us to marry soon, but I have misgivings. Jonas is a fine man, and I told William so, but he doesn't have the sense of adventure that William has. I didn't tell William that. He asked me if I would ever come back; I said I hoped so.
He asked when Jonas and I would marry, and all

at once I knew I could never marry Jonas. Not after meeting William. My distance from Jonas had reinforced my previous doubts, as I had thought it might. I'm afraid I cried and clung to William and told him I couldn't marry Jonas and I didn't want to leave Barlow Manor or Happenstance. He asked me why not. I looked up at him, tears on my cheeks, and he leaned down and kissed me. I've never been kissed like that by Jonas. We sneaked into the conservatory and shared our hopes and dreams surrounded by hibiscus and wisteria.

He said if I would go back home like a good girl now, he would come to visit me at Christmas, and if I still felt the way I did this evening, he would ask me a question. He made me promise not to marry Jonas before then, under any circumstances.

William assured me he would speak to Carlo and make him promise to protect me from Jonas and all the other young men who would be vying for my hand. I laughed at him and he kissed me again in the moonlight.

October 25, 1922
Tomorrow Carlo and I must leave. My romantic reality is about to be consigned to the place of dreams and memories. William and I said our farewells yesterday, alone, and promised each other to be patient. He said he had some work to attend to, and the time would speed by here. He didn't explain, and I didn't let on that I knew anything of the tunnels. But if I ever return to Happenstance—and in my heart I know I will—I promise myself I will find out the secret of the tunnels. I will convince William that he can trust me.

October 26, 1922
I watched Barlow Manor, and my William, until we turned out of the lane and onto Main Street.

As we passed through the covered bridge, I had the strangest sense that I would return, that I belonged there. Perhaps the future will be even brighter than this brief visit. And now I must think of home and Jonas and what to do about him.

Matt slipped the book back under the bed, aware of the subtle parallels of the present and the past. Did history always repeat itself? He lay a long time, hands clasped behind his head, staring into the darkness.

As Matt showered and dressed the next morning, his thoughts shifted to the welfare of the Barlow sisters, and he began to sort ideas for gaining customers for the hotel. They needed to advertise, but what would attract people? Maybe Roni would have some ideas. He was sure she had the sisters' best interests at heart, even if they didn't understand that. She cared about Morris Craddock too, even though he treated her with disdain.

Like Morris, everyone had a story. Even the hotel. Tunnels! He couldn't believe it.

Tunnels! He stopped in his tracks. Of course. His pace quickened and he called for Grayce and Emmaline as he approached the dining room.

"Whatever is the matter?" Miss Grayce appeared from the lobby, eyes wide.

"Nothing is the matter. I've had an idea."

"Are you seeking congratulations, Mr. Smith?"

"Miss Grayce, please. It has to do with the hotel."

She raised her eyebrows and beckoned him as she proceeded to breakfast. Emmaline sat waiting, expectant.

"I'm dying to know about your idea."

"Emm, you are not dying, although a week ago we thought it a bitter possibility."

"You know what I mean, Grayce Lorraine. Come sit so Matthew can tell us."

Matt pulled out a chair for Grayce and then sat down himself. "I have an idea for bringing customers to the hotel."

"Do tell."

"The tunnels! You were telling me about the underground railway and also of your father's use of the tunnels under the hotel."

"I'm not proud of what Papa did," said Emmaline. "If he hadn't used this grand hotel for ignominious purposes, he may have lived longer and Mother wouldn't have had to survive on her own."

"Emm, that's private business, and as I've said before, I'm sure Mr. Smith is not interested in our family problems. I believe Johanna will bring our breakfast in a minute."

"Listen!" said Matt, sitting on the edge of his chair. "What else do you know about the tunnels?"

The ladies both stared at him. "I believe this was your idea," said Grayce.

"Yes, but I need to know more details first. Not your father's vices. Tell me how Barlow Manor helped the slaves in the days before emancipation, and about the rum-running. We could use those stories to promote the hotel.

"Listen to this: *Barlow Manor Inn, the stately home of five generations of Barlows. View the tunnels used to transport escaped slaves to the forest and from there to freedom in Canada. Experience a slice of the underground world of rum-running during Prohibition.*"

"My word, Mr. Smith. We would be run out of town. We would rather keep these things quiet than have everyone talking about them, and I doubt people would wish to seek accommodation at a hotel that had been used for such questionable purposes."

"Why? Most of the townspeople already know, or their parents do."

"Perhaps Matthew has a point, Graycie. I read about a place up in Canada where they do something like that. It was in Deer Head or Moose Head—let me think—Moose Jaw. That's it. They have tours of tunnels where the Chinese immigrants lived and worked, a whole underground society. And they also have tours of the tunnels used by bootleggers like Al Capone."

"Emm, your imagination has run away with you again."

"No, it hasn't, Graycie. I read it. Did you ever hear of it,

Matthew? The tourists flock there every summer."

"I haven't heard of it, but it sounds fascinating."

"I think it's a wonderful idea," said Emmaline. "What fun we could have."

"Fun!" retorted Grayce. "Remember our age, Emm. Too much fun can kill us."

"If I hadn't promised to help the Seligs with their painting this morning, I would run downstairs right now and see what is left of the tunnels. As it is, I think we have the beginning of a plan."

"Don't do that yet, Mr. Smith. Please allow us time to process your ideas."

As difficult as it would be, Matt agreed to wait.

17

After breakfast, Matt walked to the parsonage to help the Seligs with their living room project. Annaliese had not yet decided on a paint color, so he did a bit of mudding to hide nail holes and gouges, preparing the walls for painting. He did all he could; they said they would call him when they'd decided on the paint.

Time hung heavy for Matt all afternoon, and at 5:05 he walked over to Paradise Realty to pick up Roni. She was on the phone and Karl Collins was nowhere in sight.

Roni held her hand over the mouthpiece and stared at him. "Matt?"

"Came to walk you home."

"Oh."

Into the phone, she said, "Hang on, would you?" She stood and put on a smile. Matt thought it looked forced and wished he'd called ahead.

"Matt, why don't you grab a cup of coffee and entertain yourself in Karl's office while I finish up. I won't be a minute." She set down the phone. "Here, I'll turn on the radio for you, and—" she typed in a password on Karl's keyboard, "—you can check your emails."

"Sure thing. I'm not in a hurry."

She smiled and closed the door once he had gone into Karl's office. The local oldies station pumped out the tunes and Matt sank into Karl's leather chair with a cup of stale coffee.

He clicked into Karl's computer and typed in *Moose Jaw,*

then *Tourism*, and scrolled down to *Tunnels*. Emmaline was right. He leaned back and watched a mini-film about the *Passage to Fortune*—the Chinese immigrant story—and *The Chicago Connection*. The idea fascinated him and made him more determined than ever to use the Barlow Manor tunnels to promote the hotel.

Roni pushed open the door of Karl's office. "To what do I owe this surprise?"

"You done?"

At her nod, Matt clicked out of the site and joined her in the front office. "Hope I didn't rush you. I'm bored. I spent the morning helping the Seligs."

"Looking for brownie points?"

"No brownie points. I agreed to do it because I have time on my hands. Bear volunteered me. I didn't land a job like you did. I have to fill my time somehow."

"You didn't try to land a job."

"I didn't ever dream I'd be here for more than a couple of days."

"Better start checking the ads. This place doesn't let you go that easily." Roni wiggled her eyebrows and hummed the tune from *The Twilight Zone*.

"Let's get out of here," he said, shaking his head.

She laughed and took his arm. "Do we have time for a flavored coffee at Phil's before dinner?"

"I prefer the plain stuff."

"Boring. Let me introduce you to something more exotic."

Matt and Roni settled in a window booth and she ordered French Vanilla flavored coffee for them both. He asked her about her day and she filled him in on the state of the housing market in Happenstance and area.

"But I'm putting all that out of my mind for the rest of the day. Time for one of Johanna's superb dinners and a quiet evening," Roni said.

Matt considered how to phrase the issue on his mind, then blurted it out. "Roni, I think you need to know that Grayce suspects your tea as the cause of Emmaline's collapse last week."

Roni stared at him, her cup in mid-air. "She what?" She banged her cup down and the coffee sloshed onto the table.

"Are you serious?"

"You're the one who told me I had no sense of humor. I wouldn't joke about this. Emmaline took the tea on Monday evening and Tuesday morning and then collapsed. Grayce jumped to conclusions."

"Do you believe that?"

"I thought it was ridiculous, but there's this one catch: Emmaline has more digitalis in her system than her mild meds provide."

"Digitalis! My herbal tea is a mild combination of organic herbs for enhanced health, that's all."

"That's what I assumed, but where did the digitalis come from? It was in Emmaline's system."

"I can't answer that, Matt. Maybe she's taking something she's not talking about."

"They both claim she's not, and Grayce didn't want me to mention it to you, but I think it needs to be addressed."

"Of course. I have a list of the ingredients in my suite. I'll show you what's in the tea, but I can't imagine it being harmful. In fact, to be on the safe side, I'll take my herbal tea mix and have it analyzed. The point is, Matt, as much as I love the ladies, they can't even remember where they left their glasses. How do they know how much medication they've ingested?"

"I don't think they will leave it alone until they have proof." Matt shook his head. "I don't get it. I know Emmaline is a bit scatterbrained but she's very alert. As for Grayce, I've had some terrific talks with her, and I'd swear her brain is in better shape than mine."

"Which means..."

"Hey, be nice to me. I'm new here."

Roni smirked and took another sip of coffee. "I know you think I'm making this up about Grayce, but this type of thing is on and off, and I've seen it progressing. Anyway, I'll get you a tea analysis so they don't lay charges against me or something."

"Thanks, but I know you're busy. Why don't you let me look after the analysis?"

"Oh, I don't mind. I can courier it with the realty mail. It would go to the same lab that tests water samples for the houses we sell."

"Let me know the results as soon as you find out, will you?"

"Will do. This is upsetting. I thought everything was going well and now this. No wonder Grayce looks at me with distrust. We'd better scoot back to the hotel for dinner or she'll blame me for keeping you away."

Matt checked his watch and slid out of the booth. "Listen, why don't we get together afterward on the verandah? Looks like too nice a night to sit inside playing Bridge or Scrabble."

"You're on. You know, I've become fascinated with astronomy."

"Really?"

When she appeared for dinner, Roni brought with her a labeled tea tin. She clapped it down between Grayce and Emmaline, then waited until they both turned to look at her.

"Matt said you two were concerned that the tea I made for Emmaline may have contained something that didn't agree with Emmaline's medication."

The ladies both shot Matt worried glances. Matt was surprised at Roni's timing, but realized they'd have to take care of the misunderstanding sooner than later.

"Shall I read it for you?" he asked Grayce.

"Yes please, Matthew. Our eyesight isn't what it used to be."

"It's the small-print conspiracy. Here we go: plantago ovata."

"That's psyllium seed," said Roni. "It has laxative qualities. Some say it can also help remove cholesterol from the blood."

"Foeniculum?"

"Fennel seed. Used in cooking."

"Yeah, I think I've heard of it. How about...uh...polygonatum multiflorum?"

"It's used in many herbal remedies, known as King Solomon's Seed. I don't have the specifics but it's not toxic."

"Tiliceae?"

"That would be the linden tree. Its flowers and petals can

be used to promote digestion and may also have some effect on coughs and fevers."

"And green tea leaf."

Roni smiled at the ladies and Matt thought he read triumph in her expression. He understood. He knew how it felt to be blamed for something you didn't do, and by people who had been your friends.

He was thankful to retreat to the back garden with Roni after dinner while the ladies played Scrabble.

Matt took Roni's hand as they walked down onto the lawn.

"You sure know a lot about herbal stuff. Where'd you learn all that?"

"It's a hobby of mine," she said. "I love research, and I like what herbal remedies do for me."

The trees whispered their own soft song in the calm of evening, and Matt's heart lifted in hope. He took pleasure in the feel of Roni's hand in his, in the freedom from constant incrimination, in a place that seemed to welcome him without judgment. He rubbed the back of her hand with his thumb and she smiled at him.

"Hey, Matt, you're getting distant again."

"No, I'm right here." He put his arm around her shoulder and pulled her closer, and she slipped her arm around his waist.

They settled themselves against a tree on the edge of the woods, illuminated by tiny white lights arranged in the branches above. For a while they sat in the silence of contentment.

"Now that your bike is almost fixed, are you going to ride off into the sunset and leave me here with a broken heart?"

"I have trouble believing I've made that much of an impression. Maybe the heart that breaks will be mine." His eyes caressed her face, not seeing the color of her eyes or the tone of her skin, but the wild riot of curls. He remembered the feel of Ginny's curls in his fingers and reached out.

She tilted her head to look into Matt's face. "My heart is as vulnerable as the next person's, but I hadn't met anyone here who interested me in the least. Until now."

"Until now? I'd ask who, but I think I might get slugged." She grinned. "Got that right."

Matt heaved a sigh, his fingers entangled in her hair. "Well, as much as I hate to say it, you'd better not get too attached. Things don't seem to work out well for me."

"Too late. I think I'm hooked, Matthew Smith. Even though I don't know much about you. I don't even know where you come from or what you do—did—for a living. Kind of one-sided, don't you think?"

He was tempted to dodge the subject, but decided it was time to answer at least some of her questions. She seemed to sense his hesitation and moved to sit with her back against him. He put his arms around her shoulders and rested his chin on the top of her head.

"I was, and still am, an educator. I've taught kids and teens for more than fifteen years and loved it all, until last term. Something happened that turned the staff and students against me, and then the parents, and pretty soon, the whole town was accusing me of something I hadn't done. It was a set-up, but I don't expect you to believe that. Not even my church believed it. They all hung me out to dry."

"Don't lump me in with the rest of them. If you say so, I believe you. What happened to create all the fuss?"

Matt blew out a breath of air and looked up at the white lights. "Nothing. I was accused of doing something inappropriate. Let's leave it at that. Thanks for believing I am innocent of whatever I was accused of. Let's soak up the beauty of the evening and leave the past behind."

Roni was silent for a time, then turned in his arms to face him. "Matt, I will honor your wish, but I hope you will too. Leave the past behind, I mean."

He tapped the end of her nose and smiled. "Mind reader. I'll try. And thanks for giving me space. Spending time with you makes me forget the past and everything else."

He knew as he said the words they were unwise. He was thinking of the familiar pleasure shared in a strong marriage, but he knew nothing about this woman.

Before he could rephrase his words, she answered him with a kiss that brought both comfort and promise. And passion. When Roni kissed him again, he broke away, heart hammering in his chest. He was pretending this was Ginny. This was not Ginny.

"What's the matter, Matt?"

"I...ah...don't think this is wise."

"Wise? Who's talking about wise? Why are we talking at all?"

Matt ran a hand through his hair and stood, leaning against the tree. Roni stood with him, holding onto his arm.

"Isn't this what you wanted?"

"I think I might have misled you."

"I can make you forget everything else, Matt."

"I'm sure you can. I'm sorry, I didn't explain myself and of course you don't know me from Reed—from back then."

"What are you talking about?"

"I'm one of those old-fashioned guys who puts marriage before intimate involvement."

"Old-fashioned? Try extinct."

Matt rubbed his hands over his face. "I'm sorry, Roni. I wanted something I can't have right now. Forgive me. I believe in love and commitment, and marriage is the best and only place for that. I do enjoy being with you, but it can't be more than that right now. It's a commitment between me and God."

"Sometimes the best is unattainable. Sometimes you take good because it's better than nothing. And what's God got to do with anything?"

Matt shoved his hands into his pockets and kicked at the grass at his feet. "A lot. I thought I'd lost my connection with Him, but this place has been drawing it out again, and I can't jeopardize that."

She turned away from him, her hair falling forward to cover her face.

You are such a jerk, Sadler. He put a hand on her shoulder and turned her around. She let him hold her as she cried.

"I'm sorry, Roni. Can we start over, now that you know where I stand?"

"I don't know, Matt." She sniffled and wiped the tears from her cheeks. "I'm not sure I will ever understand you."

"Would you give it a try?"

She leaned back and traced the pattern on his shirt, then attempted a smile. "I guess I can. But you will need to trust me with a few things too, open up a bit, you know?"

"Okay." He kissed the top of her head. "I'll try, too."

She pulled away and smiled. "All right then. Tomorrow is work, so I'd better get some sleep. Talk to you then. Hey, and maybe one of these days you can take me for a ride on that Harley. It's been years since I've ridden on one. That shouldn't be against your rules."

Her words were tinged with bitterness, and he didn't blame her. "Let me know when it works into your schedule."

They walked to the house together and said goodnight at the foot of the stairs. Matt went to his room shaking his head. What had gotten into him? He'd been without Ginny for five years. Why did he lose it now? He could feel the pangs of conscience when he stepped off the path, but he sorely missed the love he'd shared with Ginny.

She's gone, Sadler. You won't ever find a love like that again.

"Lord," he said as he sank into the chair by the window, "I'm tired of being alone."

He needed to talk to someone. Tomorrow.

18

Next afternoon, Matt cycled down Bridgeway Avenue to Beresford Gas Station. Bear poked his head out from under the hood of an old half-ton clunker.

"Hey, Matt. What can I do you for?"

"Came to check on my bike. Say, you got a minute?"

"Sure. Bike's finished too. Want a coffee?"

"Yeah. That'd be good."

Bear nodded toward his office, a room about ten feet square filled with dilapidated file cabinets, sagging cardboard boxes, belts and pulleys, and a rickety old desk under a pile of papers. "I made a fresh pot a little while ago." He grabbed the carafe and poured the thick brown liquid into two styrofoam cups. Matt took a sip of the tepid brew and choked.

"You sure you didn't get your coffeemaker mixed up with your used oil pail?"

"What are you talkin' about? It's even decaf."

"Decaf motor oil?"

"Careful or you'll hurt my feelings and I won't offer you no more."

Matt shook his head and grinned. "I know what to get you for Christmas: a new coffeemaker with a manual." *Christmas in Happenstance! What am I thinking?*

"What did you come for if not the coffee?" Bear asked, leaning back in his torn orange leatherette chair.

"Just a few questions. I'm trying to piece together a puzzle."

Bear rubbed his big greasy hands together. "I love

puzzles. Do 'em all the time."

Matt raised his eyebrows in surprise. "Who'da thought?"

"Oh yeah. See, I puzzle over ticks and shimmies and thunks and whines, all those nasty noises a ve-hicle tends to make over time. I'm right good at figurin' it out and fixin' it."

Matt snorted.

"You have to give me a few clues before I can solve a problem. More coffee?"

"No! Thank you. Okay, first question: how well do you know Roni?"

Bear shrugged and frowned. "How well do I know her? I'd call her an acquaintance, although there was a time I thought it might be more. Why do you ask?"

"You had something with Roni?"

"Ain't nothin' now, so it don't matter."

"You sure?"

"Course I'm sure. Now look Matt, you got as long as it takes me to drink my coffee."

"Okay." Matt took a deep breath. "We were getting to know each other and then she is way ahead of me, and I slow it down and she's hurt and I'm a jerk."

"It's easy to do that with women, Matt. They don't always hear what you say, and they 'spect you to read between the lions, you know?"

"How do you know so much about women? You ever been married?"

"Me? No, I never pursued that career. Figured I had enough to puzzle on in my line of work. I observe, you know, watch how it goes. You can learn a heap by watchin' and listenin'."

"What have you observed about Roni?"

"You keen on her, Matt? You lookin' for a relationship?"

"I'm not sure. It's been a long time since I was in this situation, and then I was young and foolish. We both were, so it evened out. I'd like to know a bit more about her, how she deals with people, that kind of thing."

"Well, maybe I can give you a few pieces of the puzzle." Bear looked past him out the large window fronting his office and started to talk.

"First time I met Roni, she had a flat tire a mile or so outta

Happenstance and had called her roadside assistance club. They picked me as the nearest tow truck and I met her on the road. She had one of them little toy spare tires, one that wouldn't even hold up your bike. Didn't pay to put it on, so I towed her in here and fixed her tire."

He smiled. "I 'member as we pulled off the bridge and she saw the sign and read it out loud: *'HAPPENSTANCE: A TOWN YOU CAN TRUST'*. Said she'd been lookin' for a place like this for a long time. That's what I know for sure. She was real friendly with me at first, flirtin' and carryin' on. I was flattered, you know, but then she met Phil and I kinda got dumped like a sack of potatoes."

"Phil? From the Waldorf?"

"One and the same. She went after him, but he didn't want nothin' more than friendship. He's what you call a concerned bachelor."

"Conf...whatever. Anyone else I should know about?"

"Matt, what Roni does is Roni's business. I ain't no busybody. They don't ask me to write local gossip for *The Village Voice*. I'm a mechanic, man, not a peeking Tom."

"Peeping Tom."

"Am not!"

"No, I mean...Okay, this is a puzzle, right?"

"Don't be jumping to confusion, then. It ain't no way to figure out a puzzle."

"Sorry, Bear. I'm trying to connect the dots. I don't mean to jump to confu...conclusions."

Bear fidgeted in his chair. "Listen, Matt, I'd love to visit some more, but I got a business to run here. Guy's comin' to pick up his truck this afternoon yet, an' I still have a few pieces to put back together."

"Sorry for keeping you, and thanks for the talk."

"No worries. I ain't always this busy."

Matt dropped his cup, still half full of sludge, into the wastebasket and followed Bear outside.

"Thanks for the coffee."

"You're welcome. Here's the keys to your Harley. Hit the wick and get outta here."

"Thanks. It's been too long away from this baby." Matt cracked the throttle and chugged back to Happenstance

Hotel, leaving the old bicycle beside the gas station.

"How was your day, Mr. Smith?" Grayce asked him when he returned to the hotel for dinner. "We heard the distinct rumble of a motorcycle."

"Yes, ma'am, and it's great to ride again. I had a cup of coffee at Bear's office before I came back."

Both ladies turned horrified eyes on him. "Coffee at the gas station? Oh dear, Mr. Smith. Would you like an antacid?"

"I'm fine. I dropped it in the wastebasket without him seeing it."

"That was a good idea."

"How was your day, ladies?"

"Fine, thank you," said Grayce. Matt noticed Emmaline throw her sister a troubled look. *Everyone is hiding something.*

"We decided to take a little drive, since we haven't been out for a long time."

"Great idea. Where did you go? I could have driven you."

"Don't worry too much, Mr. Smith. We have always looked after ourselves and will have to do so in the future."

"I know, but I want to help when I can."

"We appreciate that."

"Has Roni been around at all today?" Matt heaped his plate with chicken and dumplings and twice roasted potatoes.

"We haven't seen her here," answered Grayce, "but we were away for some time. Were you aware of her plans, Emm?"

"Ask me; I don't know," said Emmaline, shaking her head. "Do you need her for something?"

"No. Just wondering."

The ladies exchanged glances again, and Matt tried to read their eyes.

"Now that you've brought it up," said Grayce, toying with her fork, "we spotted her in Athens this afternoon, speaking with a man who looked somehow familiar, but we couldn't place him."

Matt swallowed his mouthful half chewed. "Someone from here?"

"We don't know, Mr. Smith. I'll think about it some more, but they did appear rather chummy."

"Chummy? You mean—"

"Oh, I'm sure it was nothing. They seemed deep in conversation. And people are more familiar with one another in public these days than we used to be. By the way, Mr. Smith, we were wondering if you would accompany us to see Dr. Percy tomorrow. It has been almost a week since Emm returned from the hospital, and we were supposed to come in for another appointment."

"Of course. Just tell me when."

Matt finished his meal in silence, the taste lost on him as he pondered what the ladies had told him.

Matt escorted the sisters Barlow into the clinic the next day. Sylvia asked them to be seated.

"Dr. Percy will be right with you. I have to leave for a few minutes to pick up my daughter from her piano lesson and take her home."

The sisters chatted while Matt leafed through a *Popular Mechanics* magazine. The door leading from the reception area to the examining rooms burst open and Matt glanced up, expecting to see Dr. Phineas Percy. Instead, he saw a tall woman with straight black hair to her shoulders, and brown eyes that looked right through him.

"Ah, ladies, how wonderful to see your sweet faces again. I've missed you." She advanced on them and hugged both, then shook Matt's hand.

The depth of her dark eyes captivated him. He hadn't seen this nurse here before. "We're waiting to see Dr. Percy."

"I am Dr. Percy."

"Whoa. Not the Dr. Percy I've met." He still held her hand.

She chuckled, drawing her fingers from his grasp. "I suppose the resemblance is faint. I'm his daughter. And you are?"

His daughter? "Matt Smith. I'm staying at the hotel."

"Ah, the one the sisters dub their knight in shining armor. Nice to meet you, Matt. Now ladies, would you come with me, please? How is the old hotel doing?"

"But the shingle outside reads Doctors Phineas and Paul Percy. You can't be Paul."

She turned back and tucked a strand of hair behind her ear. "I'm Paula. The *a* fell off the shingle and we haven't had a chance to replace it. Dad insisted on putting up the sign as soon as I graduated from med school, and the letters weren't secured. Everyone knows who we are—except you, I guess—so it's not a big deal."

"Paula. No one mentioned it."

"I'm not surprised. I've been away at school and interning. Just got back from the east a couple of days ago, and Dad already has me working. I'm taking his patients while he's away fishing; he needed a break. Quite a schedule for a man his age."

Matt wanted to keep her talking. There was something warm and engaging in her eyes, in her friendliness. "How old is he by now?"

"Going to be sixty-six this fall, but he has no intention of retiring. I'm not sure this town has room for both of us, but I would like to see him taking more time away." She ushered the ladies ahead of her.

Matt stood and paced the small reception area, waiting for another glimpse of Dr. Paula Percy, but he was disappointed. By the time the ladies returned to the reception area, Sylvia sat in her receptionist chair once again, and he didn't get another chance to see the doctor with the smiling eyes.

"Matt! Where have you been? I've missed you." Roni breezed into the parlor where Matt visited with the sisters after dinner, and gave him a peck on the cheek.

He stood and offered her a seat. "Here and there. How about you?"

"Oh, work, as usual. Nothing too exciting."

Out of the corner of his eye, Matt saw Grayce's eyebrows rise and knew they were in for what Ginny would have called a scene.

"Did you find what you needed in Athens, Miss

Wilkinson?"

"Athens?" She adjusted her suit jacket. "Oh yes, I had to make a quick trip in to pick up some brochures. Did you stop by the office?"

"No, we were in Athens ourselves, Emmaline and I. We had some business there also."

Roni seemed at a loss for words. She worked up a smile that didn't reach her eyes. "How nice. Where did you see me? You should have stopped and said hello."

"We would have, dear, but you appeared to be otherwise occupied. We didn't want to disturb you and your friend."

"Not to worry, ladies. That was the guy who works at the print shop. He met me to check over the brochures, thought he'd save me some time."

Matt sat back and listened as the women sparred politely. He too, was interested in who Roni had met. He asked himself why. He and Roni had no commitments. She could see whoever she chose, as could he.

"Matt, did you know the ladies had gone to Athens alone?"

"Not until after the fact. Why?"

"Well, I don't think they should be driving outside of town limits alone, with Emmaline's health as it is."

Grayce lifted her chin, her lips pursed. "We managed, thank you."

"Athens isn't a megacity," said Matt.

Roni looked from one to the other. "All right, then. I'm off to bed. Good night." She stood and walked toward the door.

Matt sensed her hurt. He had learned, in the years he had been married to Ginny, that now was the time to intercept her.

"Roni, wait. Let's take a walk."

She stopped but didn't turn around.

"Come on. Down the lane and around the circle. I think some fresh air would do us both good."

When she didn't refuse, he glanced back at Grayce and Emmaline. "Please excuse us, ladies. We'll see you later."

Emmaline wore a confused expression, but Grayce's disapproval was obvious.

Matt and Roni walked in silence for the first few minutes, and Matt decided not to push the matter. He recognized hope in the fact that she had allowed him to hold her hand.

As they turned out of the lane and across the street onto the large oval of grass, shrubs and flowers, she spoke.

"I can't believe you would all stand against me, when I spoke from concern."

"I don't remember speaking against you; I just differed in opinion."

"It's the same thing. Humiliation."

"Differences of opinion are refreshing. It would be pretty boring if we all agreed on everything."

"It all depends on the way you present yourself."

As much as he didn't like what Roni was saying, he wasn't ready for a confrontation. Maybe he could make her smile. He placed his palms together and said, "Please forgive me for humiliating you. Could we be friends again?"

She swatted his arm and then tucked her hand through it. "Don't be cute. I thought you were a mature, dependable kind of man."

"So did I, I mean, I am. Hey, you'll never guess who I met today."

"No, I'm sure I wouldn't. Who?"

"Dr. Paula Percy. I thought she was a nurse and it turns out she—"

"Paula Percy?" Roni jerked to a halt and stared at him.

"Yeah, do you know her?"

Roni seemed to pull herself together with great effort and resumed walking. "I've heard of her, but I've never met her. Is she here for a visit?"

Matt tried to keep up with the changes in Roni. Was she jealous? "I don't think so. She wants to join her father in the clinic, give him more time off. He keeps a hectic schedule for someone his age."

"You learned a lot in a few minutes."

"I had no idea who she was. The sign said Doctors Phineas and Paul, and I knew she wasn't Paul."

"Good eye. Listen, Matt, I don't want to sound jealous because I know we decided to just be good friends, but I care about you. Maybe more than I should. Watch yourself around

Paula."

"What do you mean? She's a doctor, seems to be a nice person. What's to watch?"

Roni threaded her fingers through Matt's and sighed. "There's no nice way to say it. She's a hustler. I know what your values are, and you don't want to hang around with her."

Her words disappointed and surprised him. "Where, pray tell, did you gather this information if you don't know her?"

"I've been around town almost half a year and I've heard a few things. Listen, I don't want to implicate anyone else. Take the advice for what it is: sincere concern."

A car cruised by and he waited until it had rounded the end of the oval. He leaned over and kissed Roni's forehead. "Thanks for the warning." Her eyes glowed with something more than friendship as she reached her arms around his neck and kissed him on the lips. He didn't fight it, but something didn't feel right. Something he couldn't quite figure out. A puzzle, as Bear would say.

19

"Matthew, I have a favor to ask of you," said Emmaline on Saturday morning after Roni had gone to Belvina's to visit.

"To half my kingdom, Miss Emmaline."

She giggled. "You are a gentleman. Your parents raised you well."

"My grandparents raised me, but Gramps and Amma were the best substitute for the real thing I could have wished."

"Well, bless them for it."

"What was it you wanted?"

Emmaline concentrated for a moment. "Oh yes. Dr. Paula telephoned that she ordered in the heart pills I need, and I wondered if you would fetch them for me. She has them at the clinic. I'm sure Graycie and I could walk over, but I'm feeling rather tired today, and I thought perhaps you wouldn't mind going."

"Not a problem, Miss Emmaline. I plan to take a ride on my motorbike, see how it works now that Bear's done with it, and I'll stop by the clinic and get them."

"Thank you, Matthew. I do appreciate it." Her smile was demure, and he thought what a lucky man her Bruce had been.

He fired up the Harley, listened to the rap of the engine. It sounded steady, so he kicked up the stand and pushed forward, twisting the throttle. He'd idle it through town, then let loose on the 85.

He drove to the clinic and parked the bike nose out. He

shut it off and pulled open the door of the office. Before he could say "Doctors Phineas and Paula Percy," the younger of the two pushed through the half-door into the reception area.

"Do you have a bike? I heard a Harley just now."

Matt's eyes popped at her enthusiasm and he pointed over his shoulder. "Yeah, it's right out there. I came to pick up Miss Emmaline's pills."

She spotted it through the front window. "Whoa, baby, that is a sweet bike. Mind if I take a look?"

"Not at all." Matt grinned like a kid. "Just don't let me forget the pills."

"Wait a minute and I'll get them right now." She trotted behind the desk, unlocked a drawer, and produced a package. "I had to run into Athens yesterday and thought I'd save the ladies a trip. Emmaline shouldn't be without them." She handed Matt the bill, which he paid with money Emmaline had given him, and slammed the drawer shut with her hip.

"Let's go take a look at the old girl. I don't have another patient until this afternoon. Got a couple of cancellations this morning."

Matt was still grinning, feeling like the boy with the newest toy, and someone to admire it. "You like bikes?"

"Do I like bikes? Is the Pope Catholic? I ride bikes."

"What do you have?"

"Nothing right now. Long story. I haven't ridden in ages. Hey, could we go for a bit of a spin?"

"Sure. I just got a coil job and I want to see how it runs out on the open road."

Paula glanced back at the clinic. "Let me lock up and grab my jacket."

She was back in two minutes flat, eyes blazing with excitement. "My car is out back," she said. "Follow me home and I'll pick up my helmet."

The Percys lived on the prestigious west side of Happenstance, the west side consisting of a few streets of ostentatious homes. Paula parked in her driveway and Matt waited as she ran inside.

She fastened her helmet as she locked the house door and ran to the bike. "Old money," she commented, waving her hand at the house and yard in general. "Not mine, but it's nicer than my apartment in the city."

"You ready?" How many times had he asked that of Ginny?

"Hit it!"

Bingo. Where had this girl been hiding?

They crawled past the town square, then picked up speed on Parkview Drive going north, but when Matt opened it up on the 85, Paula shrieked with joy. Her grin filled the rearview mirror, and Matt had trouble keeping his heart in his chest. It was the thrill of the ride, he told himself. He loved his Harley, and didn't mind sharing the experience with a fellow biker.

Later, Matt left a note at the hotel that he wouldn't be staying for lunch and headed to the Waldorf. Bear and Donald were both there, and they beckoned him over when he walked in.

"You win the lottery or what?" asked Bear, studying Matt's face.

"Nah," said Donald. "It's a woman."

"Wrong on both counts," said Matt, trying to convince himself. Something about Paula appealed to him, but he pushed the thought from his mind. "Got my bike fixed. Just took a little spin up the 85 and it's working like a charm. Many thanks, Bear."

Phil walked over with the coffee and menus just as Roni and Belvina entered the restaurant. They waved and approached the men's booth.

"Hey there," said Roni. "How was your morning? Not eating Johanna's cooking today?"

"Thought I'd get out and visit with the boys. See you at dinner though."

She winked at him and moved to a table across the room where Belvina waited. Phil called after her. "Veronica, I thought you didn't like bikes. You didn't ever ride with me."

Roni turned back without sitting down, questions in her eyes. "You didn't ask me, Phil. What are you talking about?"

"Were you not riding with Matt this morning? There was a woman on the back—" He turned away from her abruptly and said, "Would you like to place your orders now?"

Matt heard an "ooh boy" from Bear and a hissing sound from Donald. They ordered burgers and fries all around and Phil slunk back to the kitchen.

Throughout the exchange, Matt's comfort level dropped. He had not even thought of Roni when he had agreed to give Paula a ride. Remembering how upset she had been about his brief meeting with Paula the day before, he knew she would go ballistic about her riding on his bike with him. Roni had warned him but he hadn't taken her advice. On the one hand, it was his life, but on the other, was he leading Roni on or did he have feelings for her? It was all too complicated. Whatever the case, he was in deep weeds here.

Roni leaned over and whispered something in Belvina's ear, and the two of them left the restaurant without a backward glance.

Phil watched them go as he brought out ketchup and vinegar for the fries. He stood in front of Matt and swallowed. "Listen Matt, I'm truly sorry about that. I assumed it would be Veronica. I have opened a can of worms."

Matt blew out his breath. "It's okay. I didn't...I wasn't meaning to...I had no idea. I didn't think it would create such a problem."

"I'll get your meals."

Bear and Donald fiddled with their cutlery and drummed their knuckles on the tabletop.

Bear looked at Matt and shook his head. "You really stepped in it this time, man. How could you?"

"How could I what? I went for a ride on my Harley."

"With another woman."

"What do you mean, another woman? Roni and I are just friends."

"Didn't look like it last night in the park," said Donald.

"How'd you...?" Matt remembered the car that had driven past. He pursed his lips and started drumming the table himself. "Yeah, well, I don't think there's any more to it than that."

"You don't sound too sure."

Matt rubbed his forehead as he spoke. "I like her, and it's nice having a female friend, but she's not that easy to get along with."

"Who was riding with you?" Bear leaned forward, intent on the truth.

Matt winced. "Dr. Paula. I stopped to pick up some pills for Miss Emmaline, and when Paula heard my bike, she asked for a ride. What could I say?"

Bear nodded. "Yup, I see how that could happen. She's always been everbody's sweetheart."

"What do you mean?"

"She's born and raised right here in Happenstance," said Bear. "Daddy's pride and joy since she was a wee thing. Lost her mama when she was in her teens. All through those years when her friends were free and easy, she was makin' meals and keepin' the house tidy. They did have some help, but Phineas and Paula managed pretty well theirselves. They're as loyal to each other as two peas in a pod."

"Peas aren't loyal, they're alike," commented Phil as he served their platters. "Paula was always mature beyond her years, yet still capable of living life with gusto. I admire her."

"Has she always lived here?" asked Matt, wanting to hear more about the little girl from Happenstance who'd grown up to be a doctor.

"Not for a while," said Donald. "She became a cop right out of high school, and a darn good one. Met and married another cop, but that went sour real quick. Didn't hear for a while, then she went to med school and now she's here."

Bear interrupted, pointing his fork at Donald. "The rest is hers to tell, McDonald. Best not to drag out the past. She's started a new life and we owe it to her to keep our traps shut. She can tell who she wants what she wants and it ain't none of our affair."

Donald held up both hands. "You're right, Bear. You'll have to ask her, Matt. I didn't mean to gossip. She's a treasure, and that's the truth."

Matt trudged home, avoiding Paradise Realty, and wondered if he should pack up and leave town before he had to face Roni. He hated that he'd caused her pain—again. Life was complex sometimes.

You're a real winner, Sadler. Not satisfied with the

problems you already have, you create more. Way to go.

He pounded his fist on the railing as he climbed the steps of the hotel and burst through the door muttering to himself.

Grayce poised with one foot on the stairs and stared at him. "Whatever is the matter now, Mr. Smith?"

"I've done it this time, Miss Grayce. Is Roni in?"

"Why no, she planned to spend the morning with Mrs. Rampole and then work at the office in the afternoon."

"I thought maybe she'd stopped here after lunch."

"We haven't seen her since this morning. Has something happened between the two of you?"

"Not yet."

"Oh dear." Emmaline joined them from the front desk.

"We had a little misunderstanding is all. I have to think through how I'm going to correct it."

"Yes, you'd better, Mr. Smith. Now, if you will excuse me." Grayce continued up the stairs.

"What did you say to her?" asked Emmaline.

Matt ran a hand across his head and tugged on his ponytail. "It wasn't anything serious. I'm sure she'll get over it if I give her some time. It will all work out."

Emmaline shook her head at him. "You men don't understand a woman's heart. If you want to continue the relationship, you have to make it up to her, Matthew. If you don't, then tell her the truth. She deserves to know."

Matt knew from experience that she was right, but he didn't want to tackle the complexities of Roni's psyche. He tried occupying himself with other projects, but couldn't get Emmaline's advice out of his mind.

He relented and hiked over to Paradise Realty. Roni, on the phone in her office, stood and pushed her door shut in his face. He saw the hurt in her sea-green eyes just before the door clicked, and kicked himself mentally. Karl looked from the closed door to Matt and smirked.

"If you've come to walk her home, I wish you luck, buddy."

"Thanks, I need it. Is she almost done for the day?"

"Should be, but I can't guarantee when she'll come out. You must have pulled quite a stunt; I've never seen her so upset." He stood and gathered his papers. "I've gotta go out to

Athens yet. I'll see you later—I hope." He threw a wicked grin Matt's way as he left the building.

Matt sighed and settled into the extra chair. Why did he even bother?

Because that's how you were raised, Sadler, and because you have a responsibility to make things right.

At that moment, Roni's door opened and she stalked out. Matt stood to meet her but he didn't have a chance to say a word.

"What do you want? There's no one here to humiliate me in front of."

He prepared to jump in and thought better of it. He'd let her blow off some steam and then maybe they could talk reasonably.

"Why aren't you out riding with your new friend? Or did she ditch you like you did me? I can't believe it. I mean, after last night in the park, I thought we had an understanding. What happened to loyalty, to faithfulness, to trust? You can't think I don't—"

Matt closed his eyes and held out both hands. "Let's sit." He offered her a chair and she sat down with a huff.

"You are angry with me because I took someone for a ride on my bike this morning. You have not even asked me who it was. It could have been Emmaline."

"Don't be ridiculous. I know who she was. Other people besides Phil see what's going on in town."

"Belvina?"

"Better hope she doesn't write about it in the paper. I warned you Paula was trouble."

Matt tried not to speculate about Belvina's column in the next Village Voice, but rather to concentrate on the subject at hand. "Roni, I didn't think anything of it. Paula likes bikes, she saw mine, and she asked for a ride."

Roni folded her arms across her chest and looked out the window, but Matt continued. "We took a little drive up the 85 to see how my bike was working and returned within the hour. Doesn't mean I'm taking up with her. I don't even know her. You can't visit on a Harley."

"I like bikes. You haven't taken me for a ride."

"My bike was in the shop. You were at work and...listen,

can we just forget this? I didn't mean to hurt or humiliate you."

Roni swiveled her chair away and swiped tears from her cheeks. "I knew it," she choked out. "Our relationship is ending before it even begins. You promised you wouldn't break my heart, Matt."

He took her hand and tried to get her to look at him. "What do you want me to do, Roni? How can I convince you there's nothing going on between Paula and me? We only met yesterday."

"I have tried to understand you, to respect your values, but you haven't given anything back." She pulled her hand away. "You can't have it all, Matt."

"What does that mean?"

"You can't take up with whoever walks into your line of vision. I think I deserve better than that."

"Cut me a little slack here. Besides, I don't remember us talking about a commitment at this point."

She sniffed and dried her eyes. "I would like to come out in first place sometimes."

"This isn't a matter of winning something, Roni. I could be hurt that you spent your afternoon with a strange man in Athens yesterday, but I assumed you had your reasons. I don't want to be afraid to speak to another woman for fear of reprisals from you."

"I guess I know where I stand then." She stood and pulled her hair together with one hand in that familiar gesture that always stirred his memories of Ginny.

"Roni, get a grip." As soon as the words were out, he knew they were wrong. Double-wrong. He could imagine Bear groaning and shaking his head. "What I mean is, don't take this too seriously. Maybe you need a good night's sleep. My grandma always said things looked better in the morning."

"Good night, then," she said, her words clipped. "We'll see what the morning brings." She grabbed her purse from her office and left without another word. Matt's hopes of a brighter day deflated like a birthday balloon at a pin-cushion party. He pushed himself out of the chair and slunk from the office, unable to imagine Paula reacting as Roni had done. He found himself thinking about camels and last straws.

20

Matt accompanied the ladies to church again on Sunday morning. Reverend Selig's sermon encouraged him to consider his spiritual state, so he went for a pedal to the park. He needed time to process the reverend's words.

Finding a comfortable place under a linden tree, he settled himself. This time, instead of talking aloud and arousing the resident spirit of the woods, a.k.a. Sandy, he pulled a notebook and pen from his pocket. He began as Amanda Rutherford Barlow had done, with the date and the facts.

> *August 3*
> *I arrived in Happenstance more than two weeks ago. Call it accident, call it coincidence or call it plan, here I am. I thought to escape my grief and frustration, to leave it behind in Reedport, but it followed me here.*
> *Everything reminds me of Ginny. Don't get me wrong, I love the memories. It's the subsequent pain that cuts at my spirit until my emotional arteries are severed and bleeding. Then I find Roni and she attracts me and drives me crazy all at the same time.*
> *And the school fiasco! Every time I think of it the anger is as fresh as ever. How could people who have known me for years take her word over mine? They drooled over the rumors like dogs*

over a bone. Only Jim believed me. What kind of
life can I ever have in Reedport now?
Why don't I go back, pack up and get outta Dodge
for good? I've tried for two weeks to leave here
and haven't managed it, that's why.
God, why couldn't you have left me Ginny? Could
she not have been part of Your plan for me?

The pen slid off the page and Matt sat in silence contemplating his own questions. He didn't want Ginny's face to fade, but how could he keep her memory alive without it sucking the life from him? And how could he go back to Reedport and face them all?

He wept in the privacy of the forest, a thousand trees standing by his side like soldiers of solitude.

Matt had shed few tears after Ginny's death. He had been numb. When he'd sat in the blessed peace of Our Redeemer this morning his anger had begun to melt, but the melting, the thawing, hurt more than frozen fingers coming back to life. Perhaps it was safer for him to remain numb, but he'd promised Ginny he wouldn't do that. She had told him, with a pathetic attempt at humor, to have the decency to mourn for a while, but then to get on with life. He knew she meant he should find someone else, but neither had the heart to say it out loud.

Maybe Roni was the answer to some of Ginny's secret prayers for him, but she was so moody. Maybe he should work harder on their relationship, but he only seemed to make things worse. And how was he supposed to handle the growing gap between her and the Barlow sisters? His loyalties were divided.

Matt scribbled again in his notebook, then pocketed it and hiked farther until his muscles began to complain. He was surprised he hadn't come upon Sandy. The man always sensed the presence of an outsider in his domain. Matt kept his eyes and ears open to an approaching phantom, then decided to give it up and relax. He had written through some of his grief about Ginny, but he hadn't finished with the life-shattering accusations at work. There seemed to be no hope in that quarter of ever reconciling his unjust sufferings. He pulled out the notebook again and began to lower himself to a small spot where some sunlight penetrated the foliage.

"Wouldn't sit meself down there if I were you."

The voice shocked Matt's self-absorption right out the soles of his feet. "Sandy Fitzpatrick, you magician! Where did you come from?"

"Me mother said I was born in a small thatch hut near Dun Laoghaire, but me dad insisted it was nearer to Bray."

"Aagh! You know what I mean. You're like Mr. Bean. You never do what's expected, but the moment a person lets down his guard, you appear like a lean, green sprite."

"Mr. Bean? You compare me to a vegetable?"

"No, he's an actor...never mind, it doesn't matter. The thing is you succeeded, again, in nearly scaring the pants off me."

"Best cinch up your belt another notch then Matthew. We don't care for that sort of thing around here."

Matt shook his head and grinned. "Tell me why I should not sit here, if you please."

"Ants."

"Ants?" Matt leaned closer to see the ground alive with the busy creatures. He shuddered at the thought of them crawling up his legs and arms and down his back. He would have shed his pants if that had happened. "Thanks for saving me, Sandy. By the way, how long have you been following me?"

"I was not followin' ye. I look out for me friends."

Matt decided to leave it at that. "I do appreciate it, but someday you're going to have to take a course in the etiquette of meeting and greeting."

"I'll check the syllabus when I return to the university."

"What are you busy with today?"

Sandy settled himself on a fallen log and Matt joined him, after a close inspection of the seat. "I'm checkin' out me main hypotheses before organizin' the material. Then it's off to the east again to write it up and defend it."

"How long will you be gone? It won't be the same without you."

"I'm thankin' ye fer that comment, but I may be gone fer a year or more. Much work ahead, ye see?"

"Yeah. I remember my university days. Life goes on hold while you aim to please the professors."

"Right ye are. I will miss this place like I'd miss me left hand, but it must be done. An' I've discovered many pleasant haunts in the midst of the smoke and fog o' the cities, quiet little places where birds still congregate and trees are brave enough ta grow. Even in Boston."

"Do you have friends there, in Boston?"

"Ye know, Matthew, there are friends everywhere waitin' ta be found, if ye open yer eyes. I never worry about lack o' friends. Fact is, I'll be buried up to me eyeballs in facts an' charts, an' I'll have little opportunity ta think about it. Don't ye worry about me now, Matthew Smith."

Matt smiled at his friend. "I won't worry, Sandy, but I will remember our visits, even if your unexpected appearances have shortened my life."

They shared a laugh. "Ye're travelin' alone today. Lost yer love, have ye?"

"If you're talking about Roni, she drove out to Foggy Plain today. When I showed up for breakfast, the ladies said she had already gone. Well, I'd better be off. Thanks for saving me from an *ant*-agonizing situation."

Sandy saluted him with a smile. "Don't be *ant*-isocial, now. Come again."

Matt bent to tie his shoe, and when he stood up, Sandy had disappeared. "He must be a sprite. Too tall for a leprechaun."

Matt met Bear at the Waldorf for coffee Monday morning. Roni had left without breakfast and he had not seen her. Although he was relieved, he knew it was only a postponement of the inevitable. Why did he put himself through this?

"You look a tad blue today, Matt. Havin' trouble with a piece of the puzzle?"

"I guess you could say that."

"I got time. Got the old truck fixed Saturday night after dinner and I got nothin' pressing this morning."

Matt stirred more cream into his coffee and laid his spoon on the napkin. "Roni's mad at me."

"The ride on the bike with our Paula? You expect me to be surprised?"

"First she was madder than a hatter, then she started to cry and—"

"She was cryin'? Oh man, you're in trouble when they do that. Ain't much you can make right once they start cryin'. Did she make demands?"

Matt stared at Bear. "You ought to take up counseling; you have a gift. Yeah, she made demands. It's all or nothing. Either I'm her friend and no one else's, or I can't be her friend. Reminds me of third grade."

Bear sat pondering, his mouth scrunched up, his grizzled chin in his hand. "Exclusivity. One of the harder things to handle. I'd say you might be up a creek without a' oar here."

"Paddle... Why does it have to be an ultimatum? Even if we were a couple, which we're not, she's not about to lose me to someone I just met. Am I not allowed to have female friends?"

Bear shook his head. "I don't got all the answers, man."

"Why can't women be more like men? I don't go stomping off if she has a visit with Sandy, or a discussion with Phil. What's this deal about exclusivity?"

Phil came around with more coffee. "Woman problems again, Matt?"

"Seems so. Same woman, too. Should have never chased her around the park in the first place."

Phil's eyes widened, and Bear started to snort, spilling his coffee onto the table. Phil pulled a cloth from his back pocket and mopped up the mess. "Don't create a scene now, you two, or I'll have you thrown out."

"Right," said Bear. "We'll keep it down." He set his mug on the table with a straight face, then started to chortle. A hoarse chuckle escaped Matt, releasing some of the tension, and soon they were both holding their sides. They decided they'd better leave before Phil made good on his threat.

Just then, Roni marched in with Belvina. She took one look at them, and Matt could almost see the smoke coming out of her ears. "It's nice to see you're having such a good time. We won't dampen your fun. Come, Belvina."

"Oh geez," whispered Matt as he watched them go.

"You're a dead man, now."

"Thanks for the encouragement."

"Don't let this get you down," said Bear, wiping his eyes. "It ain't over till—"

"Don't say it!"

"Mr. Smith, I would like to speak with you in my office, please."

The tone of Grayce's voice reminded Matt of being summoned to the principal's office in grade school for a prank. Even though he knew he hadn't done anything wrong— heaven forbid; he'd done enough already—he still felt like a condemned man. Why did he drag this legacy along with him wherever he went? What was it about him that invited trouble?

"Please sit down, Mr. Smith. Emmaline and I need to ask you something."

"Whatever it is, I didn't do it."

The ladies did not appear amused. "We need your opinion, Mr. Smith. This is serious business."

"Of course. Pardon me for making light of it." A teasing twinge of the unfortunate humor that had assaulted him and Bear in the Waldorf still nudged him.

"Now then." Grayce took a seat behind the oak desk while Emmaline perched on the edge of an armchair near Matt. "You offered to speak with Miss Wilkinson about our financial records, which had been locked up in this desk."

"And I did, Miss Grayce, but she has not responded to me about that."

"Thank you for your efforts on our part. Miss Wilkinson brought me a folder this morning containing what she said were the books she had taken to the realty office for further consideration." She patted the folder on the desktop and continued. "These, however, are not our books."

"Not yours? If they are someone else's, I'll take them back at once. They should be kept confidential. I'm surprised Roni was so careless."

Grayce held up a hand for silence. "What I mean, Mr. Smith, is that these papers have been made to look like ours, but they are not. I am aware of what they should look like; I compiled them myself. These, however, have been tampered with. The totals are inconsistent with what my figures were, and the complete picture is unhealthy indeed. We are in a state of alarm, my sister and I."

Matt glanced at Emmaline, who nodded in agreement. "Yes, a state of alarm, Matthew. Roni's trying to break us."

"May I see them?"

Grayce turned the ledger around for Matt to read, and he began to peruse it, with explanatory comments from Grayce and the odd clarification from Emmaline. He wasn't an accountant, but if what the ladies said was true, entries had been added and deleted to show a shaky viability.

"We have no proof that Miss Wilkinson did it," said Grayce. "She must have hidden our actual records somewhere."

Here we go again, thought Matt. "How do you arrive at the conclusion that Roni has doctored the books? What purpose would that serve her? She wants to help you."

"We don't want to lose the hotel, Mr. Smith. It is our home and our livelihood."

Matt stood to pace the office. "No, you won't lose the hotel. I'll make sure of that."

"How do you propose to guarantee that?"

He stopped in front of Grayce and patted her hand. "I will make sure, Miss Grayce. Don't worry. I will find out what happened to your records. Perhaps she has been plugging in numbers to check out various scenarios. Perhaps she has left you with the wrong set of documents. Let me figure that part out.

"In the meantime, we could promote the hotel, bring in more customers, and keep you afloat. I've been thinking of our promotional ideas."

"Oh Matthew, I knew we could count on you." Emmaline beamed at him, all worry dissipated, but Grayce narrowed her eyes.

"What ideas are you talking about, Mr. Smith? They must be feasible and achievable, and not completely destroy our integrity."

Matt sat down again and leaned over the desk. "All right,

listen to this. We go with Miss Emmaline's idea of using the tunnels to advertise. We can use the ad channel on TV, the radio, the newspapers in surrounding areas, maybe even blanket ads to reach farther out."

Grayce sat shaking her head. "Mr. Smith, we have been through this."

"Yes, I know, but we should rethink it. You said the good your great-grandfather did using the tunnels to help slaves to freedom had been muted by your father's misuse of them. We can make it right again by overshadowing the past indiscretions and promote them for the good of the economy, both of Happenstance and of the hotel proper."

"Meanwhile, what happens with the financial records?" Matt saw weariness in Grayce's eyes.

He grimaced. "I'll talk to Roni again. But the two of you might want to send up a prayer or two for me in that respect. She's pretty upset with me for taking Paula for a ride on my Harley—"

"You gave Paula a ride on your motorcycle?"

"Yes, and I'm not sure Roni will even grant me an audience."

"She is not the queen," stated Grayce.

Indeed. He needed to look at the situation from an objective point of view and think of the ladies' best interests. After all, whom did they have except him?

Matt tried calling Roni on her cellphone to arrange a meeting, but she was either busy on the phone or didn't have time to talk. He tried intercepting her after work, but she had driven off to Athens on business and wouldn't be back for dinner. He contemplated driving to Athens himself, in hopes of seeing her, but he realized it was chance that the ladies had seen her, and his luck wasn't that good these days. He left a note on the door of her suite upstairs, and retired to his room that evening with thoughts of the hotel and Roni hovering in his brain.

About 10 p.m. a soft knock sounded on his door and when he opened it, Roni stood contrite on the other side.

"Hi. May I come in?"

He hesitated, glancing back to the bed and single chair. "How about we sneak over to the chapel and talk there."

She narrowed her eyes but nodded.

Matt had not yet set foot in the chapel, in fact, he had almost forgotten it was there. He searched for a light switch and located one that lit up the wall sconces along both sides of the room. It was a tiny chapel, set with six short pews and a podium on a raised platform at the far end.

"Quaint," Roni commented.

Matt took a moment to observe the room, then ushered Roni to a seat. He sat down next to her and bowed his head, trying to put together words that would fix the mess he'd created.

"Listen, Roni, I'm sorry I hurt your feelings the other day. And I was not laughing at your expense when you walked into Phil's the other day. It was a tension reliever and—"

Roni put a finger on his lips. "Shh. Don't apologize. I overreacted and I realize it now."

"You did? I mean, you do?"

She smiled and dropped her eyes. "I've been stressed with work. Karl's had me coming and going, and with the exercise classes and the studies I'm doing on-line, it's been too much."

"I didn't realize you were doing an on-line course. What are you taking?"

"It's an accounting course, so I can help the ladies. Not a big deal, but an extra thing to schedule in. Anyway, I realize I came on kind of strong, and that you need room. I won't bother you anymore. If being friends is what works for you, then that's okay. How does that sound?"

Matt tried to adjust his expectations. "Can I still kiss you once in a while?"

"Matt, you mess with my mind. Let's keep it simple, okay? Let's build the trust again."

"Okay." He picked up her hand, then released it.

"I'd better go then. I wanted to straighten that out with you."

He watched her walk away, then remembered his promise to the Barlow sisters.

"Wait, Roni. There is something else I need to talk to you about. I was wondering if you'd finished looking at the hotel's financial records."

"Oh yes. Didn't Grayce tell you? I returned them to her—with the key. I won't lock them up again if it upsets her so much. I'm still working on the insurance document, though."

"She did tell me, but there was a problem. She said they weren't the originals."

Roni frowned and walked back to where Matt stood. "I made a copy for our records, and she must have got the one on new paper. Don't worry; it carries the same numbers."

"But she says it doesn't. She's a pretty sharp cookie, and she noticed a number of entries that were not as she remembered them. And the bottom line was different, on the negative side."

"Matt Smith, what are you implying now? That I tampered with the books?" Her eyes darkened like the sea when a storm brewed. "I have way too many things on my plate already to waste time with something like that. Besides, what do you think I am, a thief or something? I can't believe it!" Her voice raised in anger.

"I'm not saying anything, just asking on behalf of Grayce. Maybe if she had the originals too, she could compare and see that she's mistaken."

"You know, I'm sick and tired of pussyfooting around that woman. She can't even remember where she left her glasses, and now she says I tampered with her financial records. What kind of thanks is that for all I've done for them?"

Matt sighed. "You're right, Roni. I shouldn't have doubted you. Grayce can be a bit distracted sometimes. I'll try to smooth things over."

Roni reached up and touched his face. "Thanks for doing that. I'm about at my wit's end here. I decided that if things didn't improve, I'd move out to Belvina's for a while, but I'd rather stay here. Even if we're just friends, it's good to have a friend."

"Good. Glad I could help."

"Well Matt, I'm tired. I need to get to bed. Will you excuse me?"

"For sure. See you tomorrow."

"I have a breakfast meeting with a client tomorrow morning. I guess I'll see you when I see you."

She walked out, leaving behind a scent of flowers, and Matt's senses reacted. How could one woman arouse so many opposing emotions in him? One moment he was ready to send her packing and the next he wanted her to stay.

He still faced the problem of the financial records, however. Grayce seemed bright enough, but she had momentary lapses. How was he going to handle that?

After lunch the next day, Matt set out for a walk downtown. He pulled open the front door of Wuppertal's General Store and stepped into a chaos of customers, clerks calling for support, and merchandise piled almost to the ceiling. Must be another sale. He looked around for someone who was not busy and instead opted to stand in line at a checkout to ask his question.

"Good afternoon. Is Mr. Wuppertal in please?"

"You mean Dad or one of my brothers?"

The clerk was a nice-looking, efficient girl of about seventeen or eighteen. He'd watched her as he waited his turn. There were several younger look-alikes working in other areas of the store.

"I'm looking for Josiah."

"My little brother Josiah is over there," she pointed to a boy stacking jeans, "but you must mean my dad." She turned and hollered, " 'Siah, where's Dad?"

The boy looked over and yelled back, "Shipment, Hannah."

"He's out back sorting a shipment, sir. Go down this aisle and then over two, then around that bunk of shoes and follow your nose. You can't miss it."

Matt thanked her and started out for the rear of the store, wishing for a GPS, or at least a compass. General stores needed a bit of everything, but it seemed Wuppertal's had a *lot* of everything. He moved around the shoe center and faced two doors. He tried one and a female voice answered, "Occupied. I'll be right out."

He tried the other door and it opened into a storage area even more crowded than the store itself, if that were possible. "Josiah? Josiah Wuppertal? Senior?" Clerks dodged Matt, carrying bundles of clothing and other merchandise. Some of them looked like taller, sturdier versions of Josiah Jr. How many Wuppertals could there be?

"Here. Keep coming. Oh, it's you, Matt. How are you today? Great day to be doing business, isn't it?"

"Looks like it. You have quite a supply of merchandise."

"Taught by my father who was taught by his father. What kind of deal can I make for you today?"

"No deal. Just a couple of questions about a matter concerning Happenstance." Matt looked around him. "Is there a quiet place somewhere?"

"No, I don't think so," said Josiah. "Sit down there on that bale of shirts. They won't get any more creased than they already are."

Matt sat while Josiah took a break on a carton of running shoes.

"Since I'm the mayor here—by the people's choice, not my own—I like to know everything that goes on. Tell me what you know."

"It's about the ladies, the Barlows, that is. By the way, they don't know I came to talk to you."

"My lips are sealed. You were saying?" The mayor looked more interested.

"I'll get right to the point. They're afraid of losing the hotel. They haven't had any business this season besides Roni—Veronica Wilkinson—and me. They are worried they won't be able to keep it running and will be out on the street."

"Out on the street they will not be, I can assure you of that. Losing the hotel, I don't know about that. I know a lot of things that go on, but not all the details, you see. What is your part in this, Matt?"

"The ladies are depending on me to help them come up with some kind of solution."

"And have you found any?"

"I have a couple of ideas, but they aren't well received." He continued before Josiah inserted his comments. "One idea is to advertise on the highway across the bridge, the main road, and on the internet, invite people to stop by and stay awhile. I think Bear put the sign back up on the highway.

"Another idea is to use some of the hotel's interesting

features to advertise, but the ladies are hesitant about that."

"You mean the shady past of Barlow Manor during Prohibition?"

"You know about it?"

"Matt, I told you I know most everything. Why don't they want you to talk about the tunnels in the advertising?"

"Bad reflection on their father, I guess."

"A reflection is created by the one who looks in the mirror, am I right? What damage could it do now? I like the idea."

He rubbed a hand over his thinning hair. "We have a council meeting tonight; I will present your idea. No, better yet, you will present it. Come to the meeting and tell them what you told me."

"Me? At the town council?"

"Why not? Tell them you want to save our hotel. They'll jump on the bandwagon. Am I right? Of course, I'm right."

Matt wondered what kind of wife lived with a man who was always right. He pictured an Edith Bunker. He thanked Josiah and fought his way to the front of the store, wishing for a pith helmet and a machete. He waved to Hannah and young Josiah and walked back to the hotel to talk to the sisters and to prepare a presentation for the council meeting.

21

"Miss Emmaline, is Miss Grayce here too?" Matt had located the younger sister in the parlor, crocheting squares for a blanket.

"Yes, she is, Matthew. She may have stepped into the library at the end of the hall, but I'm sure she'll be back soon."

Grayce entered the room as Emmaline spoke the words. "Emm, the other journal—oh, hello Mr. Smith. I was saying to my sister that the second journal of our mother's is still missing from the library. I don't understand the disappearance."

"Maybe it was misplaced earlier," suggested Emmaline. "Matthew was looking for you, Graycie."

Grayce turned to him again. "May I help you with something?"

Matt led her to a seat and sat down on a chair across from them. "I believe so. And you will be helping yourselves at the same time."

"This is an interesting puzzle. Please carry on."

"It's about the tunnels."

Emmaline stopped knitting and Grayce opened her mouth to speak, but Matt held up his hand for silence.

"Please give me an ear before you speak. I want you to reconsider using the tunnels to promote the hotel. I talked with Josiah—please forgive me, but I needed another opinion—and he assured me it was an excellent idea, and that he is well aware of the stories, and that I should present it to the town council this evening. I'm here to ask your permission. We need to do something, and as yet I haven't thought of anything else. Whether we offer actual tours of the tunnels or simply use the stories is something we can decide later."

"Yes, I think you should go ahead," said Grayce.

"You think I should go ahead?" Matt stared at her.

"You think he should go ahead?" sputtered Emmaline.

"Well, yes, provided that the tunnels are still open. I haven't set foot in them in at least sixty years," said Grayce. "I don't see any other options at the present time. I've been thinking it over, and I agree that no more harm will be done than has already occurred. As long as it's all right with Emmaline, you have my permission."

"Miss Emmaline?"

"Well, yes, if Graycie says it's all right with her."

Relief flooded through Matt. He had anticipated a challenging argument. He thanked them and excused himself to prepare for the evening meeting. Now that he had their permission to speak of the tunnels, he wished he had time to inspect them. But that would have to wait for another day. Maybe he could convince Roni to come with him.

After dinner, Matt walked to the town hall situated between Wuppertal's and Estelle's. He still hadn't figured out where Estelle's got its name. Maisie McDonald ran the place and he'd never met anyone named Estelle. He'd have to ask.

Matt's footsteps echoed on the hardwood floor of the empty hall. A long table stood near the front with metal folding chairs set around it. There were half a dozen chairs off to one side, along the wall, which Matt assumed were for visitors.

A line of light escaped from under a door off the main auditorium. Matt peeked through and saw a pretty young woman making coffee. She turned to greet him.

"Hello." She dried her hands on her apron, smiled and reached out to shake his hand. "I am Abigail Wuppertal."

"Matt Smith. Your father invited me to make a presentation tonight at the council meeting."

Abigail's pleasant laughter bounced between the walls of

the small space. "My father would be honored, but he passed away fifteen years ago. My husband will be here any minute though."

Matt was astounded. "You mean all those fine strapping boys and beautiful girls belong to you?"

She laughed again, humor radiating from her eyes. "Yes, they are all mine, mine and Josiah's. He never knows when to quit, that man."

The door opened and Josiah himself walked in.

"Matt. Good you came. Abigail, my dove, thank you for the coffee. We will need it tonight, I'm sure." He kissed her on the cheek and she patted his face.

"You're welcome. I'm going home now to check on the children."

He watched her leave and said, "I worship that woman."

Matt grinned and followed Josiah to the meeting table.

"You should maybe sit there on one of those chairs until we see who shows up for the meeting. If Wesley doesn't come, which I doubt he will, you can sit in his chair." The man continued to talk while he unpacked his briefcase. Matt only half listened, preparing himself for a long meeting.

The council members trickled in one or two at a time: Maisie McDonald, Harold Haskins, "Phil" Philatopoulis, Bob Rampole, Reverend Selig, and a few more he hadn't met. At 7:58 p.m. Morris Craddock appeared. He took his seat and checked his wristwatch. Josiah banged the gavel on the lectern and each member took a seat.

"Matt, come over and join us," said Josiah. "No use sitting alone. I figured Wesley wouldn't show up."

They were about to begin when the door crashed open and Karl Collins rushed in. He jogged over, dropped into the chair beside Matt, leaned over and shook his hand.

"Order!" shouted Josiah. "We will begin. Minutes please, Mrs. McDonald."

The meeting carried on with more order than Matt expected. When his turn came, Matt stood and presented his request that the council help the Barlow sisters keep the hotel open. He explained their situation, with the added burden of Emmaline's hospital stay and the cost of constant upkeep of the hotel. He emphasized the importance of the hotel in the history and the future of Happenstance and suggested they allow the sisters to advertise, and perhaps other businesses could play on the tunnel theme.

He sat down to applause. "Well done! Good job! Hear, hear!"

Josiah stood up. "We've heard the story, now what are we going to do about it?"

Several offered opinions and ideas. Then Morris Craddock rose to his feet and Matt tensed with the rest of them.

"Your Honor, fellow council members, Mr. Smith, I believe we are going about this in the wrong way altogether."

Matt heard groans, but these were silenced by Craddock's frown. "There are other ways of handling this. I taught at the school situated on Barlow property for many years before I moved on to the high school. Never in all my tenure was I aware of any remuneration given to the Barlows for use of their property or their gatehouse. I move the town council of Happenstance apply to the school board and/or the government for some form of compensation, to be paid at regular intervals. By doing this, we could provide a small additional income to help with the running of the hotel."

Josiah popped up behind the lectern again. "You heard the man. Any seconders for Morris' motion?"

"I'll second," said Harold Haskins.

"Discussion?"

The group discussed the motion in detail and then raised their hands to make it unanimous.

After the meeting, Bob Rampole approached Matt. "Say, Matt, word about town says you have teaching experience. Would you consider stepping into Morris' position?"

"Me? Who have you been talking to?" He'd told no one but Roni.

"Oh, Belvina hears everything. It isn't a rumor is it, you being a teacher?"

Matt tried to sidestep the question, but hesitated too long. "I have taught in the past, but I'm not looking for a position. I'm here temporarily and will be gone long before the new term begins."

Bob smirked. "Been there; said that. Do me a favor and

think about it, would you? We were hoping to have the position filled by now."

For some reason, Matt agreed to think about it and found himself whistling as he walked home down the well-lit streets of Happenstance. He couldn't lie, even to himself. He'd always loved teaching, until last year. He wished he could have some closure on the fiasco in Reedport, but he had lost faith in the powers-that-be and bolted. He supposed he should at least notify Jim as to his whereabouts.

When Matt arrived home the lights were off, except the one in the lobby and a light in the hallway to help him find his way to his suite. He'd drunk enough coffee to keep him awake through the meeting and then some. He needed a bathroom and a good book, in that order. He wished he had the second journal.

As he walked past the basement door, it pushed open and almost knocked him over.

22

Matt stumbled back and stood staring at Roni, and she at him. She looked as bewildered as he felt.

"We have to stop meeting this way," he said, recovering himself.

She put her hand to her chest and heaved a deep breath. "You scared the heck out of me, Matt. What are you doing here?"

"I live here. You?"

"Don't be smart, Matt. I was putting my laundry in the dryer. I thought everyone was asleep already."

He noted she wore an old sweatshirt full of small particles, and he couldn't hear the dryer. He could give her some tips on doing laundry. They stood in awkward silence until Matt said, "How was your day in Foggy Plain? Missed you at dinner."

"Foggy Plain? Oh, uh, it was good. How was your day?"

"Great. The town council is interested in promoting the hotel by advertising the tunnels, and they—"

"Tunnels!" Roni's voice rose and her eyes widened. "What on earth are you talking about?"

Matt took her hand and led her to the parlor where she perched on the edge of a sofa like a bird ready to fly. He sat on the coffee table facing her. His heart wrenched at the sight of her, looking like Ginny did when she was afraid.

"I know it sounds ludicrous, but there used to be tunnels under this hotel before it was a hotel, and if they are still in good shape, we can use them to promote the hotel and save it from financial ruin. And think what it could do for the town. We could—"

"Matt, stop. Have you thought through what you're saying? For one thing, how do you know there are tunnels under this place?"

"I read about them in an old journal the ladies gave me. They weren't happy to let me in on the secret, but it's out now."

Roni took hold of his shoulders. "I wasn't going to tell you this, but I read about them too when I first came here, in another of the so-called journals. I decided to check out the story and was disappointed. There is no trace of them, just a room full of dirt. Someone must have collapsed them if they hadn't already fallen. They would be generations old, unsafe to use."

Matt listened and looked down at his hands, disappointment nagging at him. "Are you sure? I thought they'd still be open, just neglected. I can't believe I didn't check it out myself."

"Sorry, Matt. We'll have to think of something else. I hope the ladies aren't too disappointed. They need encouragement right now."

"Yeah, and I was the one to build up their hopes. Well," he looked at his wristwatch, "it's too late to do anything about it tonight."

"Even if they still existed, it would cost an arm and a leg to renew them."

They sat in silence, and then Matt remembered the other high point of the meeting. "The council—to be specific, Morris Craddock—did come up with a couple of options to keep the hotel open: appeal to the county for remuneration for decades of use of the Barlow Manor Gatehouse as a primary school facility and/or regular rent, retroactive, for the gatehouse."

"There, that's much more realistic. Trust me. Stick to the other options, whatever they are, and leave the tunnels out of it. These are the kinds of stresses that will finish Grayce and Emmaline."

Matt pulled the elastic from his ponytail and toyed with it, thinking. Roni reached out and combed through his hair.

"It's quite long. I like it."

"I've let it grow. Bit of the rebel in me, I suppose. You'd think I'd have conquered that by the time I turned forty, wouldn't you?"

Her smile was sad. "You don't solve all life's problems in the first forty years."

"You're telling me!"

"We'd better get some sleep, Matt. It's late."

They stood for a moment, not knowing what else to say.

"Thanks for listening and setting me straight. We'll try another tack."

"Good plan. Goodnight, Matt."

He prepared for bed and started into a novel he had found at the library, but he couldn't concentrate. What was Roni doing in the basement at such an hour and why was she so vehement in her opposition to the tunnel idea? *The Secret of the Midnight Laundress.* He sighed in disappointment as his plans of promoting the tunnels crumbled into nothing.

Matt came to breakfast the next morning hoping he and Roni could begin to feel at ease with each other again. They had talked through their disagreement about the tunnels and settled things. It was a start.

"She isn't coming," said Emmaline when he asked. "She said she would stop at the Waldorf Café for coffee and a muffin before work. She seemed unhappy about something."

Matt cringed. "Here we go again."

"Whatever did you—"

"Emm, mind your own business," said Grayce. "This is a private matter between Mr. Smith and Miss Wilkinson."

"Better not talk about minding our own business, Graycie. We've gone past that."

Grayce sent her sister a withering look, but Emmaline continued.

"I think we need to confide in him."

Grayce looked uncomfortable, but after a few moments and another sip of coffee, she pressed her lips together and nodded. "Very well. Mr. Smith, we have proceeded on a course of action by which to verify the actual scientific contents of Miss Wilkinson's supposed herbal infusion, and we have unearthed some startling results."

Matt raised his eyebrows and looked to Emmaline, who said, "We confiscated a jar of her tea leaves and had it analyzed in Athens."

Matt leaned forward with his elbows on the table. "And?"

She glanced over her shoulder as if to make sure they were alone. "It contains digitalis, Mr. Smith."

"You're kidding! How could that be? I have to tell Roni before she offers it to someone else or drinks some herself. I wonder where she got it."

"Mr. Smith, you don't seem to understand our implications. We believe Miss Wilkinson included the toxic ingredient in the tea on purpose, knowing full well that together with Emm's pills, it would cause a collapse—or worse."

Matt shook his head in amazement. "I don't believe the two of you. You must be watching too many detective movies or something. This is real life. By some terrible fluke, there is digitalis in the tea. That does not implicate Roni. We have to find out where she bought it and go to the source."

The ladies sat tight-lipped.

"She even offered to have an analysis done of it. I've forgotten to ask her what the results were."

"Would you mind asking her then? We would like to hear her explanation."

"I will, as soon as I locate her." He could imagine Bear saying something like, "Better nick this in the butt, Matt." He left the room without another word and launched down the lane on one of Bruce's old bicycles. Best not to warn Roni with the noise of his Harley. He pedaled past the clinic and took a side street to the realty office, but Roni wasn't there.

"She's sick," said Karl. "Went over to Belvina's for a bit."

Why Belvina's and not her own suite at the hotel? Matt rode up the driveway to find Roni and Belvina sitting on the porch swing with sweating glasses of lemonade in their hands.

" 'Morning, Belvina. Roni, I missed you at breakfast and at the office. Karl told me you were here."

Roni adjusted her dark glasses and said, "Belvina, would you excuse us while I talk with Matt?"

Belvina nodded, frowning at Matt, and closed the screen

door behind her. Matt knew she wouldn't move out of hearing distance but he didn't care. He needed to talk to Roni. She remained sitting on the swing and waited for him to begin. Matt faced her, leaning on the porch railing.

"How are you feeling? You look a bit under the weather."

"Migraine coming on. I should move inside where it's dark, but I was hoping it would pass if I relaxed."

"I hope it isn't too debilitating. I had a friend who suffered from them."

Roni grimaced and leaned her head back. "What did you need to see me about, Matt?"

"I need to ask you some questions."

"Fire away, but I don't promise to be too coherent."

"I'll get right down to it. Did you ever get the results of the analysis on your herbal tea?"

"Oh, I forgot to tell you. Yes, it's fine. Nothing illegal or life-threatening. Why?"

"The ladies have done some investigating of their own into the cause of Emmaline's sudden illness and they've discovered some interesting facts."

"Good. It's about time they did something on their own instead of expecting you and me to protect them."

Matt waited for her to finish. "They had an analysis done on the herbal tea also."

"And?"

"And it contains digitalis."

"That's ridiculous, Matt. It's perfectly safe. I showed you the list of ingredients."

"The lab in Athens found digitalis in the product, Roni. Where did you buy it?"

Roni paused. "I got it in a health food store in Athens, but...I added a bit of something."

"You what?"

"I dug the herbs in the forest. Sandy showed me what was what and I added a bit of comfrey. Thought I might try to market it on the internet if it worked out."

"I wouldn't advise it. It's lethal."

She sat forward, holding her head. "Did it ever occur to you, Matt, that if what you say is true, they may have put digitalis into the mix themselves to implicate me? Grayce has been trying to get rid of me for weeks now."

"How would they find digitalis?"

"You're saying I acquired some; then so could they."

"Yes, but they don't know about that kind of thing; you're the herbal genius. Besides, I can't imagine them scouring the forest for herbs."

"Don't underestimate them, Matt."

"Wait a minute. First, they're daft, then they're outwitting us. Which is it?"

Roni fidgeted. "This is getting tiresome. I'm not up to it today. Do you know where they got the sample? How do you even know it's my tea?"

"I didn't ask where they got it. The point is the product is extremely toxic to someone already on medication containing digitalis."

Roni blew out her breath and tried to stand. Matt took her hands and helped her.

"I...can't think right now. If I promise not to touch the stuff in the meanwhile, would you let me get this migraine under control? Then I'll deal with it. I'm sorry it turned out this way. I had no intention of hurting anyone."

Matt saw a tear escape the corner of her eye and trickle down below her sunglasses. He reached out to brush it away, but more followed. He took her into his arms and held her steady, his hands in her fiery hair. Was this the beginning of love or was it nostalgia? And what of his attraction to Paula? Was that pure friendship because of the way she challenged him, listened to him? Happenstance seemed to magnify the emotions, and he needed to use his brain.

"It's okay, Roni. Go inside and rest now. Is there anything I can do for you?"

"No." Her voice had become a whisper and he imagined the pain had increased with this new development.

"Stay here for now and call me when you feel better. We'll figure this out together."

He helped her to the door and Belvina opened it.

"Take care of her. I'll pick her up later."

"How's Roni, Matt?" asked Bear when he met him at the

back door of the parsonage later that morning.

Matt frowned. "Word travels fast in this town. I talked with her at Belvina's earlier. She's not feeling well."

"I hear you've upset her again." Bear shook his head. "You're a nice fella, Matt Smith. How do you manage to keep upsetting that woman?"

Matt shrugged. "Special gift, I guess."

"Bit of a roller-coaster, that one. I'd watch my back."

"She's a nice person, Bear, like you said. Rough background, from the little she's told me. Used to taking care of herself, but she has a good heart."

Bear met his eyes but did not comment further. "Let's go paint."

Matt knocked on the parsonage door and the two men entered the warm, spice-scented kitchen.

"Just in time for cinnamon rolls fresh from the oven," said Annaliese Selig, bustling up to them in her large gingham apron. "I make them for you special. Now come. We eat first, then work. My husband, he goes out to visit Mr. Wachsman but he should be soon back."

Matt and Bear each consumed a couple of rolls, and Bear prepared to scarf down another when Matt suggested they get to work. They moved all the furniture again, laid plastic sheets around the edges of the floor and stirred the paint. Then, as Matt brushed around the ceilings and corners, Bear rolled on the tinted primer in large diagonal strokes. In less than two hours they had primed the entire room and cleaned their brushes and rollers.

"We'll be back tomorrow to do the topcoat," said Matt. "I like the color you've chosen." He stepped back to survey their work. Harvest taupe. It added some warmth to the room, and now the old country lace curtains would highlight the decor instead of disappearing into it.

"Iss beautiful," said Annaliese. "We thank you both, my husband and I. Good workers you are. We leave the furniture all sitting in the middle now, until you have done. Come tomorrow for tea."

"Thanks, Mrs. Selig," said Matt, "but we don't need to be fed each time."

"Speak for yourself," said Bear.

Annaliese patted Bear's arm as she followed them to the door.

Matt met a flustered Roni when he entered the hotel at lunch.

"Matt, oh Matt, I'm glad you're here." She guided him into the far corner of the solarium and pointed to a wicker sofa. She sat down close beside him, her eyes distraught. "I've been thinking about what you said this morning and I may have made a terrible mistake. I...I feel horrible. If it was my fault, I'll never forgive myself."

"What are you talking about, Roni?"

"You'll never believe what I've done, or at least what I think I've done." She sniffed and brushed tears from her face. "You said the tea contained digitalis, but I denied it."

"Yes. What are you telling me?"

"Well—I think the ladies may be right."

"What?"

"Wait. Let me explain." She slipped her hand into his. "I spend a lot of time hiking in the park, and the forest beyond, and I have a real interest in herbs and what they can do for the body. I found some comfrey. It helps the body dispose of excess fluid and eases bronchial and intestinal disorders. Emmaline was complaining to me, before you came, that she was too fat and wanted to lose weight. I thought it would be simpler for her to lose some fluid, and she would feel better. I included some comfrey in my tea infusion. I didn't try it myself because I don't need it, but it wouldn't have affected me because I'm healthy and not on any medication.

"But Emmaline is," she continued. "When you emphasized that yesterday in our conversation at Belvina's, I started to think about it." She glanced at him, then looked down and spoke in a whisper. "I think I may have mistaken the comfrey for something else that's not safe."

Matt took her shoulders and turned her to face him. "Roni, are you sure? This is serious."

"I know. What should we do?"

23

Matt thought for a minute, then stood and brought Roni to her feet as well. "We'll go see Sandy. He'll know what's what. Do you have some of the herb?"

She nodded. "I have a bit more in my room. I'll get it."

"Do you feel well enough to go out to the forest and find Sandy?"

"Yes. My pills kicked in soon after you left, and I've been resting since then. I'll feel better once we get this settled."

Roni phoned Karl to tell him she'd take an extended lunch hour and stay later in the afternoon, then she and Matt took her car out to the park in hopes of locating Sandy.

"Sandy! Answer me, you stubborn Irishman," called Matt.

"Professor Fitzpatrick, show yourself. No games today."

They walked on a few minutes. Matt said a silent prayer and shouted again. "Lysander Patrick Joseph Fitzpatrick the Third, appear at once!"

"What are ye bellerin' about, man? Ye're hollerin' fit to scare away the animals and wither the leaves on the trees."

The voice came from behind him, and Matt whirled around to see Sandy standing there.

"Sandy, it's about time. We've got serious business here."

"Believe it or not, me friend, I have a life. I've been over to Foggy Plain makin' arrangements for me departure. Now if ye'll calm yourself and tell me what it is ye want, p'raps I'll be able to help ye." He bowed to Roni. "Afternoon to ye, my lady."

Matt didn't waste time. "Sandy, it's urgent. Come with us

to the place where Roni digs her herbs."

Sandy frowned. "What business would that be of yours?" He glanced at Roni.

"Please, Sandy," she said. "Let's start walking and I'll tell you."

Sandy said little as Roni and Matt explained the situation. As they reached a particular spot near the lake, Sandy bent and examined the plants at the edge of the clearing.

"What are they?" Matt looked at the large hairy green leaves of the tall plant and at the pinky purple bell flowers.

"Symphytum officinale. Blackwort. Comfrey."

"That's what I was digging," said Roni.

"Tell us about it," said Matt to Sandy.

"Ye can make a poultice of it ta help heal sores and such. But it's more commonly used for tea. Good for the stummick and the breathin'. But it can be highly carcinogenic if taken over a long period o' time."

"How much did you give to Emmaline, Roni?"

"Two or three doses."

"Sandy, is there anything here that Roni could have confused with comfrey that would be toxic?"

Sandy paced the circumference of the marsh and frowned. His eyes narrowed and he looked at Roni. "Have ye been diggin' 'round this side of the marsh, ma'am?"

Roni's eyes widened. "Yes, a bit. I found some comfrey here too." She pointed it out.

Sandy gasped. "That is not comfrey, milady. It's foxglove. Witch's bells. Deadmen's bells."

"Oh no!" Roni gasped as the truth hit her. "I've been poisoning Emmaline. Grayce was right. What have I done?"

"Sounds ominous. Are you sure, Sandy?" asked Matt, although he knew the answer. "It looks like comfrey."

"This is most assuredly foxglove, and so is what ye be holding. Easy to confuse it with comfrey in the flowering stage."

Sandy rose to his feet, a stalk of foxglove in his hand. "This plant is the source o' digitalis, which is used as a cardiac stimulant. An Englishman by the name o' William Withering discovered it in the late eighteenth century and it's been used ever since. Very valuable. Very effective. And very deadly." He held the plant out for Matt and Roni to see. "If ye were to chew up and consume one o' these leaves, it could paralyze ye or cause sudden heart failure."

Matt and a weepy Roni sat side by side on the sofa in the parlor, facing Emmaline and Grayce.

Roni spoke through tears. "I made the mistake without knowing it, and then I gave it to you, intending to help. Can you ever forgive me, Emmaline?"

Emmaline reached out and patted Roni's shoulder. "Of course, my dear. Don't think about it again. I'm alive and well, and will not drink any more of your tea, so there's no need to worry about it. Earl Grey is much better anyway."

Emmaline smiled at Roni, and she mustered a smile in return. Matt could feel the relief at having solved the puzzle, as Bear would dub it.

Grayce said nothing, and Matt thought her expression hard, even cold. She seemed unconvinced by Roni's plaintive explanation. He, on the other hand, did not doubt her sincerity. A person could not put on an act like that. Besides, why would she admit it if she had done it on purpose? She could have denied the facts. He admired her strength of character. He shouldn't have doubted her.

"Well," said Roni, drying her tears, "if I don't get back to work, Karl is going to fire me and then I'll be in more trouble. Thanks for listening and forgiving. See you all later."

She gave Emmaline a peck on the cheek, Grayce a pat on the shoulder, and Matt a tremulous smile as she left the house.

After she had gone, Matt sat down with the ladies.

"Okay, let's start with you, Miss Grayce. You must realize how much it took for Roni to confess and ask forgiveness. Yet you gave her the cold shoulder. Aren't we supposed to forgive?"

Grayce lifted her chin and gave him a calculated look. "You don't know all the facts, Mr. Smith. There is more to Miss Wilkinson than meets the eye, and what meets the eye is not what it seems."

Matt frowned. "Why do you say that? Do you still doubt her sincerity?"

"I can and I do. But I don't expect to convince you of that without further evidence. I hope and pray you do not become her next victim. Be careful, Mr. Smith. In spite of your naiveté in this situation, we care about you."

"What are you saying, sister? Didn't you hear Veronica? She is sorry. We cannot hold a grudge; it's not Christian."

"Neither are attempted murder and fraud and whatever else is going on. She may have pulled the wool over your eyes and Mr. Smith's, but she has not fooled me. Mark my words, Miss Wilkinson is trouble with a capital T."

Trouble, right here in Happenstance. Matt completed the line in his head. He refrained from rolling his eyes at her dramatic monologue.

Grayce continued. "I already have some evidence and will continue to compile more. In the meanwhile, please be careful and don't do anything that would arouse her anger." Here she focused on Matt. "I am concerned for you, Mr. Smith, since you are blinded by romantic feelings. Let common sense be your guide."

"Wait, wait," said Matt. "What evidence are you talking about?"

Grayce hesitated for a moment. Then she said, "I'm not sure you're ready to see it. You doubt my mental capacities, and believe instead what Miss Wilkinson has been telling you. She is using you, Mr. Smith, and until you recognize and acknowledge that fact, I cannot confide in you."

She rose to her feet and left the room, leaving Matt and Emmaline to stare at each other.

"Miss Emmaline, do you know what she's talking about?"

She seemed flustered. "I...well, oh dear, Matthew. I don't know if I should tell you, considering what my sister said. She has a relevant point, you know."

Matt sighed. "I'm sorry for putting you on the spot, Miss Emmaline. I am confused by all this. Do you think Roni's lying?"

Emmaline's lips tightened. "I would like to believe her. You see, I have a weakness in that area. I like to give people the benefit of the doubt, believe the best of them. But I am not the best judge of character, as my sister has often told me...except for Bruce." Her eyes misted even as her smile broadened. "I judged well with my Bruce."

Matt couldn't help but smile with her. "I wish I could have met him."

"He would have liked you, Matthew," her face clouded, "but I'm not sure he would have liked Veronica. He would have been polite, of course, my Bruce was always polite, but he would have cautioned me about her, I think. Perhaps I should heed Graycie's warning. By the way, Matthew, did you know our Dr. Paula is coming for dinner this evening?"

"No, I didn't. Does Roni know?"

Concern crossed Emmaline's features. "I don't know if she does or not, but it doesn't matter, because she informed me she would be absent this evening. Phineas is coming too. Graycie thought it would be a marvelous idea to invite the Percys."

"If Roni's away, we can avoid World War III, for now anyway. Have you always known the Percys?"

"Oh yes, but we haven't visited with Paula in years. She used to play in our yard and beg for cookies. Then she grew up and met that nice-looking young man, who it turned out wasn't nice at all. Poor girl. We were concerned for her."

"She married him?"

"Yes, she did. She misjudged him." Emmaline leaned conspiratorially toward Matt. "He was a user and a pusher." Her eyes darted to the door as she whispered the words, but she seemed quite satisfied with herself.

Matt's eyebrows lifted. "You mean he was into drugs?"

"Oh yes. And poor Paula didn't guess it at first. He was with the police force too, you know, and they were working to crack a drug ring in Athens, but every time they closed in, the perps would clear out. They never caught them, but Paula grew tired of the way he treated her—we were all afraid for her, you know, but we thought she should be able to handle herself, being an officer too—and then she left him. He disappeared and no one's heard of him since."

"You have your terminology down, Miss Emmaline," commented Matt. "You must have followed the story closely at the time."

"Yes, we did. Belvina kept us informed of the details in her column and in person. We knew everything there was to "know and more."

"I'm sure you did. After—what was his name?"

"Daniel. Daniel Sherman."

"After Daniel left, did he and Paula divorce?"

"Yes, they did. I'm always sorry when a marriage ends like that, but we were afraid for her, Matthew. You must understand that."

"I'm not judging, Miss Emmaline. Just wondering."

"Yes, they divorced and then she moved to another state and worked her way through medical school. And now we have our Paula back, and a doctor of medicine at that."

"You must be very proud of her."

"Indeed, we are."

"Well, I have a few things I should do, if you'll excuse me."

"Of course, Matthew."

Matt whistled his way out of the parlor, then turned toward the basement door, intent on slipping unnoticed down the stairs to investigate the place for tunnels. Enough waiting and conjecture; he was going to find out a few things for himself. He grasped the doorknob, but it wouldn't turn. He tried again. It was locked, and there was no key hanging at the side of the frame.

He banged his fist against the door and walked away, not wanting to ruin the wood by prying it, or bother the ladies with more problems. He walked out the front door and down the lane to the library, where he picked out a couple of Louis L'Amour novels to pass the time.

When he arrived back I time for dinner, a well-used pickup truck sat in front of the hotel. Laughing voices drifted in his direction as he entered the foyer, making him feel like he'd come home. In a few short weeks, this old hotel had become to him what no other home had been since Ginny died.

"That sounds like our Matthew," Emmaline's voice said.

"He isn't ours, Emm."

"Oh yes, he is. Matthew, is that you?"

Matt grinned and called back, "You bet it is, Miss Emmaline." He joined the group in the parlor, surprised at his elation at seeing Paula again. He shook her hand and that of her father.

"Quite the vehicle you have there, Paula."

"Me! That's Dad's fishing truck. I have better taste than that."

"I beg to differ," said her father. "That rattletrap you drive isn't fit to be called a car. Bad for business if people see you driving it around town."

She laughed. "Ah, but I won't be driving it much anymore." She turned to Matt. "Got myself a bike, Matt."

"You did? When? What kind?"

Her grin almost split her face. "You'll have to come over and see it."

"You're on. I—"

"Excuse me, Mr. Smith, dinner is served." Grayce took his arm and led him and the others into the dining room.

Matt tried to stay objective about Paula, to consider some of the things Roni had warned him about, but he failed. Dinner that evening was a pleasant occasion. He enjoyed hearing Phineas' fish stories, which Paula referred to as fishy stories, and managed to get Paula onto the topic of bikes once again.

When the others retired to the parlor for coffee, Paula and Matt excused themselves to look at her new acquisition. "Let's take my bike," he suggested.

"I don't have my helmet here."

"Wear mine."

"I will not. Come on, let's take Dad's truck. We'll bring it back by the time he's ready to go."

"He seems to know the ladies quite well," Matt commented as he climbed into the passenger seat of the old truck.

"Sure does. Lifelong friends. My grandfather was Grayce's number one man back in the day."

"Really? What happened?"

"It's a long story. Quite the intrigue. Her mother was a rather formidable woman, and Grayce tended to comply with her wishes above all. My grandfather had met my grandmother in the meantime, and when Grayce refused him yet again, he closed that book, so to speak, and carried on with life."

"But there are no hard feelings in this generation?"

"Not anymore. Miss Grayce and Grandpa were always cordial. I think she regretted her decision, though. I'm glad she's had Emmaline as a companion all these years."

They puttered along in silence, each lost in thought, until Paula pulled into the driveway of her father's west side home.

"It's in the garage."

They hopped out and Matt waited as Paula unlocked the door and turned on the lights.

"Whoa, I am impressed." He inspected every inch of the bike, admiring the spit-polished chrome and the red leather seat. "I thought you were going for a Harley."

"I was looking into that, but I saw this one in Foggy Plain yesterday, and fell in love with it."

"What was the deciding factor?"

She shrugged. "I tried out a Rebel, four-stroke, air-cooled, easy handler, thought it might be the one, but then I hopped onto this Nighthawk and it felt right, you know? It's lightweight. My old bike was a bit heavy for me and I didn't want to be afraid of it. After you gave me a ride on your bike the other day, I knew I needed to get my own two wheels ASAP."

"Have you always ridden your own?"

"Yeah. My...this guy I knew loved bikes, but he didn't like passengers. If we were going to ride together at all, I had to have my own machine."

"That's great. Ginny never wanted to ride her own, and I kinda liked her behind me." He lost himself in his memories until Paula's voice brought him back.

"Who's Ginny?"

"She was my wife. She died about five years ago."

"I'm sorry. What was she like? You must have had a good thing going."

"Oh yeah." He sat there on a crate near the bike while she settled onto the steps that led to the house. Arms resting on his knees, he started talking about Ginny. Paula leaned up against the railing and listened, inserting questions and comments now and then. To Matt, she felt like an old friend he hadn't met until now. Was that real or just happenstance?

And what of Roni's warnings?

Matt glanced at his watch. "Oh man, we should get back. Sorry for talking your ear off like that."

She smiled and stretched. "I enjoyed it. It's rare to hear true and lasting love stories anymore these days."

"You're a good listener. Thanks."

They walked out to the old truck and climbed in. Paula revved the motor and backed out of the driveway, using her rearview mirror. With a glance over her shoulder, she pulled into the street and headed back to the hotel. "When do we go for a ride, or is that forbidden?"

"I'm still my own man, Paula." He looked at his watch again. "I guess it's too late tonight, right? How about tomorrow?"

Paula laughed, and Matt laughed with her, forgetting Roni's words, forgetting Grayce's suggestion to use his common sense. He liked Paula's style.

"I have to work tomorrow, and then Dad and I are spending the weekend in Athens, but next week would be wonderful."

"You call the day; my schedule is so flexible it's almost non-existent."

"Okay then. Let's set a date for next Tuesday and I'll call to confirm. Good?"

"Good."

"You're staring."

"Sorry." Matt trained his eyes on the houses along the street.

When Matt opened the front doors of the hotel and ushered Paula in before him, he heard Roni's voice. She was regaling the ladies and Dr. Percy with some sort of adventure story. The thought of Roni's response to the plans he'd just made hit him like a fist to the solar plexus. Why did any thoughts of Roni disappear whenever he was around Paula? And yet he thought about Paula when he was with Roni.

"It sounds like she has Dad wrapped around her finger," commented Paula after they had listened a few moments. "He's always charmed by a pretty face."

"Lonely, huh?"

"Yeah. I'm glad I'm home now to provide some company. And being a physician as well, I can share his stories with understanding."

They had again become engrossed in their discussion, and failed to hear the pause in the conversation in the parlor, or to see Roni standing in the hallway watching them.

"Well, well, the two wandering bikers."

24

Matt jerked to attention, then caught himself. He had told Paula he was his own man. Was he?

"Hey, Roni. This is Dr. Paula Percy. Paula, this is Veronica Wilkinson."

Paula stepped forward and reached out a hand to Roni. "Nice to meet you. I was showing Matt my new bike."

Roni ignored her hand. "Doctor. Impressive."

Matt sensed things going south rather swiftly.

"Well, I'm off to bed. See you later." Roni threw him a withering look as she passed on her way upstairs.

Paula turned on him. "What was that all about?"

Matt sighed. "I'm sorry she was rude to you."

"Why are you apologizing for her?"

At that moment, much to Matt's relief, Phineas appeared from the parlor with Emmaline on one arm and Grayce on the other. He seemed pleased with himself and Matt could understand why.

"Ready to go, my dear?" he addressed Paula.

"I am. Thank you for dinner, ladies. Matt."

"Are we still on for the bike ride next week?"

"I'll call if I have time."

That's it? I'll call if I have time? He hadn't expected a relationship with either woman, but now they were both upset with him. How did one ever understand the female mind? Even Ginny, after years of marriage....

"Matthew?" Emmaline eyed him.

"I'm sorry, what did you say?"

"Phineas asked if you were a fisherman."

"Oh." He turned to Phineas. "I have fished a few times, but I've never gotten into it. It is relaxing though."

"Yes, it is. You'll have to come with me sometime."

"Thanks. That would be great."

"Good night all."

Paula gave each of the sisters a hug, but when she shook Matt's hand, her eyes were full of questions.

"Thanks for a great evening," Matt said, meaning it.

Phineas assumed the driver's seat in the old truck. They waved as they left, and the ladies exclaimed about the wonderful evening, each taking one of Matt's arms as they had done with Phineas. How did one adjust from jerk to knight in a matter of moments?

"Matthew, we must speak with you in private."

Matt looked around him and saw only Emmaline and Grayce at the breakfast table. Johanna's appearances were rare, except to serve the meals, and Roni had gone off to work already.

"Whatever you wish, ladies. Your office?"

"Yes, please." Grayce stood and moved in that direction.

He waited until they had seated themselves, then took a chair, something his grandmother had drilled into him.

"What's up?"

Emmaline looked to Grayce, whose lips were compressed into a tight line. "We have made another discovery."

"We had to do it, Matthew."

"Someone had to do something, Mr. Smith."

He scratched his head and adjusted his ponytail, trying to be patient at their roundabout approach to a problem. "Can you tell me what this is about?"

Grayce unlocked the front narrow drawer and pulled out several pieces of paper, which she pushed across the desk toward Matt. He picked them up and studied them. "Tax notices? These are dated two months ago, last month, and yesterday. This last one's stamped in red."

"We are well aware of that, Mr. Smith. What we were not aware of was their presence, seeing as they were hidden in

Miss Wilkinson's bureau drawer."

Matt stared at Grayce, uncomprehending. "You found these in Roni's room?"

Emmaline nodded. "Well, Graycie did. I was running interference at the top of the stairs."

"What were you doing in her room?"

Grayce sat even straighter than normal. "We were looking after our own interests. Several months ago, Miss Wilkinson offered to help with our bookkeeping—"

"—we've since asked her to stop," Emmaline added.

"We should never have agreed to it," continued Grayce. "I believe that woman is out to destroy us and our hotel."

"You're kidding, right? She must have forgotten to return these to your office."

"Mr. Smith, you fail to understand. The taxes requested on these notices have not been paid. Miss Wilkinson has been taking care of bills, but she failed to pay this amount. I took the liberty of telephoning our solicitor—"

"—that's Joseph Mendosa from Athens—"

"Yes, and he said that we will be charged interest because even if we pay now, we are late. We have never failed to pay bills on time, Mr. Smith, even in our most difficult circumstances. This is more than an inconvenience for us. But that aside, why did she steal and hide these forms?"

"Why indeed?" echoed Emmaline.

Matt couldn't negate the conclusion at which the ladies had arrived. He had to admit it was strange that Roni would overlook tax notices, that she would keep them in her room. He didn't understand her intentions.

"I'll talk to her about it."

"Mr. Smith, with all due respect, your talking to her has not to this date resulted in positive change in Miss Wilkinson's behavior. We would like to suggest another approach."

"And what would that be?" He needed to hear them out.

Grayce continued. "We are asking that you not speak to Miss Wilkinson at all about this problem. We would like you to make copies of these papers so I can return the originals to Miss Wilkinson's room without her knowledge."

"Could you do it now, Matthew? We would feel much better if this intrigue was completed well before lunchtime.

We are shaking in our boots as it is."

"We are not wearing boots, Emm, and you may be shaking, but I am quite at liberty to do whatever I please in my own home." Grayce kept her hands folded, masking any quaking they may have been doing.

Matt's heart went out to her.

"I'll run downtown right now and do it. Don't worry, okay?"

"We will try not to," said Emmaline.

"Guess I'd better not ask to have them copied at Paradise Realty."

His attempt at humor plummeted into the ensuing silence. He cleared his throat. "I'm on my way."

"Thank you, Mr. Smith. We are counting on you, my sister and I are."

He nodded as he walked out and to his room for his helmet. He donned it, feeling like Sir Matthew, Knight of the Helpless, but this situation was getting stickier by the day.

Matt had the forms copied and back to the hotel in less than half an hour. The Barlows were grateful beyond words as he helped Grayce replace the originals in Roni's room. He had not yet set foot into her space, and it surprised him. She was not, by any stretch, a person of meticulous personal habits. The room was a stopping point, not homey at all. He wondered what she did up here on her own, besides sleep. Housekeeping had not been one of Ginny's favorite things either, but she would not have put up with this kind of mess.

"Doesn't look like she'd miss the papers for a while."

"She would notice the important things."

Matt marveled at Grayce's bravado, entering Roni's room, never knowing when she might return. Her schedule tended to be unpredictable.

"Psst. Psst."

Grayce froze. "That is Emm's warning. My goodness, gracious. Miss Wilkinson must be back early."

Matt followed Grayce from the room, locking it behind him. She hurried toward her suite, while Emm scurried from the top of the stairs toward hers. They wheeled and considered

Matt.

"Go that way and through the door at the end." Grayce pointed toward the far end of the hall.

Matt did as she said and disappeared through a door he'd never seen before, wondering where it led. A backstairs entrance, of course. This was an old estate home; it would have servants' access out of the main hallways and entrances. He was thankful for the light of the small window high in the wall as he made his way down the stairs to the floor below. He came out in a narrow hallway. To his right he saw a small bedroom with the door ajar, to the left another door. He eased it open and peeked through.

The kitchen. Johanna, working away over her stove. How would he explain his sudden appearance without scaring her into tomorrow? He backed off, closed the door and knocked. Hearing her exclamation of surprise, he pushed open the door again.

"Hello, Johanna. Sorry to barge in on you. I was exploring and found myself here."

Her face reddened and she wrung her hands.

Try charm, Sir Matthew.

"May I enter your kingdom, my lady?"

"Jah, jah. Komm." She motioned him in and pointed to a rack of cooling chocolate chip cookies. He raised his eyebrows in question and Johanna nodded. Grabbing two warm cookies, he offered a "Danke", and ducked out of the kitchen and out through the dining room.

He didn't know if he could stand much more of this intrigue. While others his age were investing money in the stock market or negotiating with dignitaries from other countries, he, Matthew Sadler, was skulking around an old hotel in a town he'd never heard of three weeks ago, avoiding a beautiful but confusing woman who inspired fear in two of his favorite elderly friends.

This was ridiculous. He would talk to Roni, tell her what was going on, and they would reach a reasonable conclusion. All this covert activity was pointless.

He shrugged off the pleas of the sisters to keep the current situation quiet. All this pretending was for children, not mature adults. After all, he had never promised not to talk to

Roni; they had assumed he would acquiesce to their request. He wouldn't tell her about the ladies' clandestine dealings. He'd think of a safe way to convey the situation.

That evening, after a double helping of Johanna's tantalizing tortellini with German sausage and layered lettuce salad, Matt asked Roni to accompany him outside to his verandah. As he had hoped, she seemed to have come to terms with her anger or jealousy of the night before and mellowed into controlled friendliness. He missed the consistency of Ginny's love and acceptance, but he'd decided there would never be another relationship like his with Ginny. Perhaps Roni was right, that good was better than nothing.

They carried their black forest cake and coffee, settled back in the padded deck chairs and relaxed.

"Why do I eat so much?" Roni asked the question of herself, Matt thought, but he asked himself the same.

"I think it has something to do with Johanna's culinary expertise and our lack of resistance."

She smirked. "Why does food consumption have to be connected to weight gain? Eating is such a comforting and enjoyable process."

"I suppose there have to be limits of some kind or we'd harm ourselves. How was your afternoon?"

"Same as ever. I like to be able to get away often enough to take the sameness out of it. This week's been slow that way. How about you? Did you paint today, oh friend of the needy?"

"Don't mock, Roni. I enjoy helping the Seligs and they always appreciate it. Bear was busy today, but I think we'll go tomorrow and finish up. Today I hung out here and helped the ladies."

"With what?"

Matt phrased his answer with care. "They've run into another snag: found out from their solicitor that they are being charged interest for not paying their taxes."

"Oh brother. Don't tell me they let that get past them?"

"They said they didn't receive any notices."

"The tax people always send more than one, Matt. The ladies asked me not to interfere anymore, so I left them to it, and they blew it. I told you they were unable to manage on their own."

"But the original notice came two months ago, followed by another last month, and a final, red-stamped copy yesterday. They hadn't seen any of them."

Roni scraped the last crumbs of chocolate from her plate and ate them. She set the plate and fork on the little plastic table beside her half-empty mug of coffee and turned to face Matt.

"Then how did they know they had missed them?"

"I told you: they talked with their solicitor."

"How did he know?"

"The notices had been sent to him, I suppose. How else would he know?"

"You're a poor liar, Matthew Sadler. I'm sure you can do better than that."

"I haven't told a lie. I was helping—what did you call me?"

"I called you by your real name. What were you doing in my room?"

She had called him Matthew Sadler. What else did she know? He clamped his mouth shut, not trusting himself to speak. Sure, he'd been snooping, but on behalf of the ladies, and they had every right to their financial information.

Roni sat back and watched him. Her face and form were Ginny's, but that was where the similarity ended. He couldn't take much more of this particular rollercoaster.

Before he could think of a suitable comeback, Roni said, "I hear you're considering stepping into Morris Craddock's shoes. I wonder what the school board will say when they find out you've been let go for molesting one of your students."

Matt jerked out of his chair so quickly, it toppled sideways. He stood over her and spoke in measured tones. "First of all, the details are none of your affair, but since you pretend to know, at least get them straight. I was not let go. I left because of false accusations and misunderstandings that impeded my ability to teach the students. And secondly, I did not touch any of my students. It was a setup. It's slanderous for you to bring it up. What do you gain by it?"

She studied her nails and spoke in such a soft tone that Matt had to concentrate to hear her words. "On the flip side,

Mr. Sadler, what would you gain by telling a solicitor that you had found unpaid tax notices in my room?"

"Justice for the Barlow sisters. You can't just—"

She stood up and met his gaze, their faces so close he could smell the chocolate on her breath. "Can't just what? You," she stabbed at his chest with a well-manicured fingernail, "keep your nose out of my business, and you might yet be able to assume the role of high school teacher in Happenstance. Think about it. You won't ever teach again in Reedport. Your reputation there is shot. Don't blow it here too. Kapeesh?"

"But why did you have the notices in your room? If it was an oversight, why don't you return them and let this go?"

"Why can't you keep your nose out of things that are not your business? Let me work through this with the ladies, and you forget your hero persona for once."

"The ladies are understandably upset. I can't allow you to ruin them by your oversights or whatever caused you to keep these papers from them, no matter what you think you know about me."

"That's unfortunate. Belvina will have a heyday with this information."

"You don't even have the correct information. How can you spread false rumors like that?"

"It's not difficult. Rumors ruined you in Reedport, as they will here in Happenstance, unless you keep your trap shut. Think about it, Sadler."

She pushed past him and he stared after her in disbelief. She knew all about Reedport. How had she found out? Internet? Newspaper back-issues? Why was she doing this?

All this time he had been duped by her looks. He had believed what he wanted to believe, dictated by her resemblance to Ginny. Now she had given him an ultimatum. What was her problem?

Maybe she was scared because of the tea episode, and desperate to find something to hold over him to guarantee that he and the ladies wouldn't press charges later. Maybe that was it. She'd even mentioned it earlier.

He knew she was jealous of Paula. Maybe that had incited her against the ladies, who treated Paula like family.

Considering Roni's background, he imagined she would fight for what she thought was hers. Maybe that included being the ladies' financial advisor and his special friend, although their friendship seemed in serious jeopardy now.

Matt righted his chair and slumped into it. He should have been angry, but instead, defeat filled him. The threat of renewed animosity from yet another group of people made him feel like an old balloon, withering into a corner, the life slowly seeping out of him. Where would he go next? And even if he did comply with Roni's demands, could he trust her to keep her end of the bargain?

He ran his hands through his graying hair and it fell forward as the elastic snapped. *Pitiful old man. Some knight you are.* By tomorrow, all of Happenstance would also label him a perverted old man. He slammed his fist on the plastic table, splintering it into shards along with the ceramic coffee mug.

He got up and walked out onto the lawn, toward the trees. What would happen if he kept walking, lost himself in the woods, never to be heard of again? With his luck, Sandy would find him the next day and bring him back home, tail between his legs. No, this time he would face his demons head on.

He had known, even without contemplating it, that he could not cave to Roni's threat, could not leave the sisters unprotected against her schemes, whatever they were. What kind of knight did that? No, he would have to pull himself together, do his best for the Barlows, and worry about the consequences later.

It bothered him, though, that Paula would read the rumors without knowing the truth. He wasn't sure why he cared, except that he had enjoyed her company the other evening. She had listened to his reminiscences, asked caring questions, and respected his memories of Ginny.

For the time being, he had work to do. Since Roni knew about him, he would do his own sleuthing and find out what he could about her. He would investigate her background and figure out why it was important to her that she keep him in line. If she could do research, so could he. He wished he'd brought his laptop. He would have to go to the library, which wasn't open until tomorrow, and by then the slander would be front page news. Who could he get to help him?

Paula! He checked his watch. After 11:00 p.m. Did he dare call her now or would it wait until morning? He grabbed the phone and dialed, visualizing his face and name spread all over *The Village Voice* in the morning. He'd risk calling late before Paula read the lies and believed them.

25

The phone rang five times. Matt was about to hang up when he heard her voice. "Dr. Percy here."

"Paula. It's me, Matt. I need to talk to you."

Silence. "Are you ill, Matt?"

"No. But I might be if I can't speak to you."

"That is the worst line I've ever heard. Good night."

"Paula! Don't hang up. This is bigger than you and me. Just please listen."

She sighed. "What?"

"I need to see you, face to face. Can I come by? Take you for coffee?"

"Matt Smith! You are incorrigible. How dare you call me this late and then demand an audience. I have come between you and Miss Wilkinson twice already. I don't do triangles."

"There's nothing between Roni and me but trouble."

"The moment you break up, you call me? Well, sorry fella, but I'm not good with rebounds. Now leave me alone."

"I'm coming by," he stated before she slammed down the receiver.

Matt grabbed his jacket and slipped out the verandah door, locking it behind him. He jogged around the side of the house, borrowed one of the old bicycles from the shed, and pedaled down the lane, not daring to fire up the Harley for fear of waking the dead—and the living.

When he bumped onto the driveway of the Percy residence, the kitchen light was on. He hoped it was Paula and not Phineas. How did one explain to a father that you were stopping by to pick up his daughter for coffee at 11:30 p.m., even if that daughter was in her thirties?

Before he could knock on the door, Paula opened it.

She's ticked, all right, but at least she's dressed to go out.

She peered past him at the bicycle, then stared at him. "I ought to slam this door in your impertinent face," she said. "What is this? Let's go out, will you drive? What kind of a—"

Matt held up a hand to stop her tirade. "Please, Paula. There is a reasonable explanation for all of this."

"I've heard that one a few times too, Buster. Let me remind you that I can take you out with one hand tied behind my back. Watch yourself." Her eyes blazed, and the way her dark hair hung over one eye gave her a dangerous look.

He waited, knowing more words would weaken his position.

"There's an all-night pizza place through the back alley," she said. "Let's go. I want to get back home to bed. Unlike you, I work for a living."

"Ouch. You might want to temper your words, Paula. Makes less to apologize for afterward."

She narrowed her eyes and sidestepped his proffered his arm.

"I can walk by myself, thank you." She stumbled off the curb and went down on one knee. He heard her say something distinctly unladylike, but decided not to ask her to repeat it.

"Shut up, Matt."

"I didn't say anything."

"You thought it."

"I can't help..." He snorted in spite of himself and she joined him, unable to retain her cool disconnection. Taking his arm, she walked beside him, muttering about misplaced curbs and ridiculous ideas and thoughtless men. Matt let her get it out of her system.

By the time they arrived at the pizza place, Paula's ire had dissipated. The cool night air invigorated Matt, and he was glad—so far—for his persistence. They found a table in a corner—the place was pretty dead at this hour, except for a table of bored-looking teens, and one single person on his laptop—and ordered colas and bread sticks. *Something to do with my hands so I don't fall asleep*, was what Paula said.

"Now, what is at the bottom of this crazy call of yours?"

Matt leveled his gaze on hers. "I need you."

Her mouth and her eyes popped wide open. "You know no bounds!"

"Let me have my say and then you can smack me, okay?"

She flexed her fingers and he winced.

He looked around to make sure no one was listening, while she drummed her short-clipped fingernails on the table.

"Roni's blackmailing me," he stage-whispered.

She opened her mouth to reply but he spoke first.

"We've discovered something, the ladies and I, and I think Roni's desperate to keep me from taking it further. She's put out an ultimatum."

"And how long have you suffered from delusions of paranoia?"

"She's threatening me, Paula. You'll hear all about it as soon as Belvina gets her next column written. I wanted you to hear the truth before that happens."

It was his turn to sigh. "I need to tell you my story in order for you to understand. I don't want to, but, as I said, if I don't, Belvina will tell it without the aid of facts."

"Why do you care what I think?"

He looked into her eyes, which weren't smiling, and then down at his hands. "I don't know, I just do. And I know you care about the ladies. I think Roni cares more about herself than about them."

Paula dipped a breadstick in hot sauce and munched, waiting.

"Twelve years ago, Ginny and I moved to Reedport. I taught school; she worked in a daycare and dreamed of having our own kids one day. She died five years ago, her dream unfulfilled, and I stayed on, teaching at the high school. I was a good teacher too."

Paula's look softened, but she didn't interrupt.

"Last year, this new teacher joined our staff—Jaqueline. She was young and pretty and full of life. I liked her as a fellow teacher. She was way too young for me and I had no interest in her. I didn't want to replace Ginny.

"She flirted brazenly, so I decided I'd better tell her straight that I wasn't interested. She didn't take it well.

Avoided me, wouldn't speak to me unless absolutely necessary, started saying nasty things about me to the rest of the staff. I figured she'd get over it.

"One day a student came into my office, asked to speak to me. She was distressed, bad home situation, bad relationship with her boyfriend, the whole kit. My door was open and the secretary was at her desk just outside. I didn't realize Marge had stepped out for a cup of coffee, but Jaqueline did. I remember seeing her walk by the office and glance in, then check out Marge's empty chair. Didn't occur to me to think anything of it at the time.

"Well, she had her revenge. By the next day, everyone was looking at me like I had leprosy, and then Jim—the principal—called me into his office and told me what they were saying: that I'd been in my office alone with this girl for a long time with no one else around. Marge had to admit she'd left for a few minutes; I couldn't blame her. Jim believed my story and of course, so did Marge, but somehow Jaqueline got to everyone before I did, and my name was mud.

"Long story short, it hit the papers and I was finished there. Jim defended me, but it didn't matter."

"What about the girl?"

"She didn't speak up at first. I don't think her father would let her. It wasn't her fault either. Later on, she sent me a letter apologizing for all the trouble. She said she'd talked to the police too, and all pending charges were dropped, but it didn't change what people thought.

"Jim told me to hang in there, that I had been cleared and could come back teaching. Instead, I got a job working construction for a guy who didn't care about the stories as long as I put in my hours, but you can imagine how it felt to walk around town and have people cross the street to avoid you, to hear them calling you names I won't repeat right now. I knew it would never be over.

"One day a few weeks ago, I'd had enough. I threw a few things into my bike cases and rode out of town. Almost ran into the Barlows' car and turned in at Happenstance to avoid hitting them.

"Bob found out I was a teacher and asked me to fill Morris' place. I was almost considering it until today, but now

I know I'm history in this place too. I just want to stay around long enough to deal with Roni and protect the sisters from her."

Paula shook her head. "Quite a story. I'm sorry for what you had to deal with, but what's Roni's part in all this, and why are you telling me?"

Matt leaned forward. "The ladies confided to me that they thought Roni was trying to poison Emmaline, that she had tainted the tea she had made for her. I thought that was ridiculous, and so did Roni, of course. She offered to have it analyzed and it was okay. The ladies, however, didn't accept her word for it and pilfered a sample of the tea leaves from her room. Had another analysis done and discovered it contained digitalis."

"You're kidding!" Paula pounded the table with her fist. "That's why Emmaline succumbed to it. Combined with her pills, it was lethal."

"Right. When I told Roni about it, she went to pieces, said she'd made a terrible mistake. She'd dug her own herbs in the woods and must have picked the wrong ones. We verified it with Sandy that she had picked foxglove instead of comfrey."

"What the heck was she doing with comfrey? That's not recommended for internal use. People think just because it grows wild, it's good for you."

"Anyway, she apologized with sincerity and Emmaline forgave her. Grayce didn't and I couldn't believe she could be so cold."

"You're too trusting. Too naïve."

"What happened to 'innocent until proven guilty'."

"Whatever. Being a cop, you see the seedier side of life every day. Even quiet little towns are full of weirdos and kooks. After a while you get hardened to it; it isn't conducive to trusting. Is there more to the story?"

"I think that's what Roni's trying to keep quiet. She likes it here too and doesn't want anyone to know she was careless."

He was about to dismiss the rest, but Paula questioned his hesitation.

"Okay, I'll tell you the part I haven't figured out yet. Grayce suspects Roni of tampering with the hotel's financial records. Just yesterday, Grayce and Emmaline called me into their office and showed me three tax notices, all unpaid, that they had found in Roni's dresser drawer."

Paula laughed. "I can't believe it. Those ladies are spunky."

"Yeah. We almost got caught putting the stuff back after I made copies. In the process, I discovered the backstairs from the upper hall to the kitchen."

Paula paused with a breadstick halfway to her mouth. "I had forgotten that passage. Used to disappear there sometimes when I didn't want to go home. Emmaline would give me cookies, but Grayce always found me."

"I nearly scared Johanna into next week when I knocked on the kitchen door." He sipped his cola and held Paula's eyes. "Why would she take the tax notices? Why would she alter the books, if that's what she did? And what can we do about it?"

"Hold on there, Matt Smith. Why are your problems becoming my problems? What do you want of me?"

He sighed, his heart heavy. "For the record, my name is Matthew Sadler and I'm sorry I deceived you, but I was hoping to remain unknown. As to *my* problem, I thought you cared about the ladies too. I need to find out who Roni is and I need your help."

Paula's eyes narrowed. "How do you expect me to find out who she is?"

"You were a cop. You have ways—"

"Wait a minute, Buddy. I *was* a cop. I am now a physician. I have no clearance to access private information."

"But you know where to find it. You have to help me."

"No, I do not have to help you. I may decide to, but nobody pushes me into anything. Not anymore."

"I sense a story here."

"There's a story all right, but now is not the time for it." She bit into another breadstick and chewed, deep in thought. "What do you know about Roni?"

Matt smiled to himself but knew better than to show any victory. "Nothing but what she's told me. Don't you have anyone you could ask in a case like this?"

"You want me to ask the cops, off the record, to find the identity of some woman when all you know is her name and she hasn't been charged with anything?"

"Then there's no way we can find out who she is?"

It was her turn to sigh. "Let me think about it."

"That's all I ask. And that you believe the truth instead of whatever Belvina and Roni cook up tomorrow."

"You think they'll be at it tomorrow already?"

"Why do you think I took you out for coffee at midnight?"

"Why indeed? I'm not making any promises Matt, but I will try to be fair. Now, I need some sleep before going to work in the morning. I'm not as young as I was in med school."

Matt paid for the drinks and bread sticks and walked her home.

"I'll give you one thing, Matt," she said when they reached her door, "you are one of the more interesting men I've met in a while. And honest. I like honest."

Matt grinned. "Me too. Sleep well. Talk to you soon. Don't believe everything you read."

"Yeah, yeah. Good night already."

But her eyes were smiling again as she entered the house.

26

Matt's muscles ached after finishing the final coat of paint at the parsonage, but his reward came in the form of Annaliese's delight. "Such a wondrous color iss it," she said, and the reverend agreed. Bear returned to his shop to work on a car, while Matt lingered.

"I have to stop by the church for a bit, Matt," said the reverend. "Would you walk with me?"

"Sure."

They chatted as they crossed the grass between the parsonage and the church.

Matt sat down in a pew and rubbed his hands over his face. He kept his beard trimmed, but he was still sometimes surprised to find it there after so many years of the clean-shaven look. "What do you think about coincidence, Reverend? Is there such a thing?"

Reverend Selig sat down near him. "Why do you ask?"

"Well, Miss Grayce doesn't believe in it. She thinks there is a plan for everything that happens, that God is in control of it all. That's what I was taught as a kid, too, but sometimes reality challenges that belief."

"You think everything happens randomly?"

"I don't know. The part I don't understand is how a person ends up where he is supposed to be. I was in Reedport and now I am here in Happenstance, and it seems a gigantic coincidence to me, yet the Barlow sisters both believe I've been led here for a reason."

"Perhaps you need to look at this from another

perspective. Perhaps life happens to us because we live here on this earth, subject to time and illness, aging and circumstance, but the eventual outcome is for our good."

"If I believe that, then there was a reason for my wife's death. I find it difficult to believe that was for the best." Matt tried to remain calm but the memories threatened to engulf him.

"I can imagine that Ginny's death was heartbreaking. When we lost our only child to leukemia, we questioned whether any good could ever come out of it."

Matt's pain changed to surprise and sympathy. "I'm sorry. I didn't know."

"We are sorry too, but we believe God had a plan that would bring good from losing a little girl so young and innocent." Pain descended like a cloud over the reverend's face.

"How old was she?"

Reverend Selig smiled away the cloud and met Matt's eyes. "Sue Ellen was seven. She was a beautiful child, always cheerful and sweet. She never expressed bitterness or self-pity about her illness. She believed it to be a part of God's plan for her."

"Did you believe that?"

Reverend Selig bit his lip as if searching for the right words. "We struggled through it and then decided we would be negating her faith if we remained in emotional and spiritual paralysis. You know, Matt, when we gave up our anger and fear and self-pity, the despair lifted as well. It was as if a heavy dark cloak were lifted from our shoulders, to be replaced by a lightweight robe of peace. Of course, we would rather have had Sue Ellen remain with us and grow up to be a woman of God, but perhaps in her death, the good Lord saw an opportunity to teach us a great truth."

Matt sat back in his pew and folded his arms. "I don't mean to make light of what you've shared, but besides giving you relief from despair, which I understand, what benefits have come of the experience?"

The reverend smiled. "I've been able to share with you, Matt. If I'd never lost anyone, my words would hold little credibility with you, but as it is, you can see I have experienced some of the same kind of pain you have. To quote a Scripture, 'The God of all comfort comforts us in all our troubles, so that we can comfort those in any trouble with the comfort we ourselves have received from God.' "

"Sounds awfully sacrificial to me."

"To give up despair for peace? More like common sense, I'd say. Coming to terms with our helplessness allows us to reach for the consolation God offers."

"Coming to terms. I guess that's the clincher," said Matt. He stood and nodded to the reverend. "Thanks for listening—again—and for sharing your wisdom. I don't make a habit of unburdening myself to anyone. Just since I came to Happenstance."

"Matthew, we all have times when we need someone to listen. Don't deny yourself that. Come anytime. By the way, how are things with the Barlows?"

"We're still trying to think of some simple way to bring in customers."

"Besides seeding nails on the highway beyond the bridge?"

Matt smiled. "Should probably steer clear of that."

Reverend Selig grinned. "I will think on it, Matt. Annaliese and I love the Barlows. They have been good to us in the past and we will do anything we can to help."

"Thanks. I'd appreciate it if you'd say a prayer for them when you think of it, and maybe even for me." He shook Reverend Selig's hand. Somehow peace infused him in this place, even though his puzzles had not been solved.

"Be glad to."

Matt smiled and left, a strange peace accompanying him back to the hotel.

Matt trudged over to Beresford Gas Station after lunch and bought a pop from the machine instead of risking Bear's toxic excuse for coffee, then waited until Bear came into the office.

"Wish I could find my good wrench," the big man chirped, pouring himself a cup of sludge from his carafe. "Can't for the life of me think where it got to. You got another puzzle to ponder?"

"Kind of. I thought you might have some ideas."

Gavin Beresford stopped whistling. "Hey now Matt, I ain't no rocket scientist. I do puzzles is all. Whatcha talkin' about?"

"Well, I thought we'd do a bit of advertising for the hotel, get some more customers out."

"How do you suggest we do that?"

Matt sat back and guzzled the rest of his drink. He set the can on Bear's messy desk and leaned forward. "I'm not sure how much you know about Happenstance Hotel in the old days, but it was called Barlow Manor and it has a long, illustrious history."

"May as well give me the lowdown," said Bear. "I've heard some rumors but forgot the details."

"Well, way back in the time of slavery, the sisters' great-great grandfather, Robert Austen Barlow, dug tunnels to help runaway slaves avoid detection, and escape to Canada. Much later, during Prohibition, the ladies' father, William Richardson Barlow, used the tunnels for rum-running."

"I'm startin' to remember now." Bear leaned back and sipped his coffee.

"Yeah. At first, Miss Grayce didn't want to bring that up, but I talked with them again later, and after some thought, they agreed it would be a way to gain notoriety and business for the old hotel."

"I heard the town council decided to help with money from the old schoolhouse. Ain't that enough?"

"The money will keep them going all right, but the hotel needs exposure to bring it to people's attention. We want it to remain a viable business for years to come."

"Longer than the sisters theirselves."

Matt sighed. "It would never be the same without them, but yes, I hope it carries on for many years. I've suggested they change the name back to Barlow Manor, or at least Barlow Inn, but they need a little time to think about that. For the time being, it will remain Happenstance Hotel."

"Sounds like a terrific idea if we can pull 'er off."

"You think so? The tunnels, if they are still open, may need some work. Roni told me they had fallen in, but I'm not sure I believe anything she says anymore. If they still exist, I might be asking you for assistance here and there."

"You got it, Pontiac."

~ ~ ~

After Bear locked up the garage for the day, he and Matt jumped into Bear's old pickup truck and drove downtown to the Waldorf for iced cappuccinos. Matt's coffee preferences were becoming more exotic.

Phil walked up to their booth with the coffee carafe in one hand and a copy of *The Village Voice* in the other. He tossed the paper on the table in front of Matt. "Myself, I dislike being the purveyor of bad news, Matt, but you may want to peruse the gossip column by one Belvina Rampole. And please do not take revenge in my establishment."

Matt looked at the paper as if it were contagious. "That bad?"

Phil shook his head. "Best you read it for yourself."

"C'mon, Matt," said Bear. "If you don't, I will."

With a glance at Phil, who had walked away, and another at Bear, who tapped his fingers on the table, Matt opened the thin newspaper and paged to the section that carried the local gossip. He skimmed through the page until he found Belvina's column.

Our best wishes go out to our dear Veronica Wilkinson, better known as Roni to her many friends, who will be taking some time off work for stress-related reasons after an altercation with another newcomer to our fair town who shall remain unnamed at this time, if indeed he is going by his actual name. Miss Wilkinson is convalescing at the personal residence of this writer. Get well soon, Roni, and try to avoid unnecessary stressful encounters with questionable and potentially dangerous characters in the future.

Matt's eyes widened. He swore under his breath at the blatant accusation and dropped the paper like a hot potato.

"Lemme see that, Matt. Ain't heard you cuss since you came to town. Must be somethin' nasty."

Gavin Beresford read the column, with a reaction similar to Matt's.

"You warned me to watch my back," he said to Bear. "I

didn't think it would come to this."

Bear shook his head. "No way, Hosea," he said, his voice escalating in pitch. "I didn't think she was that mean."

"José... Nor did I. Welcome to the real heart of Happenstance."

"Hey now, don't paint us all with the same roller, Matt. She's one person, and she hasn't been here long."

"I realize that, but she's got her claws in Belvina, and that's one person with a lot of readership, in spite of the dismal quality of her writing. People believe that trash. I should have left two weeks ago, before this happened."

They stood to leave and Matt dropped some change on the table for the drinks.

"I wouldn't do that if I were you," said Phil, coming out from behind the counter. "Tips and loose change have been disappearing around here the last day or so."

"Kleptos in Happenstance?" said Bear. "I don't believe it."

"Believe it." Phil rescued the money from the table and popped it into the cash register. "I don't know what's happening, but I don't like it."

Bear dropped Matt off at the hotel. He entered, out of sorts, and almost missed Emmaline standing behind the counter, her face pale and confused.

"Something wrong, Miss Emmaline?"

"Oh, hello Matthew. I'm looking for something."

"What's that?"

"Our bell seems to be missing."

"Your bell?"

"The desk bell. The one presented to Grayce and me by the school, in gratitude for the use of our gatehouse. We never move it except to dust, and then it's lift and replace. It was here first thing this morning, but now it's gone. If someone ever does come in, we won't hear them."

"Won't people holler if they need you?"

"My dear Mr. Smith," said Grayce, coming up behind her sister, "we do not holler."

"Right, propriety. I'm sorry about the bell. Let me know if there's anything I can do."

"Of course. Now, you go on about your business and don't waste a worry about the bell. I'm sure it will turn up soon enough."

"Ladies, would you mind if I skipped dinner tonight? I don't have much of an appetite and I think I need a ride on my motorbike."

Worry lines furrowed Miss Grayce's face. "Has something happened, Mr. Smith, to cause you anxiety?" Miss Emmaline had interrupted her troubled thoughts of the bell and waited for his answer as well.

"Do you have a copy of *The Village Voice*?"

"Yes, we have it in the office," said Emmaline, "but we haven't read it yet."

"Take a look at Belvina's column. My patience is worn about as thin as it can be with that woman."

"Oh dear, not Belvina again," said Grayce. "She does not know when enough is enough."

"I think you're right about that, but I don't think she's working alone," commented Matt as he headed to his room for his helmet. It wasn't on the shelf in the closet where he had left it. He looked on the chair, on the floor, under the bed. Had he left it hanging on the bike? He never did that unless he was on a road trip.

He ran out the front door, down the steps and over to his bike, parked under an awning on the west side of the hotel. No helmet. His blood boiling, he jogged back into the house and approached the ladies.

"Excuse me, but have either of you seen my helmet?"

Grayce narrowed her eyes. "You mean that little hard hat you wear to protect your brain when you roar away on that motorcycle of yours?"

"That's the one."

"No. Emm, have you seen Mr. Smith's helmet?"

"No, I haven't. You won't go without it, will you, dear?"

Matt let out an exasperated sigh. "No, I won't, but I intend to find out what happened to it. I guess it's the old bicycle then, but it isn't at all what I needed tonight."

Emmaline quirked a smile in sympathy and encouraged him to be back before dark. He had to be; the bicycle had neither lights nor reflectors. And where on earth was his helmet? Had Roni taken it out of spite? Was she that vindictive?

Just as he crossed the hall into the entry, the phone rang and Emmaline answered. She put her hand over the mouthpiece and called after him.

"It's for you, Matthew. Bob Rampole."

Matt wondered what Bob could want. To warn him about Belvina's antics? He doubted that.

"Bob? It's Matt."

"Uh, yeah. Matt, I, uh, think I, uh, got ahead of myself the other day when I, uh, asked if you'd be willing to take Morris' teaching position. We, uh, have to advertise and everything, you know."

Matt's anger rose. Here we go again: Sorry, we have reconsidered and we can't hire you right now. Perhaps in the future...

"Matt? You still there?"

"I'm here. Funny how the timing of your decision coincides with the article in the paper. I guess I know where I stand."

"Listen, Matt, I'm sorry, but that's what the, uh, board decided."

"Thank you for your call."

"Goodbye."

The phone call quashed any hope of a future career in Happenstance. His purpose now was to find justice for the sisters and their hotel, then to move farther down the road.

The gloves were off. No more Mr. Nice Guy. Time to see what, if anything, Paula had found out.

Questions circled around in Matt's brain like the pedals of the bicycle as he pushed on down the Happenstance lane, trying to avoid potholes. He hit a new one, and the old bike jolted him onto the grass at the side of the road. After swallowing a few choice words, he raised himself to his feet, dusted off his knees and his backside, and planted the bent bicycle next to one of the trees, out of the way. He'd pick it up later. Right now he had to meet Paula.

He limped into the clinic parking lot, pushed open the

door and called Paula's name. Sylvia had already gone home, and Dr. Phineas was fishing again.

"That you, Matt?" came the voice from the back office.

"Yeah, last I checked."

"Come on back."

Matt walked through the half-door leading to the examination rooms and found Paula at her desk, writing up reports for the day. He leaned against the doorframe until she looked up.

"You have anything for bruised egos?"

"What happened?"

"You read the paper yet?"

"No. Is it bad?"

"It's not nice, and it's leading to something more, I can almost guarantee it. I got a call from Bob Rampole, rescinding his offer for Morris' teaching position."

"Oh, Matt, I'm sorry."

He grimaced. "It's not like it's the first time I've been through this. You'd think I'd be used to it."

"You don't get used to things like that." She scribbled a final note on the sheet before her, slipped it into the folder and inserted it into the lateral file beside her. "I'm done. Let's get out of here. Hey, how about a ride on our bikes?"

"Do you have an extra helmet? Mine sprouted legs and disappeared."

"Where'd you leave it?"

"I left it in the same place I always do: on the shelf in the closet in my room. It's gone, and I've looked everywhere else I can think of. It's getting weird around here, Paula."

Her brow furrowed as she shed her white lab coat and grabbed her briefcase. Just as they walked past Sylvia's desk, the phone rang. Paula cast him an apologetic look and answered it.

After a brief conversation, she hung up and frowned. "I'm sorry, Matt, but I have to go to the hospital. I'll have to take a rain check on the ride. Maybe you'll find your helmet by then."

"No problem, Doc. I'll amble on over to Phil's and drown my sorrows in a latte."

"Make me feel bad."

"You have to do what you have to do.."

She smiled. "Listen, I'll call you tonight. I have a few things to discuss with you."

"About Roni?"

"Or whoever she is."

27

The only person in the Waldorf when Matt arrived was Morris Craddock, and although he was one of the last people with whom Matt preferred to visit, he nodded and asked if he could share his table.

"Doesn't matter to me," said Craddock, looking out the window.

Matt cringed inside. This would be fun.

Phil brought coffee without his usual smile. He glanced at Matt and nodded, then filled their cups and left.

"What's with Phil?"

"Perhaps he has had a difficult day," said Morris. "For some of us, life is not a bowl of cherries."

What was that supposed to mean? He thought Matt led a charmed life? He had no idea, and wouldn't care if he did.

Matt searched his mind for conversation starters. "I appreciate you coming alongside at the town council meeting and supporting my idea to save the hotel. Your suggestion was excellent."

"My suggestion was made for the sake of Grayce and Emmaline, not you. The hotel is one of the oldest and most respected establishments in the community. It is worth saving."

Matt cleared his throat, tamping down his ire at being told off once again. "It needs a lot of work, but I'm sure it can be saved."

Craddock made no reply and Matt considered moving to another table. He thought even his own company was better than this. Then Morris spoke up.

"Don't you have a job? Why must you meddle in the affairs of Happenstance?"

Meddle? Thanks for that. "I am unemployed at the moment. I am a teacher, so I'm off for the summer. Taught high school for more than fifteen years."

Morris stared at him from beneath lowered brows. "What happened? Couldn't take it?"

Matt had to smile at Craddock's determination to be grouchy. "It was often challenging but I loved it. The opportunity to discover a student's gift or particular interest and then show them how to learn about it on their own, to want to learn, that was the best part. And to see changes in kids' lives. Not all of them, but some. It was more reward than the paycheck."

"Then why did you quit?"

Matt pursed his lips and studied Morris Craddock. Did he really want to know? Did Matt want to tell him? He looked out the window as he spoke.

"I was accused of something I didn't do. They didn't fire me, but a man can only put up with so much pressure. Every day I walked into the school wondering what my students were thinking about me, what their parents had told them, what the other teachers thought. To make a long story short, I packed up and left." He looked over at Morris, who was staring at him, judging him.

"You left your job and your family and just took off? This generation has no courage, no perseverance, no commitment. When the going gets tough, they flee."

"Just a minute there, Morris. You know nothing about my life but what you've read in the gossip columns, and I would think you too intelligent to believe that fluff.

"For your information, I don't have a family. My parents are long dead, my grandparents who raised me are dead, my wife died five years ago, and we had no children. My life has not been a bowl of cherries and I resent the judgments you're throwing at me without knowing the facts."

Morris Craddock's bushy eyebrows moved up and down and he seemed at a loss for words, even sarcastic ones. His lips bunched and straightened as if he contemplated a response, but it didn't come.

Matt winced. "Listen, I shouldn't have talked like that to you. I try to respect my elders. I guess your accusations added to the slough I'm already wading in."

Morris looked into his coffee cup and shook his head. "No. I deserved it. I'm a crotchety old man whose only pastime is making others miserable. I had no right to judge." He took a slurp of coffee and his hands shook.

"How long since you lost your wife, Morris?"

The older man hesitated before speaking, and when he did, his voice shook in time with his hands. "Nearly ten years. I've been a miserable old coot since then, but it's her fault. She never should have left me."

"Do you think she had a choice?"

"Of course not, but why would the good Lord take away the most important thing in a man's life? Madeline was everything to me. She captured my heart and then took it with her when she died. I've barely functioned since."

Morris' eyes teared up and the two men sat in silence, Matt connecting with Morris' words.

"We seem to have more in common than I'd thought possible."

"Misery loves company."

"Put a spin on that: shared sorrows weigh less."

Phil topped up their cups of coffee and left them alone.

"Were you at least a good teacher?" Morris asked.

"I put in one hundred and ten percent, if that means anything."

Morris nodded. "That's all you can do. You ought to take over my position."

Matt wondered if he'd heard correctly. "What did you say?"

"I've retired. They need to hire a replacement before September, and there are no takers as yet. I could recommend you for the job, but it would have to be done soon."

Matt stared at Morris. "I appreciate the vote of confidence, but the offer has been given and retracted, based on rumors of my past. I have no option but to move on somewhere else."

"Where else would you go?"

Matt met his eyes and then looked down at his coffee. "I don't know." He stood to leave. "Thanks for the visit, Morris. The coffee's on me."

The older man nodded as Matt left.

"Here's the coffee money, Phil. I'll let you put it in the till. Any more thefts?"

Phil eyed him. "Sure have been."

"You're kidding. What this time?"

"My collectible salt and pepper shakers."

"You don't mean Big Ben and Pisa?"

"Yes. We have a collection of them; they are made to resemble well-known tall buildings around the world. I've been collecting them since I was a lad in Greece. So far, it's just Big Ben and Pisa. I've put away the Tower of London, the Eiffel Tower and the Washington Monument. My customers now have to use ordinary shakers I purchased at Wuppertal's."

"Sounds like quite a collection," said Matt.

"No two alike."

"I'm sorry this happened to you. Since we talked last, the bell from the desk of the hotel went missing. The sisters are quite upset about it."

"I don't blame them. You can't trust people these days. You think you know people, and then something like this happens."

"Yeah. My motorbike helmet is missing too."

As he left the shop, Matt felt Phil staring at him. Did he suspect him? On second thought, why wouldn't he suspect him? Matt was new here, no one knew him, things had started to go missing since his arrival. He had just been framed, like a painting, and he was sure Roni, via Belvina, had done the framing. It was all happening again.

Matt tried to shake off the insecurity, the dread probing at him. Roni seemed to know his weaknesses and preyed on them. How far would she go with the information? Did she intend to ruin him here in Happenstance, *the town you can trust*? Maybe he should bail. Hit the road. Leave Happenstance in the dust.

Nope! This time it would be go to bat. He intended to see it through, to ferret out the truth for the sake of the Misses

Barlow, Bear, Sandy, the Seligs and Paula, and for the few others who didn't believe the rumors. If it cost him his future here in Happenstance, then so be it, but he would not allow Roni's scheming to take anyone else down. He couldn't believe he hadn't seen past Roni's exterior for the person she really was, but it was difficult to see it coming from the image of Ginny.

Matt scuffed his way back to the hotel and wandered into the sunroom. Easing himself into one of the wicker chairs, he picked up a framed photo and studied it, thinking how simple life must have been in the old days.

He sensed more than heard a presence beside him.

"That was my mother," said Grayce, referring to the photograph. "She was married for only five years when Papa died and left her with two little girls. She had nowhere to go, no way of making ends meet. What with the crash, Papa's money was all gone, and people ostracized her for a time because of the way Papa died. But she didn't give up. No, she turned Barlow Manor into a hotel in order to keep body and soul together and still be there for Emmaline and me. My mama worked her fingers to the bone, washing and cleaning and cooking for the people who came to our hotel. Emm and I had to be reminded often that the entire house was no longer our domain. My mother had a difficult life, but she didn't waste her time on what might have been."

"You are a wise woman."

"I am wiser than I once was but not as wise as I wish. One does one's best and tries to help others in the process."

"You caught me bemoaning my fate again, but I'm going to take your advice, or your mother's, and do the best I can with it. Do you know I am suspected of theft?"

Grayce's hand clutched her throat and she sat down on the bench near him. "Theft? What are you accused of taking?"

"No one said it in so many words, but I read it in Phil's face. He's missing some of his salt shakers, and tip money. I told him about the desk bell and my helmet, but he stared at me as if I'd done it. After reading Belvina's column in *The Village Voice*, people are blaming the one they know the least.

That would be me."

"Stuff and nonsense! How can they assume such a thing without proof?"

"Who needs proof when you have rumors? The fact is, I don't care this time. I'll leave, but not until we've done something about this hotel, and you and Miss Emmaline are looked after."

Matt saw Grayce's eyes fill. He stood, took her hand and helped her to her feet. "No tears now, Miss Grayce. Let's figure out what to do about our situation. What would your mother have done, I wonder?"

The door knocker thudded and Paula let herself into the lobby.

"Hi Miss Grayce, Matt. How are you folks this evening?"

"Been better, but we're on the way up."

Paula grinned. "Good to hear. Listen, Matt, I have some information you might be interested in." She glanced up the stairs and into the hallway.

"There's no one here but us chickens," remarked Grayce, "but let's go into our office." She led the way and Matt closed the door behind them.

"Where's Miss Emmaline?"

"She's resting. Let's not bother her right now."

"Okay. Matt, I did some checking on the internet to see if I could find anything on Roni that was in the public domain. It's a pretty broad search, you know. Anyway, there was nothing at all on Veronica Wilkinson."

"But maybe—"

"Let me finish. That leads me to believe it's not her real name. I mean, most other people have something on them. You wouldn't believe the amount of info out there on you and me."

Matt wondered what all she knew about him now.

"Not her real name?" Grayce frowned. "Then who is she and what does she want here?"

Paula glanced at Matt. "I called in some favors from a couple of friends in the force. I thought it pertinent that I give them a heads up, you know."

"Of course." Matt winked at her. "What did they tell you?"

"I can't give you details, but they may have found some leads, going by physical description, which already says a lot. She may have been involved in some shady dealings, but there's never been enough evidence to stop her."

"What kind of shady dealings?"

"You might not be surprised. Herbal scams, selling product that doesn't live up to the guarantee."

"Herbal scams? You mean she meant to poison my sister?" Grayce's eyes widened.

"I'm sorry, Miss Grayce, but it's possible."

Grayce's eyes were glued to Matt's. "You see what I've been trying to tell you, Mr. Smith?"

"I'm beginning to see."

"I'm going to check on Emmaline," said Grayce, and headed out the door.

"This is traumatic for them," said Paula.

"They're tough," said Matt, "but it's wearing on them."

"Okay, Matt. Back to Roni. What do you know about her? What have you observed, and please try to be objective."

He stared at her, but she wouldn't look away. He knew she thought him a pushover, but she didn't understand.

"Well, for one thing, she found out my real name isn't Matt Smith, and she seems to know what happened to me in Reedport. For another, ever since I've been here, she's been feeding me this line about how Emmaline is a sick old woman ready to kick the bucket, proven by her spell a couple of weeks ago, and that Grayce is suffering from dementia or Alzheimer's or something like that."

"Grayce? Alzheimer's? She's a lot smarter than Roni."

"Yeah, that's what I thought, but when Roni gave me examples of Grayce's forgetfulness, which now that I think of it were a setup, I started to believe her."

"And because you thought she had a thing for you."

"I think I had been trying to relive my past. I wanted to pretend she was Ginny."

"Men can be weak that way."

"Think what you will. If you saw your spouse walk into the room and smile at you, how would you react?"

"I'd take him out. Continue."

Matt fiddled with a paper clip from the desk. "That's about all I know. She's seems pretty good on the internet, but many people are these days. She lies a lot, which is common to criminals. She said she was raised in foster homes and had a rough time of it, but pursued her education and made it out of that life. For some reason, that part sounds believable."

Paula pulled out her phone and entered the information. "Anything else?"

Matt shook his head. "No, except that she looks so much like Ginny."

"Maybe she used that as part of the scam."

"There's no way in the world, Paula. I had no idea I was coming here."

"Happenstance." They said it at the same time.

"Anything else?"

Matt shook his head.

"Okay, we have a bit more to go on. Let me plug in and I'll send the information to my contacts. I can't get wireless here."

As she did so, Matt wondered aloud what more Roni might be into. He still didn't understand the connection between the tea and the tax notices. And then there were the tunnels.

At that moment, Grayce stepped into the room with Emmaline in tow. "Remember, Mr. Smith, when you suggested we use the tunnels in our advertising campaign and Miss Wilkinson was so opposed to your idea?"

"My *stupid* idea, if I recall her words, yes."

"Why would she be so resistant to your suggestion?"

"She said it was because it would take too much money for you to restore the tunnels and the cellar in order for people to venture down there."

"And since when has she shown concern over our financial situation, considering the past-due slips I showed you, or any other of our interests for that matter?"

Matt scratched his head and adjusted his ponytail. "I see what you mean. It doesn't fit."

Paula clicked off her phone and put it back in her pocket. "She was adamant about not using the tunnels? Why didn't you tell me?"

"Perhaps there is a reason why she does not want us down

there," said Grayce, "in which case...Emmaline Louise, fetch the high-powered lantern. We have business below."

28

Emmaline's eyes widened as they approached the basement door. "What if Veronica comes upon us while we're in the cellar?"

"I doubt she'll be back tonight, Emm," said Grayce. "She's moved most of her things to the Rampoles'."

"But what if she finds out? How will we explain what we're doing?"

"Emm, whose house is this?"

"Why it's ours, Graycie, but she would be so angry if she suspected us of suspecting her."

Matt turned toward them. "She already knows. Has she threatened you, Miss Emmaline?"

She wouldn't meet his eyes.

"Miss Emmaline?" Paula's voice demanded an answer.

"She warned me to be careful."

"Meaning?"

"She said I was never to repeat anything referring to the herbal tea or the tunnels or there would be consequences."

"Did she elaborate?" Matt's indignation grew with each word Emmaline spoke.

"She said I might have another spell. But I decided I would not let her manipulate me anymore."

"Record that as threatening comments," said Paula. "Miss Emmaline, shall I carry that lantern for you? It looks a bit heavy."

"Thank you, dear."

Matt grasped the doorknob but it wouldn't turn. "I forgot!

The door to the basement is locked and I couldn't find a key. I didn't want to break the door, or alert Roni."

Grayce withdrew a key from her pocket and unlocked the door, then stepped aside.

"I'll go first," said Paula, carrying the ladies' lantern. They descended the steps, then walked around the perimeter of the basement, Grayce and Emmaline following Paula, and Matt bringing up the rear with his own slim pocket flashlight. They moved from the freezers to the cast iron cookstove in the northwest corner and past the table of "almost-empty" egg cartons. As they passed the wardrobe, Matt had visions of Narnia. He could believe anything in Happenstance.

"Shine the light here, Paula," said Grayce.

Matt watched in amazed silence as Grayce felt along the rough surface and then exclaimed, "I have it." She tugged at a round iron ring in the wall.

"Let me do that," offered Matt.

Grayce moved away and Matt pulled until a crack appeared in the wall.

"It's the door all right." He opened it wide and brushed cobwebs from his face. As he aimed his flashlight at the opening, he remarked, "The bottom of the opening is a foot above the floor. You'll have to climb over it."

"We can do that much, Mr. Smith."

Matt stepped into the room and inhaled musty air. "Clothes," he said in annoyance. "There are rows and rows of clothes hanging here. Of what great significance is that?"

"Oh, for heaven's sake, let me have the flashlight," said Grayce. Matt relinquished it and Grayce pushed past him, past the racks and toward the north wall. Emmaline followed close on her sister's heels. They disappeared behind the last rack of mildewed garments.

Matt and Paula followed. The sisters had stepped through another narrow opening. It had a wooden door that stood open against the wall.

"We've never been farther than this room. Mother absolutely forbid it."

"Oh, Emmaline Louise!" The flashlight illuminated a shelf carved out of the earth along the walls.

"It's Big Ben!" said Grayce. "And Pisa."

"And my helmet."

"Shine the light around, Graycie. I'm sure our school bell is here somewhere."

"There it is. Dusty, but intact. Thank the Lord. But what is this?" Grayce pointed to a wrench.

Matt looked closer. "Bear said his favorite wrench had gone missing. What are the odds?"

"I don't understand why she would do this," said Grayce.

"It's kleptomania, Graycie, pure and simple."

"Nothing pure or simple about it, Miss Emmaline," said Paula. "It's thievery and it's a way to divert attention and blame someone else. Matt was a prime candidate."

Paula set her light on the floor and the upward beam brightened the cave room. "We'd better leave everything as is. We don't want Roni to know we're onto her."

A rickety dresser stood across the northwest corner of the tiny room. Matt pulled open the drawers to find silks and satins, scarves and handkerchiefs and fine undergarments from the past. "Must go with the clothes in the other room."

His hand fell upon an envelope at the front of the drawer and he drew it out.

"Did you find something, Matt?"

"An envelope." He waved it and stuck it into the pocket of his jeans. "We can check it later. There has to be an entrance to the tunnels from here."

Paula was already searching the ledge.

"Perhaps it's been filled in," suggested Grayce.

"Wait a minute," said Matt. "In the journal, Amanda said something about Carlo moving a board that closed the entrance. That would also open it."

He felt his way along the ledge while Paula held the lantern, then noticed the ridges in the dirt floor where the dresser had been dragged away from the wall. He pulled it out and checked behind it.

"Aha! Over here." In the dirt he felt wood, a board that slid along the shelf without much effort on his part. He smelled moist earth as an opening appeared and widened. The lamplight revealed fresh footprints in the dirt beyond.

"I believe I will wait here," said Emmaline. "I'm quite winded."

Matt turned back and looked around the room. "There are a couple of crates over there, ladies. Why don't you two have a seat? Keep my flashlight."

"Thank you, Matthew."

Paula had already climbed through the opening into the tunnel. "Matt, are you coming?"

"I'm right behind you. Would you like me to go ahead?"

"No, I've done this kind of thing before."

"Of course."

They shuffled along the low, narrow corridor for quite a distance before Paula stopped at a fork in the tunnel system.

"What do you think, Matt? Which way?"

She shined the light ahead at the ceiling of the intersecting tunnel and squealed. "What is that? Please don't let it be bats."

Matt felt her shudder. "Don't worry, Paula, no bats. I think we've found Roni's stash." He pulled out bits from some of the clusters of herbs that hung from the tunnel braces.

"Maybe we can put the pieces of the puzzle together before—" Paula stopped speaking. "What's that?"

She aimed the light beam at the dirt floor, illuminating a scattering of thin roll-your-own cigarettes twisted at the ends. "They must have fallen from the ceiling." She picked one up and sniffed it, then moved her light around. "There's more, Matt. Up there."

He pulled down a small plastic bag from the rafters. "I don't imagine this is comfrey."

He held it out to Paula, who opened it and took a sniff. "Marijuana."

"You sure?"

"Yeah. Looks like green tea leaves, smells skunky." She pinched some with her fingers and brushed it back into the bag. "Sticky too. I'm ninety-nine percent sure, and the joints confirm it." She returned the bag to Matt who put it back where he'd found it.

Her light hovered here and there, trying to pick up more hidden contraband. They moved along the tunnel until they came to a room dug out to one side. Dozens of boxes lined the walls, and each revealed bags similar to the one they'd found in the tunnel.

Matt looked around. "This place is a gold mine, or it would have been if we hadn't found it."

"Roni has to be working with someone."

"Maybe it's that man she met in Athens."

"What man?"

"I don't know who he is. The sisters saw Roni with someone in Athens one day. He looked familiar to them, but they couldn't place him."

Paula remained silent for a few moments. Then she said, "We'd better not touch anything else until we alert the police. Let's get back upstairs. I'm sure they won't leave this stuff here long now that they know we're interested in the tunnels. I suspect they have more than marijuana hidden here."

"I wish we hadn't left the ladies in the tunnel room alone."

Paula glanced at him in the dim beam of the lantern. "Let's go."

Matt followed her along the tunnel, back to the room with the clothes racks. As soon as she stepped into the room, she stopped. He tried to see past her but she held him back with her free hand. Not understanding, he pushed past her and stared, open-mouthed, first at Roni and then at the gun in her hand.

"So you two went on a little field trip, did you? Set that lantern down."

Matt checked out the corners of the room but saw no one else. "Where are the ladies, Roni?"

"You won't have to worry about the ladies, Matt. Well, on second thought, maybe you should worry a little." Her smile unnerved him.

"Roni, this is serious business you're into here. If you hurt the ladies in any way, you'll pay."

"I know what I'm doing, Matt, and this business is too serious to have you interfering. Now, if you two will make your way back down the tunnel I'll decide what to do with you."

"How are you expecting to get the goods out of here without being seen?" asked Paula.

"You don't need to know. Now move."

As they backed toward the tunnel entrance Matt asked, "Who are you working with, Roni? I'm sure you have an accomplice."

"Oh Matt, you sound like a murder mystery on TV. Just shut up and move or you'll wish you had."

Matt and Paula stumbled along the dank tunnel, Roni's threats following them, past the place where they had examined the herbs and joints, and stopped when Roni called a halt.

"There's a room to your left. In you go."

Matt turned and tried to stare beyond the light she held. "I don't suppose you'd consider being friends again?"

"Oh please."

She pitched a roll of duct tape at Paula. "Tape his ankles together—tight—and then he can tape yours. Kind of sweet, don't you think?"

They did as instructed. "Now Matt, put your hands behind your back and let Paula fasten your wrists together." Roni kept her high-powered beam directed at them as they complied.

"Your turn, Doc. Lie down on your face and put your hands behind your back. And if you try anything, you'll die in this place." She grabbed the duct tape and proceeded to wrap Paula's wrists behind her.

"What are you doing, Veronica?" The deep, authoritative voice seemed to surprise Roni and made Paula gasp.

"Mitch!" said Roni. "You startled me. I caught these two trespassing."

Matt couldn't pick out features against the light of the man's flashlight, just a tall, powerful looking figure.

"Well, look who we have here." Pushing Roni aside, he advanced toward Paula and turned her over. "Where you been, darlin'? You been avoiding me since you took my shirt and left me on the street."

"You got what was coming to you. I should have known you would be involved in something like this."

"What's going on, Mitch?"

He ignored Roni's question, pulled Paula up and kissed her on the lips while she struggled to evade him.

"You're as pretty as you always were, darlin', but I don't have time for you right now, like you didn't have time for me before."

Afraid of what the man might do to Paula, Matt kicked

out at him, but Mitch grabbed him by the collar and pulled him up till Matt could smell his breath. "Listen to me, Buster. You been nothing but trouble since you got here and I'm sick of you spoiling our plans. Now shut up."

He threw Matt against the wall, where he tumbled to the damp earth with nothing to break his fall. The air left his lungs in a rush. He spit dirt and fought for breath. "Leave her alone!"

Mitch kicked Matt hard and Paula cried out, "Stop it!"

"Move, Veronica," said Mitch, and backed out of the room.

She followed him into the tunnel.

"Why did you bring them here? We don't need to worry about hostages."

"They were in here. They came down on their own. The ladies showed them the way."

"The Barlows? What did you do with them?"

Roni's laugh filtered through from the tunnel and Matt shuddered at her response.

"They won't be bothering us anymore."

"Don't be stupid, Veronica. I didn't ask you to make decisions. Just follow orders."

"What was I supposed to do? They showed up. We can't have them jeopardizing our whole operation."

Matt listened as the voices receded, and heard Mitch's deep voice telling Roni to "take some of this stuff and dump it in his room so they can confirm he stole it."

"Paula?" Matt whispered. "Who was that?"

"Someone I hoped never to see again." Paula's voice broke.

Matt managed to sit, then wriggled to where she lay. His back hurt where Mitch had kicked him, but he figured it was minor to what might have been.

"Paula, if we sit back to back, we can unwrap each other's wrists."

They maneuvered into position and Matt pulled and tugged at the duct tape on Paula's wrists. As he worked, he asked the question again.

"Who's Mitch?"

"What is it with you guys? Doesn't anyone go by his real name anymore? He's Daniel and he's my ex-husband."

His hands stilled "The bad cop?"

"Yup. All you've heard and worse. He has the knowledge of a cop, the street smarts of a con, and the heart of a lizard."

Matt worked again, unwinding the tape. "So our odds at getting out of this unharmed may be slim."

"Don't even try to be funny. We are in serious trouble."

Taking in the pungent odor of darkness and years, Matt wondered how the fleeing slaves had felt when they hid in these same tunnels. He dragged his mind back to the present as he freed Paula's hands.

"Paula, before we came down to the tunnel, you were going to tell me what you had found out about Roni's past."

She twisted around and pulled at the tape holding his wrists. "Yeah, not that it helps much now. I didn't find out her name, but I put the cops from Foggy Plain onto it, and they are taking it from here. I sent them that text before we came down here, but they don't know anything about the tunnels."

"That's unfortunate. The only ones who know are the ladies, and we don't know what shape they're in. I'm praying they're okay." He pulled his wrists apart and picked off the remaining tape.

They worked on unwrapping their ankles without being able to see, and Paula said, "I used to believe that Jesus answered prayer, but after Daniel, I lost my conviction. I mean, if God would let me suffer under the hands of a crook like him, He was either uncaring or powerless."

Matt sighed. "That's a close match to my story. I figured I'd keep my distance from Him."

"And? How's that working for you?" She freed her ankles and rubbed them briskly.

Matt shook his head in the darkness, still fiddling with the binding. "It isn't. He keeps pursuing me and I can't get away. It's ironic. My suite here is next to the chapel. The reverend has become a friend. The sisters pray for me and thank God for me. Even Bubble Gum Cydnee sings His praises. It's a little much to fight against when it's all put together."

"I love this place and the people, and I wanted to help them, but ever since I got back, it's like everything is magnified, you know what I mean?"

"Sure do. So what happened with Daniel, if you don't

mind me asking?"

"He, ah, got a bit rough with me a few times. I chalked it up to job stress, but that was no excuse. Bear picked me up once when Daniel pushed me out of the car." She laughed with a harshness that made Matt's spine tingle.

"That was the beginning of the end. Bear was angry enough to tear him limb from limb, and he talked to my father. We pressed charges, filed for divorce, the whole nine yards. I went back to school to study medicine. I loved it. Daddy's girl, I guess."

She yanked one last piece of tape. "Done. Let's get outta here."

They stamped their feet to get the feeling back and Matt reached for her hand. They inched along the tunnel in the direction of the basement entrance, stumbling in the pitch darkness but driven by the fact that behind them, two dangerous people would soon be in pursuit.

"Sorry I got you into this," Matt whispered.

"You didn't force me to come down here."

In spite of the situation, he liked the feel of her hand in his. "Hey, you wanna go for a bike ride when this is all over?"

Her hand tightened on his. "You better believe it."

They searched along the wall for the doorway. Since they now knew the floor was level, they moved along at a steady pace. After a few minutes, they heard voices coming from behind them.

Paula's fingers bit into Matt's arm. "Hurry!" she urged in a stage whisper.

They stumbled along, falling through the doorway into the tunnel room, almost at the feet of Roni. She whipped out her gun and aimed it with trembling hands, first at Paula, then at Matt.

"Stay right there. Don't move a muscle or I'll shoot."

"Okay, okay," said Paula. "Don't fire that gun in here or you'll blow our eardrums out."

Matt cringed as he lay prone on the dirt floor. Roni must have split up with Mitch and come back here for some reason. But then who was coming up behind them? Daniel and another cohort? What could they do against three and a gun?

29

Matt sensed panic in Roni. She seemed surprised that they had escaped this soon. Perhaps help was on the way for Paula and him, but who knew when that might be? Very few people even knew about the tunnels. Meanwhile, he decided to use another tactic in what little time they might have.

"So, Mitch leaves you to do his dirty work, claims the goods, hides them somewhere unknown to you and takes off to the airport. You sure you're cool with that?"

"I'm not stupid, Matt. First of all, Mitch could never do this without me. It was my idea. And second, we have a thing going."

"Don't tell me you were two-timing me."

"You're no good at sarcasm, Matt." She kept her light and the gun trained on them.

"Why'd you pin the thefts on Matt?" Paula asked.

"It's not rocket science. All part of the blackmail thing, which didn't work, loyal friend that he is. But I'll make sure the right story gets back to our favorite reporter and he will still be blamed."

"I'd rather be a loyal friend than a lying thief and law breaker," said Matt.

"Don't be harsh. I thought we had an understanding."

"No, Roni, I never did understand you. There was a time I wanted to, but I never did."

"You sound sorry. That's quite endearing."

"Take a deep breath, babe. I'm sorry I was so dense I didn't see through you. Miss Grayce did."

"Yes, she is a pill, isn't she? If not for her, I'd be home free."

Paula piped up. "You planned to kill Emmaline with your lethal tea and put Grayce into a home. In the meantime, you would make sure they went bankrupt, putting you in a position to maintain the building until you had secured another location for your drug operation."

She shrugged. "It would have worked, if your friend here hadn't showed up."

"Maybe not," answered Paula. "You made a few mistakes all on your own."

"And you are prepared to point them out to me?"

"I'd love to. First, you underestimated the ladies. They saw through you before any of the rest of us did."

"Well, they've made their last mistake."

"I don't believe you would incriminate yourself with murder charges," said Paula. "Another mistake you made is to hook up with a guy like Daniel."

Roni's light wavered. "Who's Daniel?"

"The guy you're in league with. The one in the tunnel."

Roni glared at Paula. "His name is Mitch, and you don't know anything about him."

"Oh, but I do. I used to be married to him."

Shock showed in Roni's silence. "You?" She took a deep breath and regulated her voice. "Guess you didn't know how to handle him."

"Nor do you, Roni. No one handles Daniel Sherman. Get out of it while you can. Put the gun down and come upstairs with us. We can work something out before he comes back. In fact, I hear someone coming now."

"It's Mitch, and your attempt at intimidation isn't working."

"It's your call. I think you'll soon find out what he's all about."

Matt wondered at Paula's bravado. Did she sense something he'd missed? The voices they'd heard behind them in the tunnel stilled. Was someone there, or had Mitch returned to start hauling the loot out into the forest, thinking he and Paula were still secured in a side room?

"No one can pin anything on me, so save your words,"

Roni continued. "There are a million loopholes I can use."

Matt figured if they kept her talking, they could distract her somehow. "You seem educated about the law."

"Didn't pass the bar, but I had the qualifications, if it hadn't been for..."

"Cheating? Lying?"

"No more conversation. You're becoming tiresome."

He remembered Grayce and Emmaline, and worry descended on him. What had happened to them?

Dear Lord, help us here. We need a miracle. Not for me, but for the ladies.

He sighed, tried to recharge, and heard noises coming from the tunnel. Roni's fragile calm seemed on the verge of shattering. "Mitch! Get in here. I need backup."

Silence answered her call.

Roni fumbled for her cell phone and punched in a number. Meanwhile the light from her lantern wobbled, throwing grotesque shadows. Matt knew she would get no cell coverage down in the tunnel. He sensed Paula gathering herself for a charge and reached out to warn her. Guardian angels were immune to bullets; he and Paula were not.

Roni swore and dropped the phone into her pocket.

Matt heard a scraping sound from the direction of the basement, and they all turned toward it. Roni's gun wavered from Matt to Paula, and strayed off toward the ceiling as she turned to look. At that moment, Paula launched herself at Roni and they crashed to the dirt. The gun fired and the lantern flew into a corner.

Reeling from the reverberation of the gunfire in the now-dark room, Matt held his hands over his ears. Then he heard a grunt, followed by Paula's voice.

"Turn on...cell phone."

"Paula, there's no service down here."

"The light, Matt." Another grunt.

Cluing in, he pulled his cell from his pocket and turned it on. A faint light glimmered in the darkness, while he activated the flashlight. When he crouched down and directed the brilliant beam at the forms on the floor, he realized Paula had Roni pinned, arms twisted behind her back.

Matt grabbed the duct tape Roni had dropped and helped

Paula secure Roni's wrists, as the woman muttered curses into the dirt and cried about the pain in her ears. Paula finished, then rolled off onto the dirt floor, but didn't get up. That was when Matt noticed blood staining the shoulder of her blouse.

"Paula, you're bleeding." He yanked off his shirt, buttons flying in all directions, and pressed it against the wound. "We have to get you help."

"Matt, I'm a doctor," she said between clenched teeth. "I need to stay calm while you get help. Before Daniel gets back."

His ears pounded and echoed from the exploded gunshot, and he started to panic when Paula's eyes fluttered shut. "Paula, hang on."

He tripped over Roni in his haste to call for help. At that moment, someone burst into the room from the tunnel.

"Hold it!" said Matt. "No more trouble." He aimed his phone in the direction of the tunnel, and Bear squinted in the light.

"Put that thing down, you're blinding me!"

"Bear! I don't care how you figured this out, but we need help right now. Paula's been shot. She's losing blood."

Without comment, Bear set his own light beside Paula and checked her over. "My first aid kit is in my truck. I'll watch her while Sandy gets it."

"On me way, Gavin," said Sandy. He had slipped into the room with Bear and disappeared into the basement.

Matt walked over to where Roni lay prone on the dirt floor. "Get up." He took her arm and helped her to her feet. "I'm not leaving you here with Paula."

He led her out into the clothing storage room and out through the basement, right into the arms of two police officers.

Surprise overwhelmed him as they clicked cuffs onto her and one of them took her upstairs.

"How did you know to come here?"

"Hey to you too. I'm Constable Priscilla Rising Moon and that was Charlie Haliburton. You must be Matt. The Barlows called us. What's going on?"

Matt's head spun and his ears pounded. "The Barlows called you? I thought Roni had hurt them or at least tied them up."

"She did. They escaped and placed the call. Paula had fed us some leads, so we figured we'd better check them out."

"Glad you followed your hunch. Listen, Paula's been shot in the shoulder. I've got to get back to her. We've got a first responder with her, but…"

"Paula's been shot?" Constable Rising Moon pushed past him into the tunnel room where Paula was beginning to stir. She crouched beside her. "Hey, Paula. Lie still until we get you wrapped up."

"Where's Matt?"

"I'm here." He moved into her line of vision. "Hang on till Sandy gets back—here he is now."

"Give me some room," barked Bear as Sandy handed him his kit. "Let the lady breathe."

Matt pulled back and stood beside Sandy. "How did you get here?"

"Through the tunnel, me man. How else? Bear comes ta me yellin' about trouble in the tunnels, and since I be knowin' the way in from the woods, I leads him here."

"But how did Bear know about the tunnels?"

"The ladies told me," said Bear, glancing up from his bandaging. "I didn't want to meet the culprits in the cellar, so I roared over to find Sandy, and he led me in the back way."

"You guys are amazing. We were running out of options."

"All in a day's work," said Bear.

"Yeah, right. The puzzle thing again?'

"Yup. Now let's carry this lady upstairs and to the hospital."

"Call my dad, would you?" Paula asked as Bear cradled her in his arms.

"He's on his way," said Sandy.

30

Matt sat holding Paula's hand while she slept in her hospital bed. Her father had been the one to clean the bullet wound and stitch her up, so Matt knew she had been given the best care available.

He heard a soft knock at the door and looked up to see Grayce and Emmaline, along with Constable Haliburton. Matt released Paula's hand and enveloped both Barlows in a hug. Their eyes filled as they stepped back.

"We're so glad to see you, Matthew. We were worried sick about you."

"You were worried?" said Matt. "We thought Roni had hurt you."

"We're fine, Mr. Smith, or shall we call you Mr. Sadler?"

"All's well that ends well, they always say," said Emmaline.

"Who says, Emm? Don't generalize."

"Oh bother, Graycie. It's just a saying."

"Hey, don't leave me out of this." The words came from the bed, and they turned to see Paula trying to sit up.

Matt walked back to the bed. "Paula, please lie down. Ladies, we want the details."

Paula complied with Matt's and the doctor's orders and relaxed onto the pillow. Matt brought in an extra chair so the ladies could both sit near Paula's bed, and took up his post near her head.

"Okay, 'fess up ladies. What did Roni and Daniel do to you and where did they put you?"

The ladies seemed to enjoy the limelight and made the most of the moment.

"Well, we were sitting there in the tunnel room, as you know," began Grayce, "and then we decided we didn't want to remain there any longer, so we found our way back into the basement."

Emmaline joined in the story. "We were stepping into the basement when Veronica showed up and pointed her gun at us. We didn't know if it was a real gun, but we decided we would not tempt fate, as it were."

Matt closed his eyes in relief and Paula shook her head.

Grayce continued. "She herded us into the coal chute—"

"The coal chute? I didn't see a coal chute," said Matt.

"It's behind the furnace, difficult to see, but Miss Wilkinson knew her way around that place. Anyway, she forced us into there and locked the door."

"We thought we were doomed," said Emmaline.

"You thought we were doomed," Grayce corrected. "I had every intention of finding an escape."

"The coal chute is under the kitchen, and the ground level opening is under Johanna's window. We made as much noise as we could without completely losing our self-respect, and managed to alert Johanna."

Matt grinned as he imagined the two elderly women creating an uproar. Paula laughed and then winced. He reached for her hand again.

"As Graycie was saying, Johanna heard the noise. It frightened her, so she tried to rouse us, only to discover we were not in our rooms. She even ventured to Matthew's room, but I don't think she would like people to discuss that."

"Then why did you bring it up, Emm? Allow her to retain some of her dignity."

"Excuse me for living."

Matt chuckled while Emmaline continued.

"Our Johanna is a timid person, so it took all her determination to use the telephone, but she did. She called Mr. Beresford—she's met him a few times and he's always been most kind to her—and he came at once."

Grayce picked up the thread of the story. "He extricated us from our prison and chaperoned us to his house—"

"I'm afraid Mr. Beresford's house resembles his shop."

"Emmaline, for heaven's sake. We found safety there. We contacted the police in Foggy Plain and left a message for Phineas so he would contact us there as soon as he returned home. Meanwhile, Mr. Beresford located Mr. Fitzpatrick and he led him to the forest entrance to the tunnels."

"The police knew enough to respond because of what Paula had told them."

Matt squeezed Paula's hand. "We are both more grateful than words can express for your quick-wittedness, ladies. God used you to answer our prayers."

Paula squeezed his hand in return. The pleasure of it thrilled him.

He still had some questions, though. "Constable Haliburton, I saw you leading Roni away but what happened to Daniel?"

"We caught him with a carload of marijuana and cocaine, heading out over the bridge," said Haliburton. "He's sitting in the Foggy Plain jail right now, madder than a cornered badger. He'll be moved to the city by tomorrow to be formally charged."

"Wow. You guys covered all the angles." He put his free hand in his pocket and felt the envelope he had found in the dresser in the tunnel room.

"What's that?" they all asked in unison.

"Not sure. I found it downstairs in an old dresser. Didn't get a chance to look at it." He opened it and pulled out a computer printout of a ticket to L.A. in the name of Veronica Wilkinson. "My guess is she and Daniel didn't trust each other. This must have been an emergency measure."

"Well, she won't need it now," said Charlie. "She'll be going on a little trip, but it won't be a destination she would have chosen. I'll be on my way then. Take care, Paula."

"Thank you, Constable, for driving us here," said Grayce. "I'm sure Mr. Smith will take us home."

Charlie Haliburton nodded and left.

Grayce stood and Emmaline followed suit. "We will wait for you in the hallway, Mr. Smith. My sister and I are weary after all the excitement, and it is almost morning."

"I'll be right with you, ladies."

The sisters left and Paula smiled up at him. He sandwiched her hand between his and stared into her eyes.

Her smile faded. "You're leaving Happenstance, aren't you?"

He hesitated. "I have some things to take care of, but I'll be back."

Her eyes searched his.

"A little matter of unfinished business in Reedport, and a talk with Morris Craddock. I won't leave for a few days, till I know you're okay."

She smiled then. "You do what you have to do. I'm not going anywhere."

"You look pretty tired, Paula. I hate to leave, but you need sleep."

"So do you. Come back later?"

"Can't keep me away." He leaned over and kissed her forehead.

As Matt slipped from the room, he heard the ladies talking around the corner, where they sat waiting for him.

"What did I tell you, Graycie?"

"You did not tell me anything I didn't already know."

"I told you they were perfect for each other when they first met. You just don't want to admit I was right."

"You were right, Emm, and I approve. Does that satisfy you?"

"Not as much as the scene in that room. Don't you feel the romance?"

"Emm, he was just holding her hand. There is much more to a relationship than that."

"Yes, but it's a sign. You know nothing about it."

"I know more than you think, Emm."

Matt hid his smile as he rounded the corner. "Shall we go home, ladies?"

Two days later, Matt clasped hands with Bear and mounted his Harley.

The big man said, "Looks like the Barlows ain't gonna have to do much advertisin', what with all the media hype. The tunnels are big news now and people are already callin' for reservations."

"Yeah, that worked in their favor. Listen, Bear, will you look after them while I'm gone? They've had a traumatic time and they might need some building up."

"Don't you worry none. Everybody's pitchin' in, fixin' the place up. Volunteers thick as hen's teeth."

Matt laughed. "You're one of a kind, Bear." He revved the throttle and it powered loud and strong. He slipped on his shades, stashed his backpack in the saddlebag and booted up the kickstand.

"Thanks for everything, Bear."

Bear nodded and waved. "You come back soon."

Matt pulled his hair into a ponytail and slipped his helmet on. With a rebellious rumble, he rolled out of Beresford Gas Station and toured south down Bridgeway Avenue, the words of Amanda Eugenie Rutherford Barlow playing in his mind:

As we passed through the covered bridge, I had the strangest sense that I would return, that I belonged there. Perhaps the future will be even brighter than this brief visit.

Reader's Guide
Discussion Questions

1. We all feel like running away from our problems at times, as Matt did. Did his flight fix his problems? Have you tried to escape your problems in a similar manner? Did it help?

2. Have you ever had a second chance in a specific situation, or in life in general? What did that do for your perception of other people's problems?

3. How do you view the elderly? Do we, as a society, put them all into a box without really seeing and appreciating them? Did the experiences of Grayce and Emmaline affect your perceptions?

4. In real life, people are not always as black and white as we see them in a fictional story. Could Paula's ex have any redeeming qualities? Could Roni? Is anyone beyond God's grace?

5. We see Roni and Paula reacting to hurts they've experienced in their lives. How do you deal with people/circumstances that hurt you? Do you hold bitterness as your right, or do you let it go so it won't cripple you?

About the Author

Photo Credit: Carla Lehman Photography

Janice L. Dick is an award-winning author from the Canadian prairies. She has written six historical novels to date, as well as some contemporary stories, short stories, blogs, articles and book reviews. She is the winner of the 2016 Janette Oke Award.

Check out Janice's blog/website: www.janicedick.com
and her Amazon Author page:
https://amazon.com/author/janicedick

OTHER BOOKS by JANICE L. DICK

THE STORM SERIES

(temporarily out of stock)

Calm Before the Storm
Eye of the Storm
Out of the Storm

IN SEARCH OF FREEDOM SERIES

Other Side of the River
In a Foreign Land
Far Side of the Sea

HAPPENSTANCE CHRONICLES

The Road to Happenstance

SHORT STORIES

The Christmas Sweater

ANTHOLOGIES

Hope is Born: A Mosaic Christmas Anthology

Coming next from The Mosaic Collection:
THIS SIDE OF YESTERDAY by Angela D. Meyer

Acknowledgements

Bringing a book to life takes more ideas and expertise than one person holds.

A heartfelt thank you to my unnamed friend who helped me with initial ideas, plot points, characters and suggestions. Without you, Happenstance would never have existed.

Thanks to Wayne, my husband and best friend, for listening to the words and the ideas, ad nauseum, and for offering suggestions.

My thanks to Linda Enns and Lyse Cantin for laughing in all the right places, and for your encouragement.

My heartfelt appreciation to those who read the manuscript and offered suggestions and corrections: Eleanor Bertin, Ruth Snyder, Tandy Balson, Ruth Smith Meyer, Sheri Hathaway, Janet Sketchley, Helen F., Brenda J. Wood, Carol Harrison. If I missed anyone's name, please forgive me.

Thanks to the dear women in the Mosaic Collection, which is explained in detail in the front matter of this book. These women, especially our virtual assistant, Camry Crist, have been overwhelmingly helpful and supportive. God bless you all in your own writing careers. And thanks for *All Things Mosaic.*

Thanks also to:

— members of past writing groups, Carlton Trail Writers and His Imprint, for listening to excerpts and offering comments, especially to Jeanne Heal Osolinsky, friend and writer extraordinaire, for direction when I was floundering.

— my dear friends at WritersInk for their interest, time investment, and unfailing support, specifically Dee Robertson, Carol Gossner, Loretta Polischuk and Hazel

Kellner, who were there from the beginning.

— Constable Sterling Maffenbeier, former neighbor, now RCMP special forces, for information on police life and drugs.

— Phil Willms, friend and neighbor, for a rider's and mechanic's perspective on motorcycles.

— Dan Boehr, friend and construction business owner, for ideas on roofing.

In the story, I refer to the tunnels in Moose Jaw, Saskatchewan, Canada. These tunnels are real. I have visited them and they are truly fascinating. When I called the Tunnels desk to ask if I could mention this year-round tourist attraction in my book, they generously gave their permission. Google https://www.tunnelsofmoosejaw.com for more information.

Most of all, thanks to my Lord Jesus Christ for giving me this love of words and story, and for His faithful guidance and love throughout my life. I am His, and He is mine.

Note from the Author

Dear Reader,

This story has been in my mind and in a computer file for years, and it's a pleasure to finally set it free. I hope you enjoyed the read as much as I enjoyed writing it.

As a writer, I often discover my thoughts, feelings, and even values through my characters as I write. I hope you were able to connect with the characters in this story, and to learn from and with them.

The theme that crept through the story as I wrote was one of grace. Of second chances. Of glimpses of the God who loves us more than we'll ever know. Add to that the influence of family and friends, and the result is one of hope and joy.

I pray for each one of you, that you will allow these glimpses of glory to bring hope into your lives.

Let's Connect

Thanks for taking the time to read this story. The nicest thing you can ever do for an author, besides reading his or her books, is to write a brief review and post it on social media, as well as on Amazon.

Oh, and one more thing. If you drop by my website, you will see my newsletter sign-up form. If you take a moment to fill that in, you will receive a concise newsletter from me about once a month. It will include news about my writing, the Mosaic Collection books, and a brief personal note. I'd love to have you on board.

Made in the USA
Columbia, SC
14 February 2020